Readers love the Leader Murders series by LIV OLTEANO

A Counselor Among Wolves

"…another fabulous story in this series. I'm absolutely loving where this storyline is going and I'm really looking forward to seeing where things go next."

—The Blogger Girls

"I really enjoyed Liv Olteano's return to this verse she has created."

—The Novel Approach

"Be sure and pick up *A Counselor Among Wolves* by Liv Olteano and immerse yourself in world that is familiar and yet… not."

—Sensual Reads

A Tooth for a Fang

"I recommend it to anyone who likes detective stories, non-human creatures, hot sex, and powerful-but-loving men, served with a side of social issues."

—Inked Rainbow Reads

"It was a refreshing take for a murder-mystery fan like myself."

—Boys in our Books

"I loved Olteano's paranormal world that exists alongside ours."

—Scattered Thoughts and Rogue Words

By Liv Olteano

LEADER MURDERS
A Tooth for a Fang
A Counselor Among Wolves
A King and a Pawn

SPACE FILES R
The Heracian Affair
Sandstorm Heart

Published by Dreamspinner Press
www.dreamspinnerpress.com

A king AND A pawn

LIV OLTEANO

DREAMSPINNER PRESS

Published by
DREAMSPINNER PRESS

5032 Capital Circle SW, Suite 2, PMB# 279, Tallahassee, FL 32305-7886 USA
www.dreamspinnerpress.com

A King and a Pawn
© 2016 Liv Olteano.

Cover Art
© 2016 AngstyG.
www.angstyg.com
Cover content is for illustrative purposes only and any person depicted on the cover is a model.

ISBN: 978-1-63477-341-6
Digital ISBN: 978-1-63477-342-3
Library of Congress Control Number: 2016902330
Published June 2016
v. 1.0

Printed in the United States of America
∞
This paper meets the requirements of
ANSI/NISO Z39.48-1992 (Permanence of Paper).

One

CALL ME Clueless. It's not my name or my nickname—at least it wouldn't have been until recently. But now I was the clueless brother of a pack traitor. Even worse, a clueless beta. You might think there are worse things to be than clueless. You'd be wrong. It was worse than being the actual traitor, in my mind: my sister, Tricia Cooper, had a plan, a sense of direction, an awareness of her goals and surroundings while she betrayed us. I'd just been clueless. Forever branded as a schmuck. The sky, the earth, the wind, the gazes of everyone in the Paranormal Bureau of Investigations—including nonpack—the universe screamed at me every time I took a breath: "Schmuck!" It was always there, throbbing in the back of my mind, running in the background of my every thought. It flavored the taste of everything I ate or drank. My pack had no use for schmucks. The PBI had no use for them either. I couldn't stand to be one anymore. Couldn't afford to. Our pack was no home for the weak, particularly not as a beta.

I looked at the ring sitting on the desk of Herman Weiss—PBI director, also my alpha. The piece of jewelry had one stone: an onyx set in silver. Not tacky or anything, but I wasn't that much of a jewelry guy.

"Are we sure it works?" Weiss's mate, Timothy Sands, asked as he stared at the ring.

Weiss nodded. "And it can't be detected as a shield, I'm told. Came right out of a special vault of artifacts. It's this or nothing, anyway. So let's hope like fuck it works," he added in a grave tone.

I swallowed hard. *I volunteered for this*, I reminded myself. Since my sister had been discovered as a traitor, my status as Weiss's beta was a flimsy thing. Everyone in our pack stole glances at me when they thought I wasn't paying attention. I knew what they were all thinking: Either he's an idiot and he didn't know, or he's a traitor but he's better at hiding it. Truth be told, I needed a short break from my pack. That thought scared me. Offering to be the first Council ambassador at the Fey Court was the right thing to do. And the only thing I *could* do.

It would prove my loyalty to my pack and alpha. And clean out some of the stain of shame from my family name. My poor dad would turn in his grave if he knew what my sister, Tricia, had done. As Weiss's other beta, I should have been the first to figure out Tricia was a traitor. I should have defended my pack when it mattered, when the worms of betrayal were trying to chew us from the inside out. I had failed them. I had failed Weiss. I knew that.

This was my chance to prove I wasn't entirely useless. My alpha wanted to figure out what the Fey King was trying to do to our Council and territories—what kind of bone the fey had to pick with him, too. I was going to find out from the inside or die trying.

I picked up the ring and slipped it on my finger. "It's going to work just fine, I'm sure."

Tim frowned. "I can't sense it being a shield. I'm not sure if that's a good or a bad thing," he muttered.

As a newly turned werewolf who used to be half-fey, half-elf, Tim had the emotional grid-reading skill all fey had. Officially fey weren't allowed to use it within Council territories, let alone in the PBI HQ, but Tim had the Council wrapped around his little finger ever since the Amanda execution debacle. He was their golden boy, weighing in on all decisions regarding or involving fey. And a lot of them did, recently. We were in a state of cold war with the Fey King and his Court, pretty much. Minor details about Timothy Sands: he was the Fey King's outcast son, and the King had tried to assassinate him and openly plotted against him. When he became a werewolf, the fey officially nonfeyed him. Nothing personal, it was fey policy: once bitten by any shift-inducing creature, you were no longer fey. The fey were stuck-up assholes—that was my take on it.

"Can you read my emotional grid?" I asked, playing with the ring on my finger.

Tim cocked his head to the side. "In a way. I can get some general sense of your feelings, some anxiousness, some excitement, some fear... vague, but there. It's not throwing up a complete wall, which is smart.

Nobody being able to read anything would alert fey something was wrong. We don't want that."

I looked down at the shiny black stone. "So it works more like a scrambler than a shield?"

"Well, that depends," Tim said, blinking slowly. "Are you turned on right now?"

"What?" I snapped.

Weiss squinted. "Turned on? While talking to my mate? Are you?" he growled.

"No, man!" I squeaked. "Wanna cop a feel and see I'm not the least bit hard?"

Tim went to Weiss and caressed his shoulder, much like you would pet a restless puppy. "It's the ring. I think it projects an array of feelings and moods in natural, random combinations. It's a lot smarter than a shield or a scrambler. I'd like to know where that ring comes from," he purred, looking up into Weiss's eyes.

My alpha ignored that last part. He turned toward Tim and said instead, "Any last-minute advice for Bert?"

Tim walked over. He sat in the chair in front of me, then crossed his legs and leaned forward. "You'll be confused about them. Figure them out as you go. You need to remember some basic things. One: Kingdom fey think of werewolves as inferior beings. Don't rebel against that idea, because it's useless. Use it to your advantage instead. Two: they expect you to be simpler, more on the brutish side, perhaps even less intelligent, and therefore less dangerous. Cultivate that. Present yourself as a simpler being than they are, but without making it obvious. Be carnal, superficial, fickle. Keep up those appearances. Three: whatever any of them might do or say, never forget there are two things fey will always do much better than you—lie, and know when someone is lying. I'm not kidding with this. They will always lie better and easier, and you will never see through it. We don't know how the ring will work. So don't go out of your way to test it. Stick to truths or relative truths as much as you can. It's the easiest way to deceive them. Build contexts in which whatever you say is as true as it might get."

I gulped. "How the fuck will I find the information I need, then? If I can never trust a single fucking word coming out of their mouths?"

Tim smiled. "Because they lie so much and easily, there's an almost compulsive need to keep records about anything important.

There are official fey records in the Fey Archives about anything even remotely relevant. It's a place where you will surely find all the information ever deemed strategically important. You need to get inside there, then get oriented around the record-keeping systems and pull your info from there. You can trust whatever is written down there to be true, even if you find two accounts regarding the same thing that seem to clash. Don't worry about making sense of it right then. Just get to it, obtain a copy of it, and deliver it to us. Always carry a flash drive on you and never part with it. Not even in your sleep. Never, Bert, do you understand me?"

I nodded. "Any suggestions?"

Tim grinned. "Oh, I have one. You'll find it in your luggage. Leave with it... equipped. It's the one thing they'd never dare to search, and passing you through a scan would break protocol. They wouldn't do that so blatantly. But they might try to sneakily search any and all of your files, computers, phones. So never leave a trace of anything compromising."

A sheen of sweat covered my forehead.

Weiss turned around, picked up a tennis ball, and started throwing it against the wall. There was a dent in the spot he was aiming at.

I leaned in closer to Tim. "New thing?"

He smiled. "Stress relief. It's better than growling at everyone, right?"

I snorted. "Right. Not very Weiss-like, though," I whispered as gingerly as I could.

There was a knock on the door, and then it opened. Travis Chandler and Rick Barton walked in. They were mated lycans, the PBI agents in charge of Abuse, our most recently top-busy team since the Anti-Abuse Act had come into play, imposing all kinds of rules on leaders—alphas, sires—in order to prevent abuse. If and when they did abuse someone, the victims had the Abuse team to complain to. So Rick and Travis were the peacekeepers of our community lately, righting wrongs left and right.

At least that was their official role. I liked to think of them as two lycan nutjobs. Being on twos instead of fours, like us werewolves were, seemed to make it easier for them to stick their heads up their asses. Rick, the nonalpha of the mated pair and our Bureau's only tracker, was especially skilled at keeping his head up his ass. Despite Travis being an all-around ass and stepping on everyone's toes, Rick was the one with a real grudge against Weiss and leaders in general; the lycan tracker didn't seem to have forgiven Weiss for his involvement in Amanda's fate. Amanda Weiss had been my alpha's mate for years, had given him a lovely son—Alf, who I had been tasked with keeping safe for years until recently volunteering for this new spy gig—and had led a very good life among us as part of the PBI. She had decided it wasn't good enough for her, though, betraying Weiss and the Council, plotting to unleash anarchy in our midst by trafficking marking hormones that would counter the natural hormonal effect leaders have on their pack or clan. My sister, Tricia, had gotten involved in Amanda's plans too, turning against us, to my shock and horror. For some reason, Rick, who had been instrumental in actually catching Amanda, felt sorry for the bitch, no doubt due to some bullshit sob-story she had poured in his ear. I'm sure Rick had his reasons, sound ones in his own mind, to feel sorry for her. I, for one, thought Amanda was an ungrateful, manipulative, self-centered, traitorous bitch who had gotten what she deserved, but to each their own.

"Didn't know you were into throwing balls around, boss," Travis quipped.

Rick rolled his eyes, the general reaction he had toward Weiss.

Tim cleared his throat. "I'm sure there was something you came here to do aside from regaling us with your delightful presence," he said, batting his eyelashes.

There was always some sort of teasing going on between Tim and Travis. They had been together for a while there, a couple years ago. But Tim was totally head over heels for Weiss, I could tell. Hell, the whole Bureau could tell. My best guess was Tim liked to yank Rick's chain. I very much approved.

Travis smiled, unruffled. "Boss, if you could stop fondling that ball, we'd like to chat."

The tennis ball flew the fuck through Weiss's office door. We all stared at the round hole. Someone screamed somewhere down the hall, possibly where the end of the ball's route lay. I hoped the screamer had managed to get out of the projectile's way in time. Or at least managed to catch it with something other than their face.

Weiss cracked his neck and grinned. "Now that relieved some fucking stress."

"That's not how it was intended to be used," Tim muttered, massaging the bridge of his nose.

Rick cleared his throat. "We need more agents for the Abuse team. Complaints about abusive alphas and sires are pouring in. We're flooded."

Weiss closed his eyes slowly. "How many agents would you need?"

"How many could you give us?" Travis asked, looking serious for the first time.

Weiss turned to face the window, looking away from the room. "I'll have to take this up with the Council. Give me some fucking clue as to proportions."

"Biblical," Rick said.

"Biblical," Weiss repeated, shaking his head.

Tim's expression changed. Something dark slithered through his gaze, then disappeared. "Change is a Brownian movement," he said. "It has a pace of its own. The process needs to be helped along. I'm sure the Council will feel the same."

"It's been tough on everyone since the Anti-Abuse Act became official law," Travis said to cover the silence that followed. "There's a matings-breaking spree going on, but hierarchy doesn't seem to have suffered much so far. If anything, ex-mates work better as teams when there's a leader involved. It's a bit confusing, but things are better already, and it's only been a couple months."

Rick cleared his throat. "I'm more worried about Bert here."

I smiled. "Oh, yeah? I'm touched all over."

"I fucking hope not," Travis said.

"Don't worry, Chandler. I wouldn't dream of going for your guy. I like 'em more spirited," I said sweetly.

Travis snorted. "*More* spirited? Now that I'd like to see."

"In a voyeuristic way, you mean?" I quipped.

"I take it you're just about ready to leave?" he muttered.

"Going there this afternoon, in fact. Thought I'd settle in over the weekend. Be ready to face the music first thing Monday morning."

"So just to make it all clear," Rick said, sticking his hands in his pockets, "you're going to be our Council's first ambassador at the Fey Court?"

I nodded.

"And you're going there to do… what, exactly?"

"I'm going to support the interests of the Council, of my pack and alpha."

"That's not at all vague," he replied, frowning.

"Ambassador work, what can I say? Diplomacy is kind of a vague art."

"Aren't you worried pack members will think you changed sides while there? You know there can't be much contact or visiting," Rick persisted.

"I'll come in to report regularly. I trust my pack, and I think the pack trusts me. Why else would I be chosen to go there as the Council's ambassador?"

"True," Weiss replied.

It didn't sound convincing at all. I knew why I had been chosen: Weiss's faith in me and Tim's support. After mating Weiss and becoming a werewolf himself, Tim was deemed our Council's greatest asset aside from Weiss. A magic werewolf too, thanks to his fey and elf heritage. He was the man, vetting people as trustworthy for the Council, putting in suggestions whenever there was a trickier decision to be made. To be honest, it showed he was the son of the Fey King; he had a kind of innate diplomacy and capacity for decision-making the rest of us couldn't master quite so elegantly. I admired Tim and was very fond of him too. He loved my alpha to bits. It showed in how he seamlessly cared for him and protected their family—meaning Weiss and his now eight-year-old son, Alf. They were such an inspiration. I needed to make them proud. I needed to prove I deserved to be Weiss's beta. That I deserved the trust of living with them in their home and caring for their kid. I wanted Alf to look at me with the complete trust and admiration he used to have before the whole goddamn Tricia ordeal had happened.

The fact she'd turned against our alpha, our pack, against me, and everything we'd known and believed in still sent shockwaves through me. I ignored it most of the time, or I would go nuts trying to make some sense of it. However severe her betrayal of our pack and alpha was, she had betrayed someone worse: me, her damn brother. She looked into my eyes, smiled at me, lied to me, and fucking stabbed me in the back every minute of every day for months, maybe longer. She betrayed me with every glance, every word, every breath of fucking air. And I had had no goddamn clue.

We were still unsure about each traitor's involvement with the Leader Murders case. So far we had eight dead bodies and little clue about the real motives behind their deaths. In some cases we could guess the immediate, personal reasons. People wanted other people dead for the same reasons: jealousy, revenge, material gain. Three of the eight deaths could be explained by one of them. There had been no confessions, though. And without proof of family members being involved, we hadn't taken anyone into custody. But we wanted to. The Council wasn't famous for letting its community members off the hook when they disrespected their laws. In fact, it was famous for doing exactly the opposite. We still had to make the connections to prove anyone's involvement with any or all of the murders.

So far we knew for sure Amanda had been involved. She hadn't flipped on anyone while in custody, though, and now she was dead. Tricia was involved too, and she was still in custody. But she wasn't talking either. Morris James, the used-to-be Downtown chief, was also involved.

While we could sketch some reasons for Morris hating Weiss on account of Morris's brother being one of Weiss's exes, and then committing suicide presumably because of the pain of losing Weiss, Tricia was a complete mystery. Was it some marking hormones-induced pseudo-alpha stupor aimed at maybe Amanda, the suspected leader of the rebels in our midst? Was there something else going on between the two women? An affair? Some money thing, maybe? No one knew. There was no way to find out for sure.

We had taken some people into custody after Travis and Rick broke the hormones trafficking case. None of them had spoken. The only potential source of information at this point was the former fey ambassador, Leonard Hughes, but he had been traded to the Fey King in exchange for him stopping the pretty much hostile takeover plan aimed at our current Council. So a new leaf was turned. In an attempt to strengthen the bonds between the fey and Council territories, the Fey King had sent in a new ambassador, and we were sending one of our own out there, in his Court. This ambassador was me.

It wasn't the suicide mission my pack thought it to be, or the half admission I was a traitor too and that I needed to be punished by being sent away, like some suspected. This was my chance to prove to myself I wasn't a fucking waste of space and air. That I wasn't a phony, a useless pack member.

And I'd find out what Weiss and the Council wanted to know, even if it killed me. But I was honestly hoping it wouldn't.

two

LEAVING THE Council territories and going into the fey ones wasn't as shocking a transition as one might expect. In fact, to the untrained eye, there was no difference between the territories, no landmark and no sign announcing the border. But to any of us Council territories inhabitants, the border felt almost physical, even if it was only an administrative delimitation. There was a sort of wall of energy that made the end of our zone, or rather the beginning of the fey one, almost a blunt thing, and going through it felt like swimming through molasses.

Most of my stuff had been sent over already. A truck had arrived in front of the Hollowstar Complex, my PBI-provided residence. The truck was of the fey-owned movers, Crystalin Transports. If I didn't know the company name, the tiny fleur-de-lis contained in a hexagon would have tipped me off. All seats of power had a symbol everyone knew. Our Council's was a four-leaf clover contained in a circle. Every Council-owned business had it in its logo. Every city we owned had it on its welcome sign. It was everywhere. The territory symbol made it easy for everyone to know exactly where they were. You couldn't trespass and claim ignorance, that was for sure. Humans thought them cute little city symbols, if they even noticed them. It was shocking how much we could get away with because nobody was actually paying any real attention.

The car I was in veered off the highway and toward the main fey city. Its name was written in the same font and colors as any other, only beside the name was a tiny hexagon containing the fleur-de-lis. I was officially on fey ground now, and effective immediately, a Council ambassador with full diplomatic immunity and shit. Of course, as Tim pointed out, diplomatic immunity would mean dick squat if I seriously pissed off anyone powerful enough in the Fey Court. People disappeared all the time from all over the world; should I go the way of the dodo bird, the Fey Court could and would claim no knowledge of it. Which meant I had to watch my step and do my best to stay alive, all day, every day.

I enjoyed the tingle of adrenaline that went through my body at the thought. I might have been playing house as Weiss's beta for a while, but I was a werewolf. By definition I loved a good fight and all the excitement it could bring. If anything, I loved it more than others, particularly because I'd been Alf's guard-slash-nanny for so long. I loved the kid of course, but I missed a good fight-or-flight situation. Fey Court would undoubtedly bring some, I was sure. It didn't matter that Tim constantly told me the thrills of court life weren't the kind I was thinking about. I knew excitement was waiting to pounce on me.

My driver was a very fey-looking guy: smooth facial features, elegant bone structure, not a bulky body, though he was taller than Tim. And Tim was my standard for fey anything because he was the only one I'd known personally. This guy looked similar to Tim. But there was a definite sense of power about him, something almost slithering beneath the cool appearance. And he was just a driver, for fuck's sake. What kind of impression would powerful fey make? Not that they would trust me or pay me much attention. This guy didn't trust me much either, if the glances he was giving me via the rearview mirror were anything to go by.

Up yours too, sweetheart, I thought and smiled at him.

He blinked smoothly and looked away as if nothing had happened. I took a deep breath and tried to mentally prepare myself for the evening to come. After this asshole drove me to my new home, I had some time to shower and change, and then we'd be off again. The King was throwing me a welcome party, during which I half expected them to try poisoning me. But the Court was big on pomp and circumstance, Tim told me. They'd make an event out of picking their noses if they could. So they'd even throw a wolf a welcome party, though they generally looked on us as nasty beasts.

My driver kept throwing me glances, so I finally broke down and cried uncle. "Okay, what's the deal? Find me so attractive that you can't seem to look anywhere else? Like at the road, since you're driving anyway?"

He half grinned. "I was hoping to introduce myself. But when you got to the car, you jumped in so quickly I didn't have the time. Now I was debating if I should say something or not, because putting it off until we get to your accommodations would seem too rude. To be honest I was hoping you'd say something and take me out of my misery. I'd hate to make you feel anything but welcome," he added almost sweetly.

I was sure all of that statement was utter bullshit of course, but I smiled anyway. "Sorry, I'm not used to this having-a-driver thing. I'm Bert Cooper."

"Ambassador Cooper, then. A pleasure to meet you. Your name sounds familiar…," he said, frowning. "Cooper… oh, I know! I read about a Tricia Cooper in the *Daily Bite*," he added, smiling now. "Sad business."

I gritted my teeth. The *Daily Bite* was the only nonhuman publication in the region, and it featured all the nonhuman news—coded of course. It was a discreet addition to regular human subscriptions, carefully inserted into "paranormal people's" morning paper delivery. In this, at least, we were all as one. We got the paper, read our extra-special little addition, then had to burn it before leaving the house for work or jogging or whatever the fuck it was everyone did in the morning. Surprisingly humans had no clue. Of course they wouldn't. The few who actually looked through it accidentally were homeless people, junkies, or deemed lunatics, anyway. So far so good. Of course the *Daily Bite* did a piece on my traitorous sister. A pack beta making an ass of herself was juicy stuff to sink your teeth into, after all. Not their fault she'd given them bullets to gun the pack down with, was it?

I shrugged. "Very sad. She was my sister," I commented lightly.

He flicked his gaze back to me in the rearview mirror. "Oh my! *Was?*"

"She's been executed for treason…. I didn't get your name, sorry."

"Will," he muttered. "Execution, huh? Brutal."

"Maybe," I commented. She was alive of course, but there was no reason to share that kind of info with my driver. "But effective. Once a traitor, always a traitor, right?" I said, looking straight into his light green eyes.

He blinked but didn't reply. If I had to guess, he was trying to do the math on me being as much of a traitor as she was, or not. Becoming the Council's ambassador with their Court was probably as tough to figure out for them as it was for people back home. Was it a promotion or punishment? Was I a good little wolf wagging his tail all friendly-like, or the big bad wolf looking to tear their Kingdom down—like their former ambassador had been hoping to do with our Council, for instance?

"Do you believe people can't change?" he asked, keeping his gaze ahead on the road.

"I'm sure they can. Maybe even fundamentally if something shocking or traumatic enough happens to them. But just as easily as flipping pages in a book, and on a whim? Not so much."

"Hmm...," he replied, nodding. "So does that make you a faithful subject of your Council, and thereby wholeheartedly dedicated to their interests? Or a through-and-through traitor wholeheartedly dedicated to his own interests instead? Sent on a mission, or more like sent away to be gotten rid of, Ambassador Bert Cooper?"

"Wow. You people really like to go at it, don't you? What kind of question is that?"

"An honest one. I wouldn't want to be my King's ambassador with your Council, for instance."

"But then again, your most recent ambassador did commit treason against my Council, didn't he?" I asked sweetly.

His jaw muscles twitched ever so slightly. "Ambassador Hughes did us no favors, true. Why didn't you execute him?"

"Not ours to put down, was he? The Council upholds their end of treaties, Will." *Too bad your King doesn't*, I mentally added. Though I was hoping he'd stick to some treaties, at least. Mainly those assuring my safety while on fey ground. "You're pretty well-informed for a driver," I commented, trying to catch his eye in the rearview mirror again.

He smiled this small, enigmatic smile and went silent for the rest of the drive.

ONCE WE got to my Court-gifted residence—a pretty snazzy-looking house with a slick, modern design, surrounded by a few trees—Will got out of the car and opened the door for me to get out too.

When I did I noticed he was about as tall as I was, shoulders as wide, though he weighed less. Definitely taller than Tim. The suit he wore was a flawless black. The driver hat was off and held under his arm. It seemed curious to me because he looked more like a soldier than a driver, considering the posture and everything. If I were to bet on anything, it would be that he was no simple driver. His posture was too obviously military, his gaze too searching and hard to read. Either he wasn't just a driver, or I was royally fucked and everyone else higher up than driver was formidable. Well, I was hoping for excitement. I had a feeling I'd get even more than I was hoping for.

He went to the back of the limo and got my bag out, then handed it to me and smiled. "Would you like me to walk you in, Ambassador? I'm at your service until we leave for the reception."

Shit, reception? Of course it couldn't be a simple party, could it? I mentally rolled my eyes as I played with the onyx ring on my finger. "So what, you'll wait in the car for an hour until we leave?"

"Sure. I'm your driver for the day. Someone else will be assigned to you starting tomorrow, a permanent driver."

"Why wasn't this permanent driver assigned to me starting today, then?"

That small, enigmatic smile showed up again. "There was a family emergency, I was told. She's very sorry she couldn't be here to greet you herself."

I could just imagine how brokenhearted she was. "Sorry to hear that. Will you send her my best wishes?"

He nodded. I took my briefcase and fished out the house keys I'd been given. The house was considered Council territory, technically. A tiny bubble of home away from home. Though fey law and rules still applied, my Council's went as well here. It gave me some comfort, though admittedly not a whole lot of it.

My main hope was no fey would frisk me or, more specifically, do a cavity search. The "safe place" I had my flash drive stuck into was throbbing already from sitting in the car. It was encased in a butt plug. And I was under clear orders to always keep it on my person. Right now it was blank, so it seemed more of a joke on me. But I guessed I had to be used to it when it contained some information. So I did my best to ignore the way it almost rubbed against my prostate. Of course this meant I was constantly horny and frustrated. Not exactly a clear state of mind to do spying in, but what the hell. I needed to get laid fast. Good thing I had that ring on, or my grid would be jumping all over the place with how anxious and pissed I was starting to feel.

"Come on inside," I called over my shoulder. "Leaving you waiting outside like a dog would be barbaric," I added, almost grinning.

He came in, a study in grace as he moved. I decided he was definitely military, or military trained at least. There was no way he was a simple guy, an off-the-street driver. Come to think of it, I wouldn't send a regular guy to pick up an official, would I? But then again, we'd wait for their ambassador with a Council member, the PBI director, and other important institution representatives. Fey didn't bother with that, it seemed. They were making up for it by throwing a reception to parade me like a prize pony in front of everyone, though. So I decided it would be actually better if this Will guy was military. At least he'd be somewhat official.

We stepped inside the house after I unlocked the door. The place looked great: minimalist furniture and design, clean lines all over the place, a lot of glass walls on the first floor, a glass-and-metal staircase going up.

"Awesome place," I said, putting my briefcase down.

"You like it?" Will asked from behind me.

"Looks awesome. This level alone is at least twice the size of my apartment, that's for sure," I added, looking around.

The complex I'd been living in was great, but this was interior-design magazines awesome. Whoever paid for this baby sure didn't go easy on the budget.

"I'll go upstairs, probably where my bedroom is," I said, heading toward the stairs. "Make yourself comfortable. Grab a drink or something. I won't be too long. Just a shower and a change of clothes, and I'll be ready to go."

I felt his gaze drill into the back of my head and tried hard to ignore it. There was something about this guy that got me nervous. Something about the too-studious way he looked at me every time I said something, his focus. Maybe he was just curious about werewolves in general. Or he found me hot and wanted to try his luck.

Which he'd have plenty of, I thought as I found my bedroom and flopped down on the bed. I wasn't used to fey, that was true, so perhaps they were all equally as gorgeous... but man, this guy was beyond delicious-looking. Something about the crisp, elegant lines of his body as he moved. The hairless body I could picture underneath that neat black suit of his... yum. Then again, it might just have been the fact I'd been single for way too long. And that I had a butt plug stuck inside my ass.

I shook my head and looked around the room. My bags were here, neatly piled. My suits were arranged in a nice traveling bag, all set on hangers and pressed to perfection. I decided I'd wear a dark green one with a black shirt and a brighter green tie, plus black shoes and belt. It would go well with those beautiful green eyes of his. Not that I was dressing to match them or anything. I just happened to like green, and that was all.

Half an hour later, I went down the stairs. Freshly showered, hair still damp, and perfect suit on. My ring looked kind of cool with the whole getup, and I sure hoped it worked to hide my emotions as desire tingled through me at the sight of him.

He was sitting on a couch. His long, shapely legs were elegantly crossed and giving me a tantalizing view of his thigh and the curve of his tight ass. He was leaning his arms along the back of the couch. His head tilted to the side as he checked me out slowly from head to toe, then back up again. I couldn't tell what he thought of the view, but reading fey faces was a skill I definitely didn't possess. I might with time. Apparently these guys showed few facial expressions, and faint ones at that. Probably because everyone could read what everyone else felt, so there wasn't need for rudimentary stuff like expressing it with your face and body. Maybe not even with words.

I arranged my tie, a little agitated. "Works for this reception thing that we're going to?"

He nodded once and looked up into my eyes. "You look good enough to eat," he said in a cool tone that ruffled my metaphorical feathers. Then he went back to checking out my suit. Or me.

"Are you hitting on me, Will? I hope it's not part of your job description."

"Oh? Why would you hope that?"

"Because my permanent driver lady would be disappointed on a daily basis to see I'm not interested," I said, trying to smile in a charming rather than lascivious way.

He seemed to search my face for something. "Not into drivers?"

I snorted. "Not if they're lady drivers."

"I see," he said slowly, running his gaze up and down my body.

It made me nervous that I couldn't read much into his tone, expression, or gaze. I realized the actual words could mean anything without hints to what the speaker felt.

Tim had warned me that body language, expressions, and tone were different with fey, and it might throw me off in the beginning. To be honest I had thought he was full of shit at the time because I could read *his* body language, expressions, and tone just fine. Come to think of it, maybe that was because he'd taken them up human style, not fey. We could all read the subtext of what everyone else meant because we used the same ways of expressing our feelings. This guy just... didn't express himself in a way I could read right off the bat. I was hoping to practice my fey-reading skills on him before facing the whole cohort of them, but if things went as they had so far, I was kind of screwed—sadly not in the good way.

"So are you? Hitting on me?" I tried again, focusing on his face and eyes. *Come on, man, give me something to work with, here.*

"Would you report me if I were?" he asked, studying my face and body.

I swallowed. "You're not allowed to hit on me? What, am I outside the law or something? I'd better buy a lot of hand lotion, if so," I muttered dejectedly.

I was hoping for a smile, a grin, a laugh. He just looked up into my eyes. That focus of his was very exciting for some reason. It made me feel like I was the only important person in the world. It was the kind of gaze leaders got from their packs or clans, like the whole universe revolved around them. Like they were the sun, moon, and all of the stars. It was not how pack members looked at a beta, for instance. Nobody had looked at me quite like this. Like I was a much-coveted book, only written in a yet-unknown language. Like they were burning inside to read all of me, page by page.

None of my so-called boyfriends had looked at me like that. Maybe because I never looked at them like that either. I couldn't afford to. As pack beta and Alf's guard, I had to be available to Weiss and Alf at all times, any time. My loyalties could not be questioned or swayed, not even a tiny bit. And reading someone like Will was trying to read me, page by precious page, meant a sort of commitment I didn't dare get into. A sort of connection I couldn't afford. Much less now that my loyalty would be forever put into question. Loving someone would mean being loyal to them. And that could be taken as not being loyal to my alpha first. I would never give anyone reason to doubt my loyalty.

Besides, I was most likely imagining things. Maybe it was a sign of the same kind of curiosity I was experiencing. After all, if I couldn't read him, maybe he couldn't read me. And if that was true, then my ring worked like it was supposed to. Now if I could only get him to talk about reading my emotional grid….

"I'm not supposed to… fraternize while I work for you," he finally said.

What the hell did that mean? That he wanted to, or that he was using the excuse to brush me off? The guy was starting to be irritating. I was suddenly terrified they'd all be this impossible to read, rendering me pretty much blind and dumb. Not much could panic a wolf more than taking away his senses.

"I see," I replied in what I hoped was a cool enough voice. "Should we go, then?"

He nodded and got up, turned for the door, and walked out to the car. Then he opened the back door and stood there with his hat taken off and resting under his arm while he waited. I locked the front door of the house, walked up to him, and got inside the car without wasting time looking his way again.

I was busy enough without trying to figure out some cryptic, admittedly hot fey guy, at least for today. I might squeeze in the time to inspect matters further tomorrow, maybe.

three

THE RECEPTION was being held in one of the protocol rooms at the Fey Court, which was housed in a tall, sumptuous building and looked something like a gigantic Georgian manor. Will opened the limo door for me, then waited dutifully for me to get out before he closed the door and got back into the driver's seat, probably to park that monster of a car. I made a mental note to ask for another car, though I wasn't sure who to ask. I didn't like having a driver, and I sure as hell wasn't the limo type of guy. Maybe I could roll with a top-end car, one that was ridiculously expensive, stylish, but just not an outright limo.

I got into the tall building and followed the line of guards to a huge set of double doors, from behind which some classical music drifted off into the halls. Once I walked through the doors, I took one look around and immediately felt underdressed and ugly—something like high school all over again. It was like having a hump, wearing braces, and sporting holes in your shirt while at a supermodels' party. They were all ridiculously beautiful, slim, and wearing almost the same facial expression—or lack thereof—and I didn't fit in or make sense among them at all. So I put on my smallest polite smile and started shaking hands here and there, introducing myself because I was a take-charge kind of guy. I was kind of looking forward to going back home already.

It took a while but I met and chatted with almost everyone around of reasonable importance. I knew the King himself and his High Court would come in a bit later than everyone else. That was the etiquette. I'd be introduced to them, especially since I'd fluttered about the room already and started schmoozing with everyone worth their salt. And many of them were. These kinds of receptions weren't attended by just anyone, someone told me while I was schmoozing. All of these were important contacts, and an ambassador would get totally hard at meeting them all. I didn't, but then again, I wasn't a diplomat either; it didn't stop me from faking it to the best of my abilities. I was good at schmoozing, cooking, and adapting to any circumstances, that much I knew for sure.

Everyone fell quiet when the King and his trusted High Court entered the room. They walked almost in step, all wearing beautiful suits and large chains around their necks, each with a pendant that showed their rank and order. The King himself had the hexagon with the fleur-de-lis in its center, but I would have known it was him even without it. He looked like the meaner, older version of his son. He wore his hair long, with the power-wielding sign—the braid—hanging over his shoulder and down to his chest. Everyone gave him a small bow, and I did too.

They'd make rounds around the room, going from closest to the King and most influential at Court down to the less interesting members, and then make their way to extras, like me. If what Tim had told me still held true, the Court Historian would walk around with the King and make introductions where they were due. Which was just as well for me because that guy was the only one I actually knew here. His name was Richard Warren, and he was my source inside the Fey Court. I'd never told anyone but Weiss about his identity, but I knew for a fact he'd help me as much as he could without endangering himself. Richard was a weasel that way, but I'd take any kind of help I could get. He was my source, but he always gave me stunted information, only bits and pieces of anything remotely important. Enough to keep me coming back for more, to keep fucking. That was our deal: I fucked him, and he gave me some info on the Fey Court.

Unfortunately, knowing him wouldn't help me make sense of Court members, because he was so very, very atypical on top of being a weasel. He liked to fuck werewolves, or get very fucked by them, to be more exact. Sometimes by more than one at a time, and I had proof of that on tape, something both he and I knew. So I was sure he'd do as much of what I asked as he could without pissing me off outright, for fear of that proof seeing the light of day. But what had him coming back to me wasn't that proof; it was the fucking. I enjoyed that part too. Being single was tough for a healthy thirtysomething guy. While my proof of his debauchery might not have been terribly important before, when I was an outsider, now that I was actually here on fey ground, it weighed a whole lot more. Fucking animals like us was very much frowned upon by high fey society, especially Court members. Richard's wife was some bigwig at Court. He would do his best to keep me reasonably satisfied.

I watched the King and his High Court members making rounds through the room, greeting fey, chatting, and almost smiling. Fey mingling was a very fucked-up thing to see, I decided. There was so little feeling in everything they did, it was impossible to tell if one of them meant what they were saying or not. At least it was impossible for me, a nonreader of emotional grids. It made the whole thing very fucking irritating.

Richard walked over to me while the King was still chatting up someone.

"Welcome, Ambassador Cooper," he said, inclining his head. "We're happy to have you at Court."

I smiled. "Thanks, Mr. Warren. I trust you're well?"

He took a sip of champagne and then nodded. "Yes, thanks. How do you like your accommodations?"

"Charming," I commented. "I'm afraid I'll have to ask you where the restroom is, though."

I looked into his eyes and dared him to say no. We both knew what I was really asking for: some alone time. Not the fucking kind, at least not this time. Richard owed me something. He nodded and led me out of the room, down a corridor, then opened a door and stepped inside a huge bathroom.

I looked around and paid a lot of attention to sounds. I couldn't see or hear anyone around, and I didn't think anyone had followed us. It was as much as I could hope for. I went into the bathroom and closed the door behind me. Speaking could still be dangerous, though. There was no way of knowing where and how their security system had bugs planted.

I smiled at Richard. "Thanks for walking me here. This place is way too big for me to make any sense of," I added, reaching out to shake his hand.

He nodded and reached into his jacket's pocket. I was sure he took out a flash drive, most likely pressed between the apex of his pointer and middle finger. He shook my hand and slipped the drive into my palm. "There's no need to be this formal, Ambassador. Our Court is a large and sumptuous building. It makes sense that an outsider would find it confusing."

I smiled and closed my fist, holding on well to that drive. I knew what I'd have to do with it to keep it safe, but I wasn't looking forward to it. "I think I can make my own way back. I'd hate to keep you from the reception."

He nodded. "Very well. Let me take your glass."

It would have been creepy to leave the bathroom with a glass of anything, true. I handed it over and watched Richard walk out. I couldn't be sure, but I thought he was half hoping I'd ask him to stay. I was horny, and sexing him up would have helped my plan of leaning on him at some point. But it was too dangerous to do that here. It was probably why he didn't ask to stay either. Richard was never shy about lust, but I was pretty sure he was determined not to endanger his position. After all, it was why he had gone to such lengths as giving me this flash drive.

The deal was he'd give me all the financial information on a list of people whose names were suggested by Tim. They were people who could have been involved in the research behind the pseudo alpha hormones Amanda had so generously spread around. The lab tech who prepared them was only applying a formula. Someone else had to be behind the research, and Tim was pretty sure who that someone might be. Especially considering the fey involvement in the pentagram murders Weiss and Tim looked into.

I was looking forward to perusing whatever Richard gave me. But right now there was the important matter of putting the drive in my "vault of secrets." Of all the fucked-up things….

I shook my head and patted the pocket of my jacket. The tiny pack of lube was there. Good. I went into a stall and took my pants off. Then I inserted my hand between my legs and got the butt plug out. It was hours since I'd put it in. My ass throbbed and my hole felt loose. And I was even hornier than just a minute before. Fucking great.

I got up, held the plug in the direction where the water would flush but without touching the actual toilet with it, and flushed a few times until it was squeaky clean. I took out my handkerchief and dried it, then took out the small piece at its base that opened up the secret compartment. There was enough room to stash the drive from Richard beside the drive I had in there. I'd have to copy everything over to that drive later and destroy Richard's drive, just to be safe. But I couldn't do that here. It would have to wait until I got back to my new home. Tim said the plug was made of some sort of weird alloy that confused any tracking device a flash drive might have. I had to hope Richard wasn't trying to flip me the bird. Or if he was, the plug would work as intended. That would make wearing the fucking thing up my ass, literally, a more bearable thought.

Once the drive was in, I stuck the small piece back in to cover the secret compartment, lubed up the plug, and stuck it back inside. I had to rub one out after that because I was hard enough to show by now. It wasn't exactly helping my thought process. It only took a few good strokes, and the orgasm didn't feel like much. But it relieved the pressure behind my eyeballs and released some of the tension from my other significant pair of balls too. I shook my head, used the handkerchief to wipe myself, then threw it in the toilet and flushed until it was gone. I got out of the stall, washed my hands, looked myself over, and decided I was presentable enough to go back out there in the shark tank.

I found Richard easily.

He smiled as I got close to him and offered me a new glass of champagne. "I'll make introductions when His Highness gets to you," the weasel said, blinking slowly. Then he leaned in and whispered, "You and I know each other from a pottery class we both took. Twice a week, Mondays and Thursdays."

I smiled like he'd just told me something adorable and took the glass he offered. Those were the days he went to fuck around with weres at one of the clubs on Council territories. It was a private club, and it took good care of the members. Richard Warren had been unlucky enough to fuck with me accidentally there.

"Pottery class, right," I whispered back and held in the due snort. "We're going to meet and discuss that. Tomorrow, whenever my designated driver takes me for the Court tour I officially requested."

"Around what time?"

I shrugged. "Be there until late afternoon. I'm sure you'll squeeze it in for an old pottery classmate, hm?"

He nodded and looked away. I had to admire his lack of reaction to my thinly veiled threat. Maybe hanging around fey would help me improve my poker face. I was hoping to look over whatever he gave me and ask for anything extra I wanted tomorrow. For that to happen, I needed this damn reception to end.

About an hour later, His Highness finally made his fucking way to me. I did my best to show no feeling as he regarded me coolly and walked over with his cronies. Richard made the introductions, as expected. I made my moderate bow to the King, gave him my proper almost smile, and we chatted about how nice the weather was—despite the fact I hated it, it was too chilly—how nice the reception was—though I was bored out of my mind and hated the uptightness of it all—and how grateful I was for it—I wasn't grateful at all, in reality, but who the fuck cared about the truth, anyway?

Once I dodged that bullet, I emptied my glass of champagne and happily embarked on another. Just as I was about to run for the terrace, hoping for some alone time to breathe properly again, Richard grabbed my arm.

"There's someone else you absolutely must meet tonight," he whispered.

I smiled. "Unless it's Jesus fucking Christ himself, I don't care."

Richard shook his head. "You *must* meet him," he insisted.

I tried to pull away, but he gripped my arm harder, his gaze taking on a strange edge. "You're not listening to me, Bert," he said in a tone that made me listen after all. "You really, really *have to* meet this guy, trust me."

"You're such a social butterfly, Richard. Fine, let's meet this VIP of yours," I said in a bored tone and smiling tightly.

Whoever the hell this guy was, he had to be important. How important could he be, though, if I'd just finished meeting the goddamn King himself?

"Will you give me any clue as to who he is so I can adapt my ass-kissing routine?" I asked between gritted teeth.

Richard nodded almost imperceptibly toward a guy with his back to us. He was wearing a gorgeous uniform, the fey army one: all black, very close fitted, awesomely tailored from the square shoulder pads to the seam of the nicely fitting pants. This guy had light brown hair, and from my estimations, a strong jawline. His hair was all slicked back, though, making a lovely contrast to the uniform's black. From my angle I couldn't see his rank and order, or anything but the hair. Something about it seemed somewhat familiar, but after the probably-five glasses of champagne I'd had and the nerves and stress of meeting so many people whose faces or glances I couldn't read at all, I was beyond caring.

"And who is this hotshot?" I asked Richard.

"Court Interrogator," Richard said almost reverently. "He leads all the high-profile interrogations. His family has been doing so for generations now. Rumor has it his bloodline has more magic than most of us; maybe as much as the King himself, though nobody would officially acknowledge that, of course," he added in a rush.

"Of course," I repeated. "So what, someone from the family takes on the duty once the old one dies of old age or something?"

"Old age is not something the Simses need to concern themselves with. I've heard," Richard whispered, looking around, "that they hold some powerful spells that aren't known outside of the Sims line. A lot of the fey in this room can be... useful acquaintances, but Sir Sims is the greatest jewel of them all," he said, emphasizing *useful*. I guessed what he meant was *dangerous* by the way he stared at me.

Something about his expression sobered me up, made me realize this was important, or he wouldn't insist on it. Whoever this Sir Sims was, he scared Richard. And that made him a person of interest.

"We go over there and you introduce me?" I asked.

Richard cocked his head to the side. "If he doesn't come over in about fifteen minutes, yes. We can't risk him leaving without you being introduced. It's important that he gets your baseline here," Richard muttered.

"That he gets what?"

"Baseline," Richard whispered, and almost made a face at me. "That's how he reads people, from what I heard. He gets a baseline, then works on them until everything rings true."

"How exactly does he work on them?" I asked, frowning, then smoothing my brows in the hope that nobody had noticed.

Richard looked away. "However he deems necessary. Everyone is an open book to him, if he wants to find something out. Everyone, you understand?" he asked pointedly.

I took in his expression. He knew I was Weiss's beta and part of the Council's pack. So did everyone else in this room. Richard knew something else too: I'd been pumping him, quite literally, for information about the Court since we started our "pottering class" quite a few months ago. So he knew or could easily suspect I wasn't as much of an ambassador as I was spy, actually. If this Sims guy was the Court Interrogator, then he was the one deciding if someone was or wasn't guilty of whatever His Royal Highness wanted to charge them with.

Whether Richard was trying to help me make nice with this Sir Sims or to expose me to him, I couldn't tell. Right now it didn't even matter. I was going to meet the guy anyway sooner or later. Might as well be sooner, and I'd have some maneuvering space, hopefully. Or know that I didn't have any, which was also helpful. If Sims could read me now, then I'd know the ring didn't actually work right. And if I were to know that, then I might as well learn about it right now and do my disaster management.

"You seem quite taken with the man," I muttered and was shocked to see Richard's cheeks color. "Oh my fucking God, you are!"

"Shut up!" he snapped at me. "My wife would clip off my balls with a pair of blunt shears if she heard you. Sir Sims is... formidable. Everyone in Court is taken with him. Some are taken *by* him, too," Richard added in a strange voice.

"Lovers, you mean?" I asked, frowning.

"Who the hell knows? They never come back to disclose any information."

"What is he, the male version of the Black Widow?" I asked, chuckling.

Richard stared at me for a moment or two.

"Seriously?" I asked, losing my humor.

He shrugged. "They never come back to disclose any information," he repeated.

"Well, if he has that kind of reputation, why not just refuse him and be done with that? Don't get me wrong. I'm sure he's hot and all, but you all are hot, so there's no shortage of that."

"Power is the ultimate aphrodisiac among fey," Richard recited. "Beauty is not an asset when everyone around is beautiful."

"Hm... power over looks, makes sense," I muttered and took another sip of champagne.

"Besides, you *can't* resist him. Not once he's set his mind on you. The man is relentless," Richard said in a dreamy voice.

"And he can have you charged with anything he feels like. Powerful stimulant to keep him happy, I guess?" I ventured.

"There is always that. But there's more to it. Should anyone resist a powerful Court member like him, unattached and so readily available too because of who he is and what he can do, everyone in Court would assume you have some terrible secret to hide. Because you'd have no other reason to not enjoy his attentions."

I frowned. "Except that you disappear if you do."

Richard blinked. "Jilted lovers are said to be so devastated that they go away for a while to recover from their severely broken hearts."

"Or necks," I muttered, looking around suspiciously.

"His Highness trusts his opinion of anyone and everyone, so he's a supremely correct judge of character," Richard informed me stiffly.

"Of course he is. I'm sure he only makes the nasty ones disappear," I said, looking at the spot the man was in earlier.

He wasn't there anymore.

I looked around but couldn't see him. "Where'd he go?"

"Right behind you," Richard muttered slowly, then smiled. Actually smiled.

I knew what Richard was attracted to: power, wildness, almost abandon when claiming, owning, and occasionally when hurting too, when tormenting. The fact he was taken with this guy was bad news, as far as I was concerned. Judging by what I knew by now, he was most likely a fucking psycho.

"Sir Sims," Richard chirped and bowed slightly. "May I have the honor of introducing the esteemed Ambassador Cooper?"

I turned around in the direction Richard was beaming. *Well, fuck me sideways.* My hand froze as I was reaching out to shake this mystery man's hand. I looked into his eyes, looked his uniform over slowly, then looked back up into his impossible-to-read face, into that penetrating and eerie gaze.

He reached out and grabbed my hand, giving it a slight shake. "Ambassador Cooper, delighted to make your acquaintance."

"Sir... Sims?" I muttered.

"William Matthew Sims," he said and squeezed my hand.

"Well, I... ugh...."

I was royally fucked. I was staring at my driver, Will. My driver was the Court Interrogator. Or vice versa. They were onto me, they had to be. Why else send the fucking lie detector himself to pick me up? I replayed our discussions in my mind. What had he asked? How I felt about traitors? Or just my sister? Fuck, I couldn't remember.

I did my best to relax and focus on his face. The corners of his lips tilted upward ever so slightly, and he leaned in. "And you still look good enough to eat," he whispered. He took a step back, nodded slightly, let go of my hand, and walked away.

My hand hung there in the air for a moment before I remembered I was holding it out. I stuck it into my pants pocket and turned toward Richard. The man was staring at me with a mix of envy, reverence, and a hint of something else—maybe concern?

"I'm pretty sure you got his attention," he muttered. "I'm almost envious."

I blinked slowly. "Does he go… undercover? Or play practical jokes, maybe?"

Richard frowned. "Sir Sims would never stoop to playing practical jokes. And nobody but the King would have the rank to send him on any mission. Why would you ask that?"

I shook my head and smiled. "I'm just curious about your process. I admire fey procedures. They're so elegant, you know? My Council would slap me for thinking that way," I said in a sly voice.

"I get the feeling you'll be seeing quite a lot of these procedures you so admire," he said.

I took another swig of champagne and emptied the glass, trying to ignore the buzzing in my ears that told me someone was staring. Fuck me sideways, I'd gotten the attention of the very one I was supposed to avoid at all costs: the Court Interrogator. And if he had been undercover, then the King himself was the only one who could have sent him. I was so dead.

four

AFTER ANOTHER couple glasses of champagne, I was about ready to head home. The reception was slowly coming to an end, my head was slightly spinning, and I needed a cab. My driver had turned out to be the fucking Interrogator; not likely he'd drive me home now.

I wasn't drunk enough to sway on my feet or trip on my own shoes, but I had that floating feeling when I took a step. So I decided I was light-headed, not drunk or tipsy. Just… light-headed. And I immediately felt guilty because I wasn't supposed to get drunk, or light-headed, in the heart of enemy territory—which I wasn't even supposed to call it.

I walked out with purpose, intent on not letting on to my weakness. Someone at the front doors had to have a number for a cab. This wasn't the Dark Ages, after all, not even in fey territories.

When I got out the front doors, though, there was nobody there. No parking guys, no valets, no nothing. I looked around, close to feeling helpless, and seriously considered going back in and sleeping my light-headedness off on a chair. Fey would take it as in character with my brutish ways, no doubt.

Then I noticed the dark figure leaning against the wall behind me. He had one leg bent, his foot propped up against the wall, the other one holding up his beautiful body. The light brown hair was still perfectly combed back over his head, that piercing green gaze set on me in this unblinking sort of way that made my pulse spike.

"My driver seems to have stiffed me," I mumbled, breathing a little harder than I wanted to.

He smiled crookedly, small smile as it was. "Did he? He must be an unreliable guy, then."

"So it would seem."

We looked at each other for a few moments, and I allowed my mind to wander. In another place, in another time, under different circumstances, I would walk up to him and touch his lips with mine. I would try to touch that lean, strong body, to feel the heat of his skin, to taste that hollow spot right under his ear. In another life, maybe, I would get properly drunk on him, on his taste in my mouth, on his groans as he came, on the way he'd shiver all over as I'd suck him right after that. In another life I could enjoy all of that. I could enjoy all of him. And he would hopefully enjoy all of me, every fucking inch.

"Let me take you home," he said, blinking slowly.

"Would you?" I asked, looking at him and frowning. "Will you?"

He pushed off the wall and walked up to me, that level stare of his all-encompassing. I was defenseless as he stalked toward me with the calm and graceful movements of a ravenous feline. And for a terrible second, I wasn't that sure I wanted to run, to save myself. Something about the intensity he promised seemed tempting. Something about the absolution of a soul-shuddering experience appealed to me in that moment of senseless weakness. But I blinked, he got close enough to me I could feel the heat of his skin nearby, and I woke up from my moment of reverie. The dream vanished like the deep, dark place inside me that it was born from.

This guy would most likely get me killed. I had to push him away, not crawl into his lap.

His eyes seemed to glitter in the night, the streetlight not powerful enough to dispel the shadows in his gaze. Car lights flashed by, time trickled through me but seemed to ricochet off of him. And just like that, my moment of sanity slipped away. Something wild inside me recognized him, the look in his eyes, the ferocious need to conquer and destroy that glowed around him like a halo. He was the taste of destruction, and in that terrible moment, I wanted him. I wanted to wrap myself around his heart like a snake, sink my teeth into it, and take a good chunk of it, if not consume it entirely.

"I will take you," he said in an unwavering voice.

Take me, I thought and smiled. It seemed to freeze him to the spot for a moment. His gaze shifted into something otherworldly, a force beyond my power of comprehension; something thick, dark, and delicious I wanted to bathe in, to breathe in, to taste and enjoy until I'd be close to becoming whatever it was that inspired it.

He stopped one short step away from me, reached out, and ran his fingertips down my cheek. "Who are you?" he whispered softly.

I blinked and frowned. "Bert. I'm Bert."

He smiled, the tilt of his lips looking strange on his face. "Of course you are. Ready to go home?"

I nodded, starstruck. Hell, right now I'd have gone anywhere he wanted me to. The thought startled me and I tried to get my sense back, feeling the sharp edge of danger right at my nape, almost as if scraping the skin there.

"Ready," I muttered and nodded.

He grabbed me around the shoulders, less personal than I was wishing for in my shamefully horny state, and led me toward the parking lot. I was looking out for a limo because in my mind we'd come in one, so we'd leave in one. But there was no limo in sight. I leaned into him, pretending to need more support than I actually needed, and let him lead the way wherever he wanted. I was an expert at that, after all: following someone's lead.

I decided whatever car he'd take me to, it would be perfect. If he was going to kill me, it meant the Fey King was onto me, and I'd die even if I escaped Sir Delicious over here right now. The thought settled my nerves.

We stopped in front of a Bentley, a dark color that might have been navy, might have been dark forest green. He used some keys to unlock the alarm, then opened the passenger's door for me, let me get in, closed the door, then walked over to his side.

I watched him get into the car, watched how that sexy black uniform molded to the outline of his thigh and buttock, how it brought out the round globe of his asscheek. I swallowed thickly and thought about Sudoku. I'd been single for a while now, and wanking off wasn't the same thing as having a real sex life. I hadn't had a real sex life in a while; fucking Richard didn't count, and I hadn't done that recently either. Watching this hot guy brought that up. Brought up all kinds of things. The suit jacket covered up part of what was up, but I didn't bother covering it too much.

The drive was a blur. I didn't pay much attention to where we were going. Truth be told, he could have taken me anywhere; I didn't know my way around this city yet, I had no idea where my home was right now, and I didn't even bother to check GPS on my phone for it.

He put on some music, and the way he drove that car felt like flying off the ground, so I simply focused on enjoying that. Besides, people had seen us leave together. He was an official, and I was notorious as of tonight since the reception was thrown in honor of my arrival. So I was safe. I felt safe in the car of the fiercest representative of my enemy, the Fey King.

It was a while since I'd had champagne like the one they served at the reception. It was almost sweet, tingly on your tongue as you swallowed, and it seemed light and harmless until about the third glass. Then it all came down on you with a vicious need for a fourth one, maybe a fifth, and before you knew it, you were… light-headed. Very light-headed. The heat in the car helped the alcohol permeate my system all the more, and I closed my eyes to rest them for a moment.

"Hey," someone called.

I tried to open my eyes, but they didn't feel like cooperating. I mumbled something, not sure what. The passenger door opened and the cold air of winter rushed in. There was no snow, but it was colder up here. The city was farther north than my sweet home and PBI HQ, so the chill was more biting this time of year. It struck me suddenly it would be Christmas in a month or so, that my sister would soon be dead, and I was away from my pack and alpha, surrounded by fey whose faces I couldn't read. It all felt so depressing, sad, and lonely that I didn't feel like getting out of the car. But I did with a little assistance from my ride home.

He walked with me to the front door, watched me unlock it, and get in. He closed it behind him, walked me up to my bedroom, and said, "Good night," then went down the stairs and out the door.

I wanted to walk down and check the front door, but I was too tired to do it. I decided since it was Saturday already, nobody would break in. Even burglars took the weekend off, didn't they? And I felt relieved I wouldn't have to go into the office tomorrow since it was the weekend. I also thought I should never, ever drink more than a glass of anything around Sir William Matthew Sims… starting tomorrow.

Before falling asleep I embarked on my new bedtime routine: flash drive care. I took out the plug. Then I washed myself and the plug thoroughly and took out the drives. I powered up the notebook Weiss gave me and typed in the consecutive three passwords it asked for. They were long-assed ones too, and I had to memorize them so they'd be written nowhere. Of course someone could still hack into the damned thing if they were determined enough. But it would take a long time, and there was some temperature sensor set up to fry the whole hard drive if it was heavily used. Trying to hack it by running some hardcore decoding program would heat the notebook up for sure. This was as safe as the thing could get, and I was banned from connecting it to the Internet or any other network.

I stuck the flash drive in and looked through the files there. Financial records of the Fey Institute, mostly regarding the prestigious Dr. Vanda van Stromm—that was written in a note from Richard. It was nice of him to tell me what the files contained. I couldn't read Fey. Vanda van Stromm…. She was the lead researcher, director, and the Fey King's lover. The records apparently showed she was funded directly by the High Court and King to research something called MH. There were lots of records tracking timelines, and all of this research had taken place before the first Leader Murders occurred. But I saw no fucking note explaining what MH was.

All I could make out was there were volunteers who gave samples and were paid for it. Richard had their names written down. I recognized some of those names too. Some of them were family members of victims from the first Leader Murders cases, like Mrs. Hemington, mother of Susan Hemington—the first Leader Murders victim. I had a feeling Weiss was going to love these files. And Rick, who investigated the murders with his partner and mate, Travis, would love knowing some of those who conspired to get our vics killed could be charged with something. This was a clear connection, proof of family members being involved in this research. But I needed proof on what this MH actually was too. As usual Richard had given me half of the information I needed. He loved to play that game. And he would probably work the angle of him getting another good fuck for the rest of it. I decided I wasn't complaining. He was a good fuck. I had to see him tomorrow.

I copied the data onto my flash drive, stuck it back into the plug's secret compartment, and powered off the notebook. Then in as much paper as I could I wrapped the flash drive Richard had given me, stuffed it in a glass, and set the paper on fire. I opened up the window and stood to watch until all of the disgusting smells of melted plastic and heated metal made their glorious way into the night. When I thought it was burned enough, I doused the mess in water and let the mix cool.

I'd smash the remains to bits and burn them totally on the grill, first thing tomorrow. For now I decided I'd done enough damage to earn my sleep.

I slathered the plug in lube and got a good amount of it up my ass, then stuck it back in. On the bright side, I'd be nice and ready for any impromptu fucking that might come my way. Hurrah for that, at least. But there was no way anyone was getting to that flash drive. And hopefully starting tomorrow, it would have more info.

I DIDN'T wake up with a headache, not the way I had after drinking in the past. I remembered someone saying only cheap booze gave you headaches, but I highly doubted that was true. Though I was also sure the champagne was nowhere near cheap.

But I did still feel light-headed; not confused, just under the effect of that floating feeling, only it affected my thoughts now rather than my body. My mind kept whirring with ideas that floated about, but I couldn't quite grasp any of them.

This wasn't just a hangover. I was good with a lot more alcohol than I'd had. It was part of my werewolf metabolism, and Weiss had had us all pretty much alcoholproof by the time we were fifteen. The drinking binges us young wolves went on were epic. I could hold my liquor like a pro. So this wasn't the effect of booze.

If I were a betting man, my money would be on this being some kind of drugs. Why anyone would have tried to drug me, I couldn't begin to suspect. Maybe just to see how I'd react. These were fucking fey we were talking about, so I wouldn't put it past them.

I'd requested a tour of my office for sometime today, so I figured my regular driver would make an appearance at some point. Whenever that would happen, Richard had better be there in the office, as we discussed. I wasn't wearing a goddamn butt plug for nothing.

I showered, had two cups of strong coffee, and took the glass with the sloshing mess of that flash drive's remains. It was grilling time, and I had a craving for charred drives this morning. It took some time but finally all there was left of the thing were some twisted bits of metal. The stink was bad, but it wafted away. I took the metal remains of Richard's drive and placed them back in the glass of water with lots of salt mixed in. I covered the top of the glass and dug a nice little hole in the ground, where I stashed the glass, and then I covered the hole up with dirt. Whoever might find this thing, it would be a corroded, fucked-up piece of nothing recognizable. The whole ritual put me in a good mood for some reason.

Then I shuffled through my bedroom, arranging clothes, shoes, and whatnots. I battled a terrible craving for some chocolate mousse, but I promised myself I'd enjoy some later on. Maybe as a reward if the day went well. After all, a man needs something to look forward to while he's wearing a butt plug 24-7. No idea where to get that chocolate mousse, exactly; not like I could buy it from my favorite place anymore. I had to find a new favorite place here on fey ground.

By the time someone was finally at my front door, I was entirely bored. I walked over there smiling, opened it, and stared. "You don't look much like a lady," I muttered.

Sir William Matthew Sims cocked his head to the side. "A good thing, I imagine."

"Depends on who you're asking. I thought my driver would come to pick me up?"

"Change of plans," he replied calmly.

My pulse spiked. "Change of plans?" Just like that? I tried to think back on yesterday. Had I said anything? I'd fallen asleep in his car when he was driving me home. Had I said anything weird before falling asleep, though? Had I in any way endangered myself, my Council, or my pack?

I blinked slowly and looked him over. There weren't any explicit lines of tension in his body or expression, but if there were, would I even be able to notice? Would I know that I was in danger, if I was? Fucking fey and their body language.

"What's the new plan, then?" I asked, playing with my ring, trying my best to not seem nervous.

Maybe he could read my emotional grid, maybe he couldn't. But if I displayed signs of being nervous, which he would most definitely have an easier time reading than I might have reading his, it might tip him off something was going on. Goddammit, pack politics involved force and conviction, not subtlety and dissimulation.

"There have been some threats," he suddenly said. "We won't go into details. Whoever threatens an ambassador sanctioned and welcomed by the King is committing an act of subversion."

"I need extra security, is that what you're telling me?"

He shrugged. "I'm a better bet than a regular driver. My face is well-known. So is my rank and function. Nobody would dare go against me. Against you, either, while you're under my protection."

I waved a hand for him to come in, and once he did, I closed the front door. He walked into the living room and sat on the couch he'd sat on yesterday.

I followed, sitting across from him. "Don't I get a say in my own protection?"

His gaze shot to mine. "Have any complaints against spending time with me?"

It hit me that I couldn't really say so, even if I did. It would seem like I had something to hide, wouldn't it? Fuck me sideways, fey and their politics. I missed my pack already.

"It's not that," I said, shaking my head. "I'm just worried. What kind of threats would warrant me the protection of a high-profile figure such as you? I'm sure you understand my concerns."

"I do. Just to make it clear, I volunteered to take you under my… wing, if you will. The Court decided I would be the best option, since we already knew each other, since we connected yesterday."

Had he reported all the events of yesterday? Of course he would have. I nodded slowly, regretting that first glass of champagne at the reception. I had been nervous and alcohol had been so readily available. Today the game was over, though. It was survival of the fittest. I felt it in the pit of my stomach. The Court had decided he was the best spy to plant into my life since I already knew him now, and I might grow to trust him. My best bet was to make him think I was doing just that. In bed with the enemy, as it were. Though not quite that literally—a shame.

I nodded. "Sounds good to me. Could I see these threats for myself, though?"

"It's an internal Court issue of security. As an ambassador you have access to the factual information, not the evidence."

"I get it," I said, although I didn't.

It sounded like utter bullshit to me. The kind of thing I'd say if I had nothing to show for my claims, maybe. If they were making up reasons to stick me with Mr. Question Mark here, then someone suspected I was bullshitting them too. The more I fought it, the more suspect it would look.

"So you'll give me the tour of Court and my new office, then?" I asked trying to sound calm.

"With pleasure. The placing of your office has been... adapted too."

A cold shiver traveled down my spine. "Closer to... yours? To be safer?"

He smiled chillingly. "Exactly. Anyone daring to provoke me would provoke the entire Court and the King himself. No safer spot than close to me."

"Those threats must have hit a nerve," I muttered, feeling honestly worried. "We didn't expect this kind of... hostile reaction."

"Don't hold it against fey in general. There are some purists, some radicals, as within any community. Don't let that color your view on us all, though."

"Of course not, Sir Sims," I stated, smiling.

"Call me Will, please."

"Will. And I'm Bert, then."

He nodded.

I was royally fucked.

five

I KNEW something was wrong the moment we got out of his car. Everyone in the Court's parking lot looked at me funny. Not the "Oh, new guy!" kind of funny. The "I don't trust this creature" kind of funny. And when fey gave you looks you could actually make sense of as an outsider, you knew shit was piling up on you a mile high.

I fell in step with Will. "Any particular reason everyone is giving me the evil eye?"

"You must be imagining it."

The reply came too lightly. He seemed as relaxed as ever, his perfect hair all in order as if cemented in place. Maybe it was a hangover or the aftereffects of whatever drugs I was given, but I was pretty fucking sure everyone was giving me the evil eye.

"Anything out of the ordinary happen since last night?" I ventured.

"Out of the ordinary?"

We passed yet another control point. It must've been the third one we'd gone through since entering the Fey Court building. My diplomatic immunity didn't save me from my ID and credentials being checked every time. I suspected those threats hadn't been made against me as much as against them because of me. They sure did seem to act like it.

When we were finally inside the actual building, Will stopped walking. "We'll make a quick stop at our official medical unit. I'd like your blood work done, if that's okay."

My heart froze midbeat. "My blood work? Why?"

"No need to be worried. I just want to be sure you weren't slipped anything last night at the reception. There have been threats, as I've told you."

"Threats you won't tell me about," I deadpanned. When it became clear he wouldn't comment on it any further, I sighed. "What if I refuse to have my blood work done?"

The corners of his lips lifted up ever so slightly. "I wouldn't advise it, Bert."

The fine hairs on my nape stood up. "You can't actually make me, can you? Diplomatic immunity, remember?"

He stuck a hand in his pocket. "It may not seem like it right now, but trust me; I have your best interests at heart."

I snorted. "Right. My best interests at heart."

His gorgeous green eyes seemed to shine brighter for a second, and my ring became hot on my finger.

"You will have your blood work done right now and without further protest. You will remember nothing of protesting against it or being unwilling to cooperate," he said in a strange voice that seemed to echo.

For a moment or so, I became disoriented. I shook my head and looked around. I was in the building of the Fey Court. My name was Bert Cooper, and I was the Council's first ambassador in the Fey Kingdom. I had a sister, Tricia Cooper, who I now hated, being held in PBI custody. Everything seemed right in my head. But Will had almost certainly done something weird just now.

I frowned. "What were you saying?"

"We're going to get your blood work done."

"Blood work? Yeah. Yeah, my blood work. Let's do that."

He smiled and led the way. I knew I had to do this right now but couldn't quite grasp why. My ring was hot on my finger, which I suspected meant some magic had been done somewhere around me. Had it been Will? My head hurt when I tried to think about it harder. I put my hand to my temple, rubbing with my fingertips for a moment.

"Headache?" he asked as we entered a set of white doors.

I shrugged. "I think it's the champagne from last night. I felt kind of funny after I got home."

"That's why we have to have your blood work done. To make sure everything is okay."

Something about it didn't add up, but I felt I simply had to let it go. At least for now. A couple of fey nurses came in, and Will talked to them in their language.

I understood none of it. I became immediately suspicious of the whole situation. But my head started throbbing like hell so I tried to clear all thoughts away. They took my blood and gave me a funny Band-Aid with smiling faces on it to cover the small puncture wound where the blood was extracted from.

"I'm pretty sure these are meant for kids," I commented, staring at it.

Will gave me a small smile. "Pretty cute, though. I like how it contrasts with your skin tone."

"You have strange tastes, then. So where are we going now?"

"My office. I mean our office. Yours was arranged inside of mine."

My dick got a really kinky message out of that and stirred to life. I inhaled and exhaled slowly, trying to get my X-rated mind under control. The butt plug wiggling inside me at every step didn't exactly help me focus on non-sex-related things.

"So how about that tour around Court? Is it too risky right now?"

"I have one small issue to resolve at the office. Then I'll gladly give you a tour," he said in that terribly polite voice of his.

I was starting to dislike that tone. It struck me as either fake or intentionally confusing. People generally went that way when they had something to hide. When they were trying to bullshit someone, maybe. String them along, catch more flies with honey type of thing. That gave me pause, but I couldn't think of any one good excuse I could use to somehow get out of this situation right now.

I took surreptitious looks at everyone around us as we went up a few levels to Will's office. Fey at Court either ignored us entirely or cast strange looks my way. Now I was sure I wasn't imagining it. They were giving me weird looks. What the fuck was going on here? What was I missing?

When we finally got into Will's office, a lavish affair that looked more like some president's office, he closed the doors behind us and gestured toward a chair. I took the hint and sat down. He went round the antique-looking desk and sat in his ornate chair. He crossed his hands in front of his chest and leaned back in the chair, fixing me with his gaze.

"You have a sense of something being amiss?"

I discreetly played with my ring, feeling it heat up again. "Definitely."

"Are you scared?"

Trying to confirm his reading of my emotional grid, or taking wild guesses to make some sense of something that didn't add up?

I shrugged. "Not really."

"Annoyed, perhaps?"

I smiled. "What's this about, Will?"

He leaned back farther in his chair and crossed his long, lean legs. His knee peeked out just above the top of the desk, and I couldn't look anywhere else for some reason.

"There was something wrong at the reception last night. A few people reported feeling strange this morning. People who attended the reception."

Okay... kind of out of left field a bit, but I could run with that. "I felt weird this morning too. I felt weird last night, in fact. I know for a fact I didn't drink enough to get drunk, yet I felt like I was. If I would've been, this morning would have been a headache-fest. It wasn't."

He nodded once. "Consistent with what has been reported. I have reason to believe there was some attempt at endangering your life, or at least your reputation last night. Something must have gone wrong, though. Drinks might have been spiked. Maybe more than initially intended, or with some other substance than initially planned. I've had attendants have their blood work done this morning, to find some common substances."

Well, shit. "This job I took on will be a lot more demanding than I originally thought, won't it?"

"I'd dare say it will prove a lot more demanding."

"What makes you say that? The threats?"

He smiled slightly. "Let's go back to last night for a moment. What did you have?"

"This feels very much like an interrogation," I commented, trying to suppress the shiver that thought caused.

"In a sense it's just that. You might not think much of what happened, Bert. I wouldn't blame you. But substances slipped in drinks at an official reception that the King himself attended is no small matter at Court. I'm sure you'll realize the weight of it, if you contemplate things carefully."

I nodded, suppressing a chuckle that itched to erupt. "You're saying someone drugged part or all of the attendants last night? Someone slipped through all your numerous layers of security and got *something* in the drinks His Highness could have consumed?"

"It's exactly what I'm trying to say, yes."

"Crap. That can't look good on anyone's résumé, can it?" I muttered.

"It's a good thing we did your blood work this morning too. Whatever substances were slipped in the drinks, if they show in your blood as well, they will further clarify your state as of last night."

I frowned. "What exactly is that supposed to mean?"

He got up from the desk and crossed his hands at the small of his back, then started pacing about. "Of course I witnessed myself how incapacitated you were. My initial assessment was you were drunk. But then you needed help getting up the stairs, and you didn't smell like a drunk person would. Warning bells went off for me right then. But I hoped things wouldn't be too serious."

My heart started racing. "And yet they proved to be?"

He turned his back to me and walked toward the large windows. Sunlight streamed in, falling around his silhouette and giving him an almost saintlike glow. I couldn't deny how attracted to him I felt. Maybe I was lucky things stood as they did. There would never be anything between him and me, I was sure. Someone of his rank and importance wouldn't stoop as low as actually getting together with a Kingdom outsider.

He might play me if he sensed my weakness, though. I was entirely sure using whatever charms he had at his disposal wasn't new to him. It was nothing new to me either. I'd breezed through what needed to be done in order to get things solved, in order to find things out... like with Richard Warren, for one. And none of that felt personal. In a way I wasn't the one doing any of that. I wasn't present. And he most likely felt the same way about jobs. I was a job, clearly.

"What aren't you telling me?" I said as calmly as I could manage.

He didn't turn around. "Things will get complicated starting today, Bert. I'm not sure I could guess just how complicated, even if I tried. I hope, really hope, you'll take this chance to tell me anything you might think I should know."

My stomach clenched tight. "In your capacity as my bodyguard?" I said in a lame attempt at levity.

"In my capacity as my Kingdom's faithful subject and my Court's Interrogator," he said, turning around slowly.

"So this is an interrogation after all."

He shrugged ever so slightly. "Let's call it an open discussion for now, shall we? I hope it is, Bert. An open, honest discussion."

I got up from the chair and walked toward him. "Whatever the fuck is going on, it's you who knows and isn't sharing here, sweetheart. So if there's anyone who needs to spill his beans, that would be you."

There was a knock on the door. Will called out, "Come in."

A pretty little wisp of a fey woman walked in wearing the female version of the fey military uniform. Her eyes were bright and her complexion shiny, her hair neatly tied in a tight knot at her nape. She was carrying some folder she gently deposited on his desk. Then she turned for the door and said a monotone "sir" as she exited.

My gaze was fixed on that folder. My fingertips itched and burned with desire to reach out and open it, see what it contained. I couldn't help feeling there was something major I was missing.

"Will?"

He looked at the folder too without moving. "There are trying times ahead of us, Bert. Let's agree on something right now."

His clear gaze settled on mine, the force of it leaving me breathless for a moment.

"Sure," I replied without having the most basic clue about what he meant or what the hell was going on. "What's that?"

"It's safe to say I'm your only friend at Court, if you agree you have any."

I frowned. "O-kay…."

"I'm your only friend at Court, then. Agreed?"

I nodded, growing more worried by the second.

"And as your friend, I'd have your trust and you'd enjoy mine. Would you say that's correct?"

"If we were friends, yes. Sure."

He walked toward me slowly, his hands still at his back. For a moment I contemplated stepping out of his way, though I could see no outward sign of aggression or violence in his demeanor. But I was a beta in my pack, even if it was the beta of a ballsy alpha like Weiss. My natural instinct was to bow to someone's intense vibe of authority. And without a doubt right now Will exuded shitloads of those vibes. My heart was pounding in earnest, the plug inside my ass making me tingly all over and lusty.

"Say you needed a friend at Court," he whispered when he was but a breath away from me. "Say you needed one desperately. What would you be willing to do to gain such a friend?"

I swallowed hard. "Depends."

"On?"

"Loads of things. How much I liked that person, how badly I needed their friendship, to what end."

He chuckled. "I like your thinking, Bert. I find I like you, all in all. And you know what?"

"What?"

He leaned in even closer, rubbing his lips against the shell of my ear. "I think you like me too. Do you?"

I nodded because I couldn't help myself. And I was hard at this point, so there was no use in denying it.

"Good. I'm glad to hear that," he said, stepping away. His hands had never left the small of his back. "Now a lot depends upon what's written in that file. And upon my direct testimony. Should the file say there are traces of the drugs from last night in your blood, it would prove you'd been a victim of the attempt just like everyone else. My testimony would show just to what degree you were affected."

"And why would that be relevant?"

"Events took place last night. Unfortunate events. Decidedly unfortunate."

"You mean aside from the guests being drugged?"

He nodded. "Let's say your life hung in the balance. And let's assume how much of a friend I decide to be to you could either make or break your case."

A cold chill went down my spine. "What the fuck are you saying?"

He smiled. "I think you know. Don't you, Bert?"

"No, I fucking don't!" I shouted and just made a go at him.

I'm not sure what I was thinking. I don't think I was thinking. Rage just exploded inside me and then outward, controlling my body. I wanted to slap that smug look off his face. I wanted to mess up his hair, at least; I was almost convinced it would annoy him more than a slap to the face.

But I didn't. He easily spun me around and planted me face-first against a wall, my arm twisted to keep me in place. I growled, the loud sound booming against the walls of his office.

"Yes," he said directly against my ear. "This is the temper I expected of you. This is the intensity you were supposed to display. Yet I can't read it in your emotional grid. So tell me, growling beauty, what is it that's messing with my reading?"

I kept growling for a moment so I wouldn't seem shocked silent by the question. I'd screwed up in two fucking days. In two fucking days I'd given away the fact I had some sort of antireading thing going on, which would mean I had something to hide. And this was most definitely not the right time to be discovered as a liar.

"What's going on? What do you want?" I asked, trying to tone down the rising panic.

"I'm sad to say the Fey King is dead. He was assassinated sometime between last night and the early hours of this morning. Until matters are cleared up, everyone with opportunity is a suspect. Newcomers, and outsiders to boot, are at the top of everyone's list, as you might imagine."

The blood froze in my veins. "You're shitting me. The King is dead?"

"Very much so."

"Maybe it was natural causes," I said halfheartedly.

"It wasn't. Are you calm enough to discuss this like adults now?"

I nodded and he let go of me, stepping back. He walked over to the edge of his desk and perched on it.

"You're telling me I'm a suspect in the Fey King's assassination?" I asked in a faint voice.

"Exactly. So as I was saying earlier, you do need a friend right now. You need me as your friend. What are you willing to do in order to get that?"

My stomach tightened painfully. "What would you have in mind?"

He smiled.

six

"THINGS WILL get very tense around Court," Will said, still perched on the edge of his desk. "There's no clear heir to the throne, no officially designated successor. The High Court will be in an uproar to come up with the final list of proposed names of candidates to ascend to the throne."

"You're saying there's going to be one hell of a power struggle."

"In a way, yes. But it won't resemble power struggles as you might know them."

"Oh?"

"We do things differently," he said by way of explanation. "It will affect me more than it will you."

"How exactly will that affect you?"

He almost smiled. "The prime factor for fey power is their magic."

I leaned back against the wall, setting my hands in my pockets. "And you're rumored to have the strongest magic. Will that make you a contender?"

"Not a willing one, Bert. But once one's name makes it on that list, if you're chosen by the Kingdom's crisis assembly, the High Court, in situations like these… you don't get much say in it, if your Kingdom calls you to defend its interests."

I snorted. "You can simply say no, though. Can't you?"

He got up and started pacing around his desk, very focused on the admittedly interesting carpet. "And what would the Kingdom think about a prominent fey figure who turns down the rare honor of becoming King?"

"That the fey isn't interested?"

"In the highest role in the Kingdom? It wouldn't be conceivable."

"Yet you don't sound keen on becoming King."

"I'm not keen."

"Why wouldn't you want to be King?"

"I'm sure you've learned something of fey culture, Bert. But I see that not much. No, don't glare like that, I wasn't looking to offend you. The fey circle of power is a dangerous place to be in. The further from it you are, the safer you and your loved ones might be."

"But you're the Interrogator. You're inside that circle already, aren't you?"

He looked up, those beautiful green eyes haunted. "Yes and no. My children are safer being the children of the Interrogator than those of the King. But they're not that safe either way."

I blinked a few times. "Children? You have kids?"

He nodded. "I know you don't, but you've been the guard of your alpha's kid until recently. I think you understand that a father would go to any lengths to protect his children."

"Well, not any father," I mumbled. "Your late King didn't particularly shine in that department."

Will smiled, a small, sad smile that made my heart thump. "He didn't shine in many departments. I'm not looking for excuses for him, but being King, and having the High Court around you… it changes you in visceral ways that are entirely out of your control. The weaker you are at heart, the more it changes you."

"But the High Court doesn't have to be convened at all times to influence the King," I dared say, knowing it was clearly a fishing expedition at this point. If this discussion kept going the way it was, I was hoping I could glean some info about the High Court, at least for my own understanding, if not for Weiss's and the Council's.

Will clasped his hands at the small of his back and walked closer to me. "No, it doesn't. But once convened, it's quite difficult to actually dissolve. The members must all be willing to dissolve it, which, as you might imagine, is like a group of children willingly giving up a bag of sweets."

"Wouldn't the King be able to dissolve it, anyway?"

"Could the King think to take such a direct stand against the High Court? Sure. But would the King want to do that? Keep in mind, Bert, the order of fey power is: High Court circle, King, High Court members, lesser Court members, population at large."

"You forgot to mention where you fall in that list," I supplied sweetly.

"It depends on the Interrogator of the moment. I dare say I'd fall somewhere before the High Court members as individuals. But not before them as a collective, as circle. And they do work as circle in most, if not all cases."

"Are you telling me that the High Court is undoubtedly stronger than the actual King?"

"As a collective? Yes, without a doubt. And once you're King, you do fall in their power, willingly or not."

"Are you afraid of the High Court, Will? Is that what you're saying?" I asked, frowning.

He looked away. "I refuse to endanger my children any more than I do as the Interrogator. Becoming who I am today was not so much a choice as the only alternative. I'd save my children from the same situation, if I could."

"But how would they be in danger?"

He sighed, actually looking tired for a moment. "I had eleven brothers and sisters, all older than me. Some didn't possess enough magic; their mothers had been weaker than those of the rest. They were… expelled from the line."

"Like renounced?"

He shook his head, not elaborating. "Out of the remaining ones, a couple were too willful to be… guided by my father. They too were expelled from the line."

"Shipped off to Alaska? Expelled how?" I tried again.

"Those remaining who were considered apt began the training. It's a private version of the Fey Academy, only failing a certain amount of times results in…."

"Being expelled from the line?" I supplied, starting to get pissed off at the whole thing.

Will looked over toward the window, his expression carefully blank. "Those of us who survived the training had to duel to prove who's stronger. The losers were also…."

"Do you mean killed? Is that how your brothers and sisters were 'expelled from the line'?"

He nodded once, almost like a twitch. "The most dangerous thing for a fey family is a kid who has some abilities and a mind of their own. You have to learn to balance things in order to survive. And then when you do, your predecessor tends to be… expelled from the line as well."

"What the fuck is this, the ultimate level of hell? So once you, the skilled and not too willful successor, were secured, your father was killed? Is that what you're telling me?"

"Yes."

"And who the fuck killed your father, if all of your brothers and sisters were dead by that point? The King? The High Court?"

"I did," he informed me, looking into my eyes.

A chill traveled down my spine. Contemplating this fucked-up family chemistry, my and Tricia's story was like a walk in the park. Screw treason and metaphorical backstabbing; these guys went on a killing spree within their family home.

"So you have kids and would like to not kill them off one by one, then be killed by the one deemed fit enough to be your successor in the Sims line and in the Interrogator position. Can't you just send them off with their mom or something?"

"They have different mothers. And they could never go against the fey tradition of the Interrogator line. They would be hunted down wherever they went. If they refused following tradition, they would be killed. This is how things are done. How they have always been done, how they will always be. I can't change fey culture and society on my own. But I can try to save my children and possibly myself, if I can."

"And where do I come in in all of this?" I asked, honestly mindfucked by the whole story. "How can I be useful to you, so much so that you'd blackmail me into offering you that help?"

"Now, now, Bert. I didn't blackmail you in the least. All I did was mention you could use a friend right now. And I'm explaining to you why it is I could use one as well."

"Okay, let's assume I believe the why. I still don't get the how."

"Whoever it is who assassinated the King at this point did so intending to pin the murder on you, I think. You were lucky to attract my attention, and therefore be in my company. If you hadn't been, this discussion would have taken place in completely different circumstances. Very unpleasant ones."

I nibbled on my lower lip, contemplating possible scenarios. They all ended in me getting arrested, possibly tortured, and found guilty of killing their precious King. Not a pretty picture to contemplate.

"How exactly did I get that lucky, though? Why were you the one to pick me up? Why did you pose as my driver? Official mission?"

He shook his head. "Of course I had no way of anticipating what would happen. My initial plan was to get closer to you on a personal level. Then maybe try to work out a plan that would involve you taking my children into your alpha's custody."

"You were going to fuck me into helping your kids? You only have to ask, man. Don't go to such lengths," I snapped, irritated.

"Going to such lengths would have been a pleasure, Bert. Don't doubt that. I took an interest in you a while before you actually came here. It's why I was your driver. It's why you were in my company last night after you left the reception. And it's why you won't be blamed for the King's assassination."

"And I would show my appreciation by scratching your back too, I take it? Don't get me wrong, I'd love to not be pinned for a murder I think we both know I didn't commit."

"I'm pretty sure you didn't assassinate the King last night, yes. But if it would serve the Court to say that you did, they'd waste no time in saying so. And we execute outsiders, in case you were wondering. Especially King killers."

"You've had incidents like these before?"

He answered with a small shrug. I got the sinking feeling Fey Kings didn't often die of old age. This place was way worse than I'd expected, and I'd expected it to be tough.

"So what you're saying is that you've already done me a favor. Which is why I'm only a suspect for the assassination, and you'd clear me off the list entirely with testimony to go with my blood work."

He nodded.

"And as a token of my gratitude, I would do… what, exactly?"

"You would go back to report to your alpha and Council about what has happened here. Until the new King is crowned, there won't be much use for a Council ambassador, anyway."

"And your kids would somehow secretly accompany me back home?"

"And subsequently be taken into Weiss's custody."

"The reason why you'd trust a virtual enemy with your kids would be...." I lifted both eyebrows and looked at him.

"I'm sure Timothy would keep them safe. And Weiss is under Timothy's influence, is he not?"

I frowned. "You make Tim sound like some sort of drug. I assure you Weiss is under no one's influence. He might be convinced of this or that by different people he trusts, but he's nobody's puppet."

"And he is a father too," Will added with what I could imagine was hope. "I have good reason to believe he's no monster."

"What reason would that be?"

"Nothing to concern yourself over. I will make sure that you get out of the Kingdom unscathed, if you promise to do the same with my children. Take them to Weiss and make sure they're safe once they get there. Please," he added, looking like he was about to break into a million pieces.

It struck me then, clear as crystal, there was at least one major thing he wasn't telling me.

"Why wouldn't you accompany us back?" I asked, pushing away from the wall and walking closer to him. "That way you can be sure of their safety. And yours too."

He looked out the window again. "It was never about my safety."

"You plan to stay behind? Are you out of your mind? How would it look if you send away your children and they show up in Council territories? You'd be considered a traitor and possibly get pinned for the murder yourself."

"A traitor and a monster who has killed his children," he said flatly. "As I've supposedly killed other fey over the years, you see. Lovers I've taken right from fey imprisonment, sometimes, because powerful fey can get away with a lot of things."

Well, shit. "You're telling me you're a serial killer, and this is a strange attempt at saving your kids to get some sort of moral pass?"

"Of course not. Those I supposedly killed are safe and sound, outside of the Kingdom forever. I have killed because I've had to before becoming Interrogator. Also prisoners during interrogation, that's true. It's part of the process, if they resist."

"You mean you've been smuggling out fey? Those ex-lovers who disappeared...."

He nodded. "There's something very, very wrong about the Court. It has been so for a while now. Things need to change. And I will do my part because my father, and his father before him, were also responsible for things as they are today. I'm responsible too. I won't flee. But I want my children safe."

"Very admirable and all, but what about everyone else's kids?" I shot back. *A cheap shot*, I vaguely heard myself thinking, but I couldn't help it.

He looked at me and smiled. "I agree. But they're in less danger, as they're not the children of rebels or traitors. And I can't replace all fey parents in the Kingdom. Each must fight their own battles. I'll fight mine. Trying times are coming, but my children will be safer. And will have a brighter future."

"Rebels or traitors? What the fuck are you planning here, Will? A revolution?"

I perceived him in a different way immediately. Was he a brave soldier, wearing his gorgeous uniform, willing to fight and sacrifice himself for his Kingdom? Or was he simply a selfish traitor, rebelling against authority because he didn't like the direction things were going? And who was fit to decide what the right decision was? The Fey Court didn't seem to mind things as they were, or they would have said or done things. Fey by and large didn't seem to have an issue with their King and Court. But then again, they were on the outside of the power circle, I had to admit. And things always looked different from the outside. Tough decisions always seemed like atrocities, and collateral damage like unpardonable crimes. Yet these things sometimes ended up benefiting those who resented them.

I got a flashback of the reception last night. In my mind I saw everyone dressed up so elegantly, having impeccable manners, faces void of expression, eyes void of emotions. Could they have been worried and agitated? They might as well have been, without me ever having a clue. Maybe the whole freaking fey society was agitated and displeased. Who the hell was I to judge? I was tempted to hate rebels on principle because all of them would forever overlap with my image of Amanda and her little sect, of my traitorous sister and her mysterious allegiances.

But not all rebels were after mere destruction. Some hoped to tear something down in order to rebuild a better, more stable structure. They were agents of change. I personally resented it and feared it in my heart of hearts. I couldn't help but like the idea of it while it affected someone who was more or less an enemy of my pack and Council, though. The Fey Kingdom was still an enemy of ours, as far as I knew. And whatever hindered their plans benefited ours. Their Interrogator going rogue and working against the High Court and whatever new King they'd want to appoint would work in our favor. I decided it was a good move to help Will however I could, more so since I was helping myself right now by doing it.

"Can I ask you something?"

He blinked slowly, as if knowing what it would be before I said it. I hoped he didn't actually know.

"Did you kill the King?"

He looked away, glancing out the window. I couldn't tell what it was that he was so taken with. The sky? The moving clouds? The trees swaying in the wind?

"Do you ever consider the power of the wind, Bert?" he said in a calm, beautiful tone. "It's something you can't see directly, yet its presence leaves marks that are impossible to overlook. Common sense tells you these marks were caused by the wind. The way leaves dance in the air, the way the breeze touches your face, the way birds float on invisible currents. It drives boats over the seas for such huge distances. It powers up mills, offers us alternative sources of electrical power. And there is so much more it does that we're not even aware of. Effects of its harsh or benevolent will abound all around us. Wind does so much, yet we can't see it. We can't positively prove it the culprit of things we may or may not like. It's common sense that it had a hand in all of these things. An invisible, powerful hand formed by many individual factors and forces. A hand that will never be slapped or petted, regardless of the outcome."

Sunlight glinted in his eyes right then, his light complexion seeming to glow in that light. His expressionless face was that of a marble statue, an angel or a devil carved with much attention to detail, yet little knowledge about its true mechanics and subtle inner workings. This would be the statue standing over the grave of the former Fey King, and possibly of the entire Court. And as statues standing over graves did, he scared and fascinated me. I wanted to crawl to him on my hands and knees, to rub my cheek against his toes—the image made me shudder.

There was something so intense about him, and it made the beta nature in me shiver and submit with delight. It scared me how much he could affect me without even trying to.

"You're the wind in the King's assassination," I whispered.

He didn't reply either way. Just kept staring out that window, seemingly transfixed by the clouds. I looked up there too, allowing the image to take over my mind, to mute my thoughts for a few moments. "Are you this wind of change on your own?"

"The wind is not one, but many. A collective force that you can't stop."

"Well, the King is dead. Now what?"

"The next obstacle that must be removed now is the High Court."

"And once that's gone too?"

"New High Court members elected by the Kingdom. Then a new King. A new, cleaner power circle. I'm hoping it will bring a wave of positive change. And I'll have my children free by then. Maybe even myself, if things go well."

"So it's not an altruistic move in the name of your people?"

"Nobody elected me their representative. I'm not making choices in their name. Only in mine and my family's."

"But you made it sound as if others share your views."

"Many do, I imagine. Would they do anything to convey that message? Not unless forced to."

"You feel you're forced to?"

"I know I am," he replied, then smiled a little. "It's either Court duty, or the lives of my children. That, to me, is an astoundingly easy choice."

"Funny thing," I muttered. "You were talking about wind earlier. It made me think about clouds. We look up at the clouds, always feeling like they're slipping away, leaving us behind as they elegantly float over other cities, other lives. But they don't actually move much, do they? We're the ones slipping away, leaving them behind. Are you looking to slip away from your kids? Get rid of the competition, maybe?"

"I would never be apart from my children if I could help it. And I'd sooner die than allow any harm to come to them ever again."

I felt the heat of him before I turned to actually see him. He'd taken the few steps between us and was now standing right in front of me. He was staring at me with his lucent green eyes without blinking, his pupils blown out, darkening his gaze, his presence, the nature of his intent. His almost unnatural beauty shined in a way different from anyone else's.

The many parts of him clicked together in one picture, then quickly seemed to reassemble in some other shape or size, bringing out lighter or darker shades of something equally beautiful and fascinating, I realized. Right now I thought I could watch forever these subtle changes in the mosaic that was him. That I would never tire of observing minute changes in the general shape he was. I had never been this intrigued and terrified by anyone, ever. And I didn't want the feeling to stop. Not yet. Maybe not ever.

I wondered if he was going to kiss me. The moments grew long and tormenting as I kept contemplating that idea. I wanted him to kiss me. I wanted him to nip my collarbone, scratch the back of my thighs as he took me from behind. I wanted to nibble his inner thigh before taking him deep into my mouth. I wanted to rip off those perfect buttons on his uniform, to tear them off with my teeth. But I didn't reach forward to kiss him myself. I just stood there and waited.

And after a longer while than I thought could be quantified, he smiled and stepped back.

"So what say you, Bert? Will you do me the favor I've asked?"

"If you can guarantee me safe exit without any remaining suspicions concerning any possible involvement of mine in the assassination, then I'll take your kids with me and discuss your request with Weiss. But I can't say what he'll want to do. He probably won't have your kids killed, on that I agree. But I'm not sure he'd go so far as giving them shelter under his and the Council's authority. That might start an actual war between the Council and your Kingdom."

"It wouldn't. The Court would never sanction any strategic moves while a new King isn't crowned and the matter of the previous one's assassination isn't settled."

"Can you be absolutely sure about that?"

He nodded.

"Either way, I can't speak for my alpha and what he'll decide or agree to. So you have to understand I'm not guaranteeing their safety beyond taking them into Council territory. For that I think you should speak to Weiss yourself," I added hesitantly.

I didn't want to sound eager, though I was. For two reasons it gave me a shameful thrill to steal away the Court Interrogator and lure him to our side. One, I did like the guy in a way I hadn't liked anyone else until now. And two, it would be a pretty impressive achievement on my part as an agent of the Council. Considering my spying days were going to end pretty soon, I had to come back home with something good enough to make up for screwing up the getting-lots-of-info part.

He looked at me differently and gave me a small smile. "I find you're even more interesting than I'd initially given you credit for, Bert."

A small measure of hope took root in my heart. All was not lost. Not yet.

SEVEN

"WOULD YOU take me in as a trophy, Bert?" he asked, smiling oddly, a sort of indulgent look in his eyes.

I wasn't going to outsmart him, that was for sure. Luckily I didn't think I had to.

"I wouldn't be taking you in at all. You and your kids would simply accompany me. I'm sure you can find something of value to offer me so I'll be willing to go that way. And then you'd find something of value to offer Weiss and the Council to give you guys, say, political asylum?"

"You've thought of everything, haven't you?"

I shrugged. "I'm sure you did. I don't think you're a fool, Will. I'm sure you're not, in fact. So I'm giving you the courtesy of not treating you as one. A courtesy I hope you'll give me too."

"Implying that I have not so far?" he asked, stepping toward me again.

My pulse spiked. "I wasn't implying that at all."

We were face-to-face, a step apart at most. My mind stuttered over the few stray thoughts I managed to recognize. It was unusual someone's presence would affect me this much, this soon. Was he that special? Was our chemistry that special? Or was he using some sort of spell on me? I didn't think that was beneath him. Magic wasn't beneath any magic-wielding fey, just like changing into a wolf wasn't beneath me as werewolf. It was a natural part of who we were. I just wasn't that used to his natural part, and the very idea made me smile.

"What could I offer you that you'd like to have?" he asked as his breath touched my face with every word he uttered.

"Oh, I could think of several things," I replied.

He leaned toward me. His lips brushed against mine now when he spoke. "I could think of several things I'd like to offer you as well."

I gulped. Shit, I couldn't think with my dick. Not now at least. I so wanted to. It would be so easy to whisper it sweetly: "Fuck my brains out and I'll be on your side." But I wasn't here for shits and giggles, so I couldn't. There was no reason I couldn't hope I'd get a fuck out of the situation somewhere down the line. The more time we spent together, the better chance of that happening. That was pretty solid motivation to spin things in a way that would benefit us all in the end. There. I wasn't doing this for my selfish fuck-greedy self but for the greater good. I was a fucking humanitarian, feyitarian, whateveritarian.

"I'll only ask for one small thing for myself," I whispered softly.

He brushed his lips against mine. The touch sent little fiery thrills down my nerve endings, from the skin of my lips right to the pulsing muscle of my heart. I felt his breath hitch at the contact, and the idea it might affect him almost as much as it was affecting me sent a shiver down my spine. We could have been faking it, both of us. This was a negotiation of sorts, and now was the time to bring on our top game. But I felt it in my gut that this connection was real, that it wasn't bullshit for either one of us. I just knew it in the pit of my stomach. I wondered if he knew it too, as clearly as I did right in that instant.

His scent didn't assault my senses since he'd been hanging out in my personal space for a while now. My senses were bathed in his scent already. But I could feel the pounding of his heart as I deepened the kiss; I could feel his muscles clench and unwind with sensual tension while my body sang with it. Fuck me sideways, I wanted him right now. I wanted him so bad it almost gutted me. The feel of him languidly moving his tongue against mine made my blood turn into liquid fire, scalding my insides and bringing up my body temperature to heights I didn't think I'd felt before after just kissing. Everything in my body screamed, *This. This is it. This is what you've been waiting for, for so fucking long!*

"What do you want?" he asked after he pulled back, his forehead leaning against mine.

Fuck, fuck it, fuck! "I want all the information you can get from the Archives on a certain topic."

He was silent for a few seconds, his forehead still touching mine. But I felt him pull back from me somehow, a wall of cold between us instead of our bodies feeding off of the other's heat. I knew I'd blown something significant for me, but this was something I had to do for my alpha, for my pack, and for my Council. This was all about them. I reminded myself this was a good outcome, that I would salvage as much as I could of this fucked-up short-term mission I'd asked for with so much fervor.

"And that topic would be…?" he asked, stepping back and crossing his hands at the small of his back.

"Anything on a project called MH, from the Fey Institute. It was Dr. Vanda van Stromm's project."

"The MH project?"

I nodded. "Know anything about it already?"

"That question is actually insulting. Of course I'd know."

"Prove it. What is it about?"

"Destabilizing the current Council in order to replace members with allies of ours and of our coconspirators."

"And how would that benefit the Kingdom?"

"Fey don't mix well with others, as you surely know. So fey territories are actually limited. And on these limited territories, there are more and more powerful fey exerting their influence. Too much influence, too little territory for each, if you will."

"You've outgrown fey central, is that what you're saying?"

"Yes. The King and High Court decided the solution to that problem would be to expand our territories. It couldn't be an actual war. We don't like actual war, the death and destruction it unleashes on our ranks. Our wars are more subtle than actual fights."

"And you decided attacking our Council would be subtle?"

"You have to admit it was," he replied without blinking. "How long did it take you to realize what was going on? Who was involved?"

Well, we still didn't know who exactly was involved. He had me there.

I clenched my jaw. "Why our territories, though? Why not others?"

"A weak former member of the Kingdom had made such a cozy spot for himself among you in such a short time. The King took that to mean you were weak."

I frowned. "You mean Timothy Sands?"

"Exactly."

"He's weak?"

"In a manner of speaking. He was a notoriously weak spell caster at the Academy. A disgrace to his father, and by extension, to our whole Kingdom. Not an heir the Court approved of. We had no others."

"Which is why Tim's dad wanted him dead," I realized. "Because he wasn't strong enough by his standards. Couldn't he have other kids, though?"

"And risk them being just as weak, if not weaker? That, in turn, would make the King look terribly weak. He couldn't risk it."

I rubbed my temples. "Well, once Tim would've been dead, then what? Who would inherit the throne?"

"The King and High Court agreed it would be in the Kingdom's interest to choose someone from outside the Sands line. The selection process took a long time, but they came up with desirable options. And when they did, the King had to prove he was worth more alive than dead so they wouldn't replace him sooner than he'd have liked."

"Hence the plan targeting our territories?"

He nodded. "You were weaker than others, in his opinion. It would make him look strong to take over your territories and slowly incorporate them into Kingdom grounds."

"But you don't like hanging around with wolves or vampires."

"As much as you don't like hanging around with big numbers of fey," he pointed out in a clinical tone. "You all would have left the territories in time. The few remaining could've been interesting pets."

I shuddered. "You think you're so much better, don't you?"

"I don't. But some fey do. They think we're entitled to anything and everything we desire. Covertly taking over your Council was the thing to do."

"And when it didn't work?"

"It made the King seem weak instead of making him seem strong. It worked to the High Court's advantage. A weaker King means an even more powerful High Court. And they were determined to acquire new territories so each of them would have a bigger courtyard to play in without interference. The High Court members have become the richest, most influential fey in the Kingdom. I believe they intend to keep it that way."

"So the plan to take over the Council was to incite our community to rebellion?"

"What better way to conquer a power if not making it tear itself apart from the inside?"

"So this was the MH project."

He hummed and walked to his desk. "I was partially involved in its designs, in fact. But only partially."

"Tell me everything."

"Are we thinking ideas, pointers, or factual information?"

"All of it. But if I had to choose right now, factual information would be my priority."

He sat in his chair and gestured for me to sit in the one in front of his desk. I decided to do so, for one thing because my knees were starting to feel suspiciously like jelly. I was the kid who wanted the only kind of cake he couldn't eat because he was allergic to one of the ingredients. No substitute would do. And right now Will was the cake I couldn't have. And I wanted that cake with the passion of all of hell's fires combined.

He leaned back in the chair and crossed his legs. "Have you done information gathering before, Bert? I like your approach. You go at it from all angles, use whatever is thrown your way. I admire your dedication."

It sounded like a compliment, but it felt like a slap in the face.

"Thanks," I said and then smiled.

"And you're going to leave it at that," he stated instead of asking.

"I can say the same about you, of course," I shot back.

He inclined his head slightly. "For the record I never agreed to that project. It seemed doomed to fail from the very beginning."

"Go on."

"Will you want me to write this all down for you?" he asked as if we were discussing some mousse recipe and not a project meant to wreak havoc on my whole community.

"If you'd be so kind. That way we can be sure nothing is left out or forgotten. But I'd love to get some idea about what we're dealing with. In terms of information you have," I added coolly. I was sure it wouldn't be a good idea to let him know I had close to no fucking idea what the whole MH project really was. "Why did you think the project was doomed?"

"Too much involved that we couldn't control or influence directly," he said, shaking his head. "It seemed to me like amateur strategizing. The financial investment was more than substantial. The Institute worked hard on the research; the results were impressive, in my opinion. But the next stage... as much of it as I was privy to, it was a disaster."

"And how much were you privy to?"

"From the disseminating point, I had no actual connection with the project."

It was on the tip of my tongue, the question almost burning the inside of my mouth: "What the fuck was the project about?" In the context it sounded a lot like, say, the "Marking Hormones" project. I couldn't assume, though. I had to find out and have something more than a story to show for my efforts. Not knowing much didn't help. But I couldn't give away my hand so blatantly. So instead I went with:

"Considering the death of your former King and the uncertainty of everything, I'm sure my alpha will be more interested in the involvement of anyone from our side—documented involvement, if that's possible."

He rapped his fingertips on the desk, seeming to consider this new bit of information. I was trying to make it easier on him, at least to begin with. So he'd feel whatever he'd dig up for us would concern the Council more than it would his Kingdom. It was a first step to make future ones easier to take. When you had to make it over large distances, it helped to think of it in segments rather than a whole huge lot. Step by step instead of one giant leap. I knew he knew that as well as I did, and hoped he'd see this as a bit of a help from me. Because I did want to help him, as long as it wouldn't go against my alpha's interests.

"I'm pretty sure I can get that information. But in exchange for it, I'll want assurances that my children will be well cared for, whatever else happens."

I nodded. "I promise I'll guard their safety myself, Will. This much I can promise you, at least."

And I meant it. I was also sure Weiss wouldn't send kids to the slaughter, and that Tim wouldn't let it happen even if, by some strange twist of fate, Weiss would do it.

He nodded. "Fine, then. I know for a fact there were members of your community that participated in our research. And yes, I'm sure there are records of that at the Institute, which I will get for you. Anything pertaining to dissemination wouldn't be as easily available. Those files would only be accessible through the Archives, I believe."

"You have an in at the Institute?"

He nodded.

"Would the Archives include that information as well?"

"Yes. All information from all over the Kingdom is part of the Archives."

I couldn't contain my smile. "And you don't have an in?"

His gaze turned somewhat suspicious. "What are you implying?"

I brushed off some imaginary lint from my pants. "Nothing. I'll want you to help me get in. I'll get any files from there myself."

"Will you? And our Court Historian, working in the Archives, will have nothing to say about that? He's the only one who can access that information. It's not organized in files and folders as the name might lead you to believe. The Archives actually consist of a huge secure database. It can't be accessed from anywhere but the Historian's desk, with security codes that change on a weekly basis and that only he knows."

I thought about all the things regarding said Historian only I knew, and had on tape, so to speak, and lifted a hand. "You just worry about getting me inside. Without anyone knowing either one of us was there," I added, more as a dare.

"That last part there will be tricky," he muttered.

His gaze seemed to brighten for a moment, as if he relished the challenge. I was hoping he might. From what I knew from Richard, the security of the Archives was near impossible to sidestep. And if either of us actually went in there, we'd have even more issues than we might already. Our best option to make it out unscathed was to go in and out as smoothly as possible. With as little trace as possible. Even if Court life would be in disarray now that the former King was dead, an obvious enemy would help them get organized quicker. That wouldn't be in either my best interest, or Will's.

"Can you do it? Can you get us, or at least get me, inside the Archives undetected?"

He lifted his eyebrows a little. "Going in alone? Wouldn't you worry that I'd betray you, report you?"

I took a good look at him and contemplated that idea. Sure, it was a possibility at any point. I didn't trust him in any shape or form, just like I didn't trust anyone but my alpha right about now.

"If I do get caught sneaking in, and will use a method you devise, it would be obvious a powerful fey would have helped me. And who would that be, do you think? How fast do you think your name would come up?"

"My people have no reason to suspect me of treason," he informed me curtly.

I thought I detected a note of indignation there, which was funny considering we'd been chatting for the last hour or so about him betraying his Court.

"Oh, come on now, Will. You know as well as I do that with power comes envy and mistrust. Who better to envy and mistrust but the most powerful fey around?"

He sighed. "You seem to relish this idea that fingers would automatically be pointed at me."

I shrugged. "Do you deny it?"

"Sadly I can't. But at least it makes for grounds of trusting each other. I can expose you for a spy if you betray me, and you can expose me for a traitor if I betray you. There's a nice symmetry to that, I think."

"I guess. But still the question remains: can you do it? Can you sneak me in?"

He looked somewhere behind me, his gaze losing focus. "I loved my brothers and sisters. I trusted them. I never trusted my father. In my heart of hearts, I always knew it would come to it someday: me or him. And I always knew he'd choose himself. But later on I realized he'd been grooming me to kill him all along. All my training had that exact purpose: prepare me to kill him. And anyone else I had to, from then on. Have you ever killed someone yourself?"

I looked toward the floor, the topic making me uncomfortable.

"I take it that you have. It leaves a dreadful feeling, doesn't it? Doing the deed itself seems quite easy and quick. It's living with it that is the real issue. They never tell you about that, do they?"

I shrugged. "Why would they? It's an instinct you have, and sometimes a necessity. There's no point in telling someone who's very likely to kill people that it sucks to live with it once it's done. Where are you going with this?" I added, hating where the discussion was going.

He gave me that small, bitter smile of his. "I love my children, Bert. Perhaps that was my first sin in the eyes of fey. I truly love my children. I won't allow them to be killed or harmed. Not while I'm still alive. As the Court Interrogator or as King, it's a sure thing that only one of my children would survive. And that one will undoubtedly be groomed to kill me as soon as he or she possibly can, to replace me. I'd die willingly if it didn't mean that the same child would have first killed all of his or her siblings in order to get to me. My point is, my motivation is simple: love. You can always trust that motivation, Bert."

"Oh, I doubt that," I muttered.

He turned that inquisitive gaze to me. "You're thinking about your sister. Her betrayal. You must have taken it quite personally, I imagine."

"Of course I fucking did. She betrayed our alpha, and she betrayed me. It can't get any more personal than that."

"Would you allow me to express my opinion on that? I mean, if it doesn't bother you too much to talk about it."

Deny any weakness, my mind chanted repeatedly. "It's not pleasant, but it's not that big of a deal. Go ahead."

"I think perhaps you took her actions as meaning she didn't love you. But what if it simply meant she loved someone or something else too, aside from loving you? So much so that she'd go against her sisterly love for you, and do what she's done?"

I shrugged, showing a carelessness I didn't possess about the whole thing. What or whom could she have loved so much as to betray me? I would have put my life in her hands without any shadow of a doubt regarding her loyalty. The fault in that, of course, was mine—not hers. I'd been idiotic enough to trust love was a good enough motivation to be loyal to someone. As it turned out, though, either it wasn't, or my sister didn't love me. I couldn't decide which of the two options was actually worse. But hey, maybe they were both actually true. Even better.

"Whatever her reasons, it's her actions that matter. What we feel and why aren't as important as what we do."

"I suppose you're right," he said and smiled. "Fine, then. Here's the easiest way to prove me a traitor: my sigil ring. Only the Sims Interrogator of the day would have it. And we'd part with it only willingly or after being killed. So if you're discovered and have it on you while I'm alive, it will be clear I've given it to you of my own accord."

I lifted an eyebrow. "Or I could have stolen it," I deadpanned.

He shook his head and slipped the ring back on his finger. "Try pulling it off my finger."

"Really?"

He reached his hand toward me. Oh, very well, then, I'd play along in his finger-pulling joke. I grabbed the ring with my fingertips and pulled. A tsunami of pain rolled through my body, stiffening my spine and taking the breath right out of me. I couldn't even think, let alone scream, because of the agony. I pried my fingers off his goddamn ring and the pain subsided considerably. It took a few seconds for it to disappear entirely, and when it did, I was covered in sweat and feeling exhausted.

"Okay," I mumbled. "Now I see your point. We're sure it won't do that if you just give it to me?"

He smiled. "We're sure." And he proceeded to take the ring off his finger.

I grabbed it gingerly, holding my breath. But nothing happened.

"Don't try to put it on your finger, though. The same thing will happen as when you tried to take it off of mine."

I nodded. "You could claim I'd threatened you, or blackmailed you into giving it to me."

"No fey would believe you hold an iota of power over me in order to do so."

"Gee, thanks," I said. "How will you get me into the Archives?"

"The place is secure by means of cameras, microphones, thermo image cameras, and motion detectors. That's all in the hall of the Archives. The inside of the Historian's office in itself isn't secured in any way. There's only one way in, and no windows or other means of getting in or out."

I massaged my temples. "Well, shit. You could get one security system to pause while I go in and out, but all of that is virtually impossible to sidestep. How the hell will I get in and out?"

"Quite simple, Bert. We'll go together."

I frowned. "Because one of us can't get through, but two will manage?"

He smiled. "Who's to stop two fruit flies?"

"Is that some lingo I'm missing the point of?"

He shook his head. "No. We'll be actual fruit flies."

No way in hell.

eight

I HAVE to admit I've done some exciting things in my time. Like that threesome with the Asian twins, boy and girl, back in high school. Or the drag contests I won in college. All of the one-night stands with members from the club while being blindfolded, gagged, and sometimes tied up—the club where I eventually met Richard Warren, Fey Court Historian extraordinaire. I wasn't into BDSM as much as I was into experiencing new and exciting things, both in the bedroom and in the kitchen. Well, all over the place, actually. But anyway, I'd done plenty of things other people might think nuts or risky. But all of that paled in comparison to being turned into a fruit fly.

The notion of changing shapes wasn't that new to me; I was a goddamn werewolf, after all. But changing into an itsy-bitsy tiny flying thing went beyond everything I'd experienced. The sense of losing so much of my body, of shrinking as the world grew impossibly large around me… it was insane. How the world looked through my fruit fly eyes, how being unable to properly vocalize my thoughts or feelings made me feel—that was entirely new. I was scared, and the adrenaline rush feeling it gave me made everything seem brighter, made me feel more alive and more powerful than I'd been. Despite the fact I could be squished dead with an envelope, let alone a folded newspaper.

I followed my fruit fly partner in crime up into the corridors, through tiny cracks in the side of doorframes. We followed Fey Court members as they went through doors, slipped through the cracks of those doors as they were closing. I didn't actually remember making a longer way anywhere. In fruit fly distances, the Archives were almost at the other end of the world. And the more I flew, the more I felt like

I wanted to throw up. I was pretty sure my current anatomy wouldn't allow me that, but once turned into human form, I could almost bet my life on the fact that I would throw up. There were obvious advantages to this fruit fly form: the butt plug wasn't lodged up my ass anymore, and I had wings and could actually use them to fly without giving it any special thought. I kept thinking about the face Richard would make once we showed up in his office. That was going to be a lot of fun for sure.

After what felt like millennia, we finally were inside Richard's office. He'd gone out to take a cup of coffee, and we piggy-backed a ride in his hair into his office. His scalp smelled sweet and tasty, and I had the weirdest craving to lick at it. But I contained my impulse, mostly because Will was staring at me.

Once inside Richard's office, we waited for him to close the door, then flew down on the floor. In a second we were growing back into our human bodies as the world around us shrank. That was another top-ten weirdest moment I could add to my list.

Richard blanched. "What in the flying god's name are you doing here?" he muttered, looking at me. Then he seemed to notice Will, bowed to him out of reflex—I thought—and seemed even more shocked afterward. "Sweet flapping wings!" he squawked.

I gave him what I hoped would be a reassuring smile. "Richard, I'd like to ask a favor."

His gaze turned immediately suspicious and calculating. "A favor? Why would I grant you one?" he asked, staring at Will.

"Let's not discuss that now," I replied smoothly. "Will here is on my side, so don't worry about his presence."

"Will?" Richard parroted back at me. "You're on a first-name basis with Sir Sims?"

Will smiled. "As Bert said, let's not discuss that now. We need you to do him this favor, and be quick about it."

Richard squinted at me. "Does this mean we won't go to that pottery class together again?"

"Probably not," I admitted. "But considering all that's happened, hobbies might be the last thing on your mind for a while."

He frowned. "What do you mean? What's happened?"

I looked at Will, now confused myself.

He just sighed. "It's not yet public information. The High Court would like to have some inkling as to what happened before announcing it, so there won't be more panic than necessary."

"What isn't public information yet?" Richard asked.

Will seemed to become larger somehow and snapped, "You forget your place, Historian."

It made Richard wince and give a small nod. "Please, forgive me. But I'm worried, as I'm sure you can imagine."

"Your King is dead," I said. When Will frowned at me, I added, "I think he deserves to know. Things might change some around here," I continued, looking back at Richard.

Maybe he would be able to get out of the arrangement he'd been forced to agree to with his wife, now that Court life would become chaotic. I didn't particularly like Richard, but all things considered, I didn't dislike him either. Sure, he was a weasel, but he did what he thought he had to do. *Including betraying his King and Kingdom*, a voice inside my head taunted me. *Sound familiar?*

Richard's eyes boggled, and he kept nodding, as if assuring himself he'd just heard what he thought he did. "Dead?" he seemed to ask himself more than us. "Dead," he replied as well. "Okay. Okay. Did you kill him?" he asked, looking at me with a strange mix of fear and admiration.

I realized I'd just become more desirable to him, and I wasn't sure how to feel about that idea.

"We don't have time for a tea party, Richard," Will chastised him.

"Of course. What favor is it that you need?"

"Give me everything there is on the MH project by the Fey Institute, led by Dr. Vanda van Stromm. And I do mean all there is, Richard. Consider it a parting gift, if you will. I don't think we'll have the pleasure of seeing each other again anytime soon," I said and smiled at him as charmingly as I knew how.

His eyes darkened, a clear sign the smile did what it was supposed to. "That's a pity. Okay, I'll grant you this parting favor. But I don't have a flash drive on me," he said, frowning. "Do you?"

Fucking hell. "Yes, I do. Give me a moment."

I shook my head as I opened what I guessed was the bathroom door. Fuck, this was going to be unpleasant. I took my pants and briefs down and crouched. I found the outline of the plug's end and pulled it out, wincing. My dick throbbed. My balls felt heavy. I desperately needed to fuck, and the notion I could easily fuck Richard wasn't helping. But I was there with Will, we were going to be leaving as fruit flies, I needed to keep the butt plug a secret, and I needed to hold off as best I could.

I washed the plug, took out the safety cap from the plug's compartment, and slid out the flash drive inside. Richard would use this baby to give me the files I'd asked for. On it was a worm or something—I wasn't geekily inclined, myself—that would help us get all the info we wanted from the Fey Archives on "Amanda Weiss, Tricia Cooper, Morris James"—both in our language and that of the fey, thanks to Tim. I set the plug in the sink and turned on the cold water on it, washed myself quickly but as thoroughly as I could, then patted myself dry with Richard's towel and got dressed again. Holding the flash drive in my hand, I returned into his office.

Richard nodded and took the drive from my hand, lightly caressing my palm with his fingertips. I thought it would bring him some comfort so I allowed it. He went to his computer, stuck the drive in a freaky drawer, and tapped merrily on his keys. For a while he just frowned, but then he smiled, and I knew he'd found something.

"Here we go," he said, beckoning me closer. "Large research project, led by the Institute Director, no less. You'll be buried under medical notes and observations, plus funding proposals and grants, but what the hell. The formula is patented already, so have at it."

In a couple minutes or so, he plucked the drive from its port and handed it out. I took it, smiled, said, "Thanks," and went back into the bathroom, not missing Will's amused look and the curious glint in his eyes.

This part I wasn't quite looking forward to. My asshole felt a meter wide already. I didn't want to stick that damn plug back in. But I had to. So I took out the small tube of lube from my back pocket, took the plug out of the sink, and coated it in a generous amount. I smeared some on the rim of my hole, then gently guided it back in. Damn it. Horny level went a notch higher. I washed my hands and splashed some cool water over my face. Then I went out of the bathroom and was greeted by a grinning Will and a dazed-looking Richard.

"What's with the weird atmosphere?" I asked, staring at one, then the other.

Will shrugged. "We were taking turns guessing where that drive went. You didn't just take it out of your pocket," he supplied sweetly.

"No, that's where I keep your fucking ring," I snapped, irritated.

Richard's dazed state got even worse.

I shook my head. "Can we go now, *Sir Sims*?"

He nodded but turned toward Richard. "If you ever breathe a word of this to anyone, Richard, even a decade later, I will make sure you suffer a slow and painful death. And you should know I never break my promises."

Richard nodded, looking panicked for a moment. "I swear I won't breathe a word of it."

Will smiled, a slippery, devious kind of smile that got me half-hard in an instant. "You will never, under any circumstances, remember what happened here today, seeing Bert or me, or hearing about the King's death. You will forget whatever it is that Bert has on you, and the fact he has it. From today onward it will be as if you've only met him at the reception thrown in his honor," Will said in that weird voice that echoed.

I felt the ring on my finger getting hot, which I was beginning to understand was an indicator some high-level magic was happening. It had gone super warm when he turned us into fruit flies, and it got hot like hell as he did it again now.

We flew easily out of Richard's office, leaving behind a properly dazed Richard. Out of the crack of his office door, above the cameras and motion detectors that didn't bleep because of our flight, and through the crack of the door leading away from the Archives hall—and we escaped, just like that. It seemed so easy it almost made me giggle. Good thing I couldn't, as I was a fruit fly. The way back to Will's office seemed even longer now, my wings growing tired and my will to move diminishing by the second. When we finally got there and he turned us back into our human selves, I was out of breath and my body was strangely tired, muscles sore all over.

Will looked at me, an apologetic expression on his face. "Sorry about that. I didn't have as much energy left to sustain the transformation and form energy as I did on the way in. I can't even remember the last time I used this much magic energy," he said, shaking his head.

"When you killed your King?" I asked in a somewhat joke-like tone.

He blinked and looked away. "I didn't—"

"Like the wind, yes, yes, I know," I deadpanned and got his ring out of my pocket. "Want this back now?"

He looked at it, looked at my own ring, and said, "Maybe we could make an exchange. Give me yours and I'll give you mine? As a safety precaution for you, and as a favor for me?"

There was no way in hell I was giving up the ring Weiss gave me. I frowned. "I'm not marrying you or anything, despite agreeing to take care of your kids."

He smiled. "Well, don't rush to make that decision yet. I haven't even asked you to."

"Your ring on me is a measure of protection. My ring holds no such value," I explained, hoping he'd give up.

"Does it hold emotional value? You seem aghast at the idea to part with it," he said, turning that inquisitive gaze on me again.

"What's it to you, anyway?" I said, shrugging. "Now that you've fulfilled your end of the bargain, let's see how we'll go about me fulfilling mine."

"First things first: let me write down my statement that I drove you home last night because you were so affected by the drugs at the reception. I'll add in a note I stayed with you until early hours this morning, to make sure you'd be all right."

I sat on the small couch in his office while he wrote his statement and added it to the folder on his desk that had my name on it. He called someone from his desk phone, and the chick from earlier returned to take the folder wherever it was supposed to go. I kept a good solid grip on Will's ring, just in case that chick returned with a couple fey guards to take me into custody for espionage.

"Are we sure this is a safe place for us to talk?" I asked Will, eyeing him with great attention.

"Of course. It's spelled to assure complete safety. I wouldn't have had our talk here otherwise."

"But aren't you too magic-tired to keep up your defenses, or something along those lines?"

He did look a lot less shiny and brilliant than he had this morning, for instance. It worried me a little.

"It doesn't work like that. Once cast, a spell runs on the energy used to cast it. Protective ones need reinforcing every now and then, but I'd know well in advance when that point would come. We're perfectly safe here."

"Okay. So now what? Am I cleared as a suspect in the assassination of the King?"

"Now you should write a formal letter saying you're going back to report to your alpha and Council, especially since there have been threats made against you. Make it sound as if you regret what's happened but feel compelled to report back to your authorities until further notice."

I walked over to his desk. "Should I write that now?"

"It would be a good thing. Request someone to assist you out of the Kingdom, for good measure."

"Should I ask for you?"

"No. Just someone in an official capacity. I'll take it from there and make sure it's going to be me."

"Right," I muttered, and started writing.

Fey were pretty big on pedantic paperwork, that was my opinion. But far be it from me to deny them the pleasure of one more useless paper in their files. When I was done, I signed it. The same chick, the one I was now thinking of as Will's secretary, came in to take my "important diplomatic document" and deliver it to the proper Court officials. To my surprise they replied almost immediately, informing me they'd assign someone to escort me out of the Kingdom tonight, apologizing for the "unfortunate turn of events at the reception," and wishing me the best of health.

I gave the paper to Will to read too, and he nodded.

"Perfect," he announced, seeming more energetic than earlier. "Now we'll get you home. Take your time packing. I'll come by with the children later on and we'll leave."

I agreed. He drove me home, and I dozed off in the passenger seat of his car.

WHEN WE got to my for-now home, he informed me it was perfectly natural for me to feel tired after the whole shape-shifting thing, and that the more mass was lost or gained, the tougher it was on the body.

I didn't know much about magic by and large, so I had to agree. Once he drove away I looked over everything, checking the tiny signs I'd left before leaving this morning so I'd know if someone had been through my stuff. It didn't seem like someone had been there, so I started packing. My secure laptop was where I'd put it, still locked inside the briefcase. Everything seemed in order. Once my bags were all done, I went into the living room, determined to wait on the sofa for the Sims family to show up.

It sounded ridiculous even in my thoughts—"the Sims family," the whole day, our plan. Something about it didn't click with me, but I couldn't put my finger on it. Whatever it was, Will seemed determined to get his kids out of the Kingdom and into my care. I supposed he didn't have any safer bet, all things considered. And despite him sort of denying it, I was sure he'd either killed the King himself or was involved in a plot to kill him. Though if it was the latter option, then he had to worry about all his coconspirators betraying him, and in turn I had to worry about him betraying me as a consequence.

But I was leaving with his kids. That had to be the best thing I could have obtained. He truly seemed to love them, if he was willing to go to these lengths to protect them. And if he had wanted them dead, he could have easily killed them himself and gotten away with it; that was my distinct impression.

When someone finally knocked on the door, I was tired from all the thinking and pacing about. I was also nervous. I knew how to behave with kids, more precisely with Alf, but fey kids were a whole new area for me. For some reason I refused to contemplate, I wanted to make a good impression on Will's kids.

When I opened the door, my first thought was I was going to be arrested. But the majority of the crowd was kid sized, so I relaxed. I was staring at no fewer than three kids who were standing and two babies in Will's arms for a total count of five. Freaking five!

"Are these all of them?" I asked as politely as I could.

Will smiled grimly. "All I have left."

I frowned and looked up into his eyes. And I saw it then, as he was surrounded by the kids; I saw that shadow in his gaze, that void that seemed to float around him cloaked in a delicate bubble of despair. I understood in a way little else could have helped me understand why he was doing this. Why he was risking a position of power and the chance to gain even more, why he was conspiring with an outsider he barely knew despite his hints that he'd researched me, why he was trusting me with the lives of his five children. He had five children now, but he'd had more.

I didn't want to know how many more because I didn't want to know how many he'd lost. I couldn't imagine what it would be like to lose even one child you loved with your whole heart. Sometimes while I was taking care of Alf and watching some sad TV show with him where some kid died or was kidnapped, I would contemplate the notion someone or something would take Alf away from me, and my mind froze with panic every time. And Alf wasn't even my own, though I loved him like he was.

Will had lost at least one child. Apparently he was ready to do whatever he could to make sure he wouldn't lose any more of them.

nine

THE SIMS family came inside and I closed the door behind them. I took a few seconds while doing so, breathing in and out slowly, trying to make sure I'd have nothing but a nice, smiling face when I turned around and looked at them.

The house remained eerily quiet as they sat in the living room. I went in and sat on a chair, looking around.

Will cleared his throat and the oldest of the bunch stood up from the couch. "This is Susannah, now my oldest. She's thirteen," he said.

Susannah had the most amazing black and curly hair I'd ever seen. It was long, all the way to her waist, and the large curls made her beautiful café-au-lait skin tone shine. It also made her purple eyes shimmer and stand out; so did the look that was way too mature on the face of a thirteen-year-old girl. She didn't have the eyes of a child at all. She held herself in an almost regal way, inspecting me coolly from head to toe and standing a step in front of her brother and sister somewhat defensively. My heart tightened for a moment, reminding myself this kid had probably been playing with deadly magic rather than dolls for years already.

"Pleased to make your acquaintance," she informed me in an imperial tone.

"Hey," I said waving awkwardly. "I'm—"

"We know who you are," she dismissed me easily and sat back down after glaring at her father.

"Please excuse my daughter's attitude," Will said, smiling fondly. "Puberty is merciless on all of us poor bystanders."

I smiled back and contemplated having to go through that with Alf and a bunch of fey kids too. It took a lot of effort not to cringe but I managed and was proud about it.

The other girl stood up and gave me an honest-to-God brilliant smile, her braces doing nothing to dim that. If anything, they made her milky, freckled skin shine all the more. "I'm Sarah. Nice to meet you," she said and then sat back on the couch.

The little guy stood up but didn't make eye contact. His wavy dark brown hair seemed to have a life of its own, and his tan skin contrasted with his brightly colored clothes. "I'm Hector. Pleased to meet you," he said, staring at the carpet, and then he sat back down, looking about as awkward as I felt.

"Hey, nice to meet you all. I'm not sure what I have in the fridge, but can I get you anything?"

Susannah looked up into my eyes and said without blinking, "Get us out of here."

I swallowed thickly, doing my best to show no emotion. They didn't need me looking worried right now. They needed me to look strong and composed, like their father did.

"And these little beauties?" I asked, eyeing the kids in Will's arms.

"Meet the twins, Meredith and Samuel," he said, holding them up a little. "Susannah likes to call them Hunger and Pestilence, even knowing they are a lot tamer than she was at their age." He looked down on them, smiling.

"Jeremy always told me I was as good as a little angel," she informed him haughtily.

"That's because you always were his favorite," Will said, still watching the twins.

I looked at Susannah and read the pain in her gaze. Clearly Jeremy was the one, or one of the ones, they had lost. My stomach tightened.

"Want to know how he died?" she asked me, staring at me in a daring way.

"I don't think we should—" I tried meekly.

"He had to duel me since we were the oldest ones left. That happened a year after he had to face Cedric in a duel. They never seemed like something real, these duels. Not until we watched our brothers doing the first. In the end, Cedric.... He spelled his heart to stop beating. To spare Jeremy the pain of actually killing him."

My brain was pounding. "Couldn't they have just… stopped?"

"Duels have a Court-assigned referee," Will intervened in a dry voice. "Should any of the duelists refuse to fight, the referee kills them both. And anyone from the family trying to help or interfere is killed as well."

"That's just barbaric," I couldn't help myself from saying.

Susannah's eyes flashed with hatred. "They had to. They had to fight."

"Oh, I didn't mean to insult them. It wasn't their fault," I tried to explain.

"Of course it isn't!" Susannah declared and squinted.

All in all she gave me the feeling of a cat with her claws out, ready to tear at my throat. I found that viciousness about her comforting in a twisted way, maybe reminding me of Tricia back when she had been that age. I looked into her eyes and she looked into mine for a while, and some sort of understanding seemed to be reached. She studied my face carefully, then glanced away, picking at something on her jeans.

"Jeremy did the same thing when he had to duel Susannah," Will whispered almost voicelessly. "I wouldn't be able to survive seeing something like that happen again. And I can't intervene or they'd kill me, and then who would take care of my children?"

There was an agony in his gaze that went beyond anything I'd ever felt myself. It was so intense, so all-consuming that it choked me. It tightened my stomach in knots and made me taste bile in the back of my throat.

Sure, pack life wasn't exactly a picnic either. We wrestled and fought and pulled each other's tails and ears as pups, and as we grew up, the fights got worse and more numerous until we figured out where we fell in the dynamic of the pack. But it rarely came to death between us, if ever. Certainly not as a requirement unless we were competing for a position already filled, and by then we were adults, all of the ones involved. These fey bastards were making kids kill each other, brothers and sisters. I couldn't even properly compute the notion.

"We won't fight each other when we live with you," Susannah said in a clear, crystal tone. "And no one will come near my brothers and sisters," she said, looking at me in a chilling way.

In that instant I knew she would not only be able but thrilled to kill anyone who actually got near them or even remotely threatened them. It was an animal thing. I felt a bloodthirsty predator growl inside of her tiny teen body, her slight frame and scrawny legs ready to pounce with deadly force on anything and anyone she thought would want to harm her family. I felt a kinship with her I couldn't put into words, a deep sense of understanding that moved me from my kind of panicked state of mind into a protective one.

"I promise I'll do my best to make sure nobody does," I told her, willing her to understand just how much I meant it.

I decided right then, seeing those kids and picturing what it must have been like to go through what they had, that they weren't just Will's kids anymore. From now on they were my own personal pack, and I would do everything I could to protect and care for them. It wouldn't matter what would happen with Will or with the kids once they made it onto Council ground. Nobody would take me away from their side, and nobody would manage to harm them without going through me first.

"Are you guys ready to go?" I asked, looking back at Will.

"Definitely," he replied.

Getting my bags in the trunk went by fast, and the kids got settled on the backseat with Susannah holding the twins in her arms. She seemed used to doing so, and when she glanced at them, the ruthless predator from her gaze was replaced by a tenderness and adoration I was gutted to witness. Will got behind the wheel, I sat in the passenger side, and he drove me back to where he had picked me up just a couple days earlier.

ONCE WE got close to Council ground, my mind started working overtime. I thought I should inform Weiss and Tim since I was returning with no fewer than six guests, five of whom were minors. I was planning to neglect to inform the pack about them, at least for the moment. The pack wasn't going to react that well to their presence. We didn't like fey because of their magic and cunning ways, which they made no secret of. And since the whole treason thing had become a trend in our pack, tensions were running high at all times. This would be a great excuse to lash out and take revenge on someone.

If Weiss didn't take them in, they'd need serious protection to live among us. I wasn't sure they would make it at all, in fact, if our alpha didn't offer them his protection. But I didn't want to discuss that aspect in front of them while in the car. Being fey among fey was no picnic, I knew now, but being fey among werewolves, lycans, and vampires wasn't easy either. Even if Weiss offered them his protection, the novelty and weirdness of having fey kids around was bound to attract a lot of attention. And we didn't need it, especially not now.

I called Weiss as soon as we were inside Council territory. He picked up after the first ring.

"Why the fuck are you calling me from this number?" he growled in my ear.

"Hey, uhm, boss—I'm on Council territory."

"What?" he snarled.

"Long story. I'm coming to HQ with six guests," I said as smoothly as I could. "We'll explain everything when we get there."

"Six guests meaning six prisoners, or six friends?" he asked, a lot calmer than he'd been earlier.

I looked in the back and noticed Susannah was watching with rapt attention. "Friends," I told Weiss, and we hung up.

I directed Will to HQ and found Weiss waiting for us at the first security checkpoint of the building. He took one good look into the car and at the driver, glanced at me, then turned around and stomped back inside. That was a good reaction by Weiss standards. A good one, and a lot better than I anticipated. I suspected he talked with the security guys, because we went through all of the checkpoints easily despite me accompanying unidentified fey children and a fey adult in their car.

Once inside HQ we went in the elevator and up. There had been no one in the corridors we walked through downstairs. On our way toward Weiss's office, we encountered Naty Stein, her fidgety tail moving chaotically under her lab coat.

"He-hey, guys," she said and smiled brilliantly.

Susannah took one good look at her and said in a level tone, "Are you supposed to present yourself like that, with animal ears and a tail?"

The other two kids, smaller than Susannah and not in raging-teen mode, just stared wide-eyed all around and at Naty every now and then.

To my surprise Naty just shrugged. "Are you supposed to talk like that to your elders?" she said, seeming calmer than I thought she could be.

Susannah squinted. "I take it from the white coat you're supposed to be a doctor of some sort. You won't touch any of my siblings or me, if that's your purpose."

Something about the deadpan threat made Naty frown almost comically, and she looked up at me and Will for the first time since we arrived.

"What have these kids been through?" she asked.

Will prepared to reply, but I cut in. "We'll discuss that later. Just make sure they're okay. Maybe they'd like something to eat and drink?" I asked, focusing on Susannah and not on Will.

Susannah regarded her brother and sister in her arms, then the bigger ones, and said, "We would all welcome a meal. The twins will have...."

She kept instructing Naty as they made their way toward a conference room with Will's accord. Weiss obviously wanted to keep their presence as contained as possible.

Will and I went to Weiss's door, I knocked, and when he shouted, "Get your ass in here, Bert!" I smiled and breathed out a sigh of relief.

Home sweet home.

Will seemed tense, and I figured it was a bad sign that I could tell, but he was not as worried as I might have imagined him to be. We got inside, where Weiss was pacing back and forth behind his desk and Tim sat calmly at his. He looked up, saw Will, and smiled.

"What's the meaning of this?" Weiss snarled.

Will flinched, but I patted him discreetly on the arm.

"After they threw me the welcome reception, the King was assassinated," I started explaining.

Weiss snapped his head around to face me, and Tim opened his mouth to say something that didn't make it out.

"What the fuck is going on?" Weiss asked, bewildered.

"If I may," Will intervened. "The reception guests were all drugged. Sometime after that the King was killed while in his chambers."

"By?" Tim managed to finally articulate.

"Person or persons unknown," Will replied smoothly.

I turned to look at him but tried not to be conspicuous about it. How naturally he chatted with Tim, as if they'd known each other for so fucking long. Yet from what I knew, it was the first time they'd met. Neither had bothered with introductions. I assumed Tim wouldn't need them. He'd probably know someone from the higher-up circle like Will, but still... something didn't fit in.

"You're sure? My—the King is dead?" Tim asked.

Will nodded, giving him a look I didn't manage to read. Was it regret, was it joy? I just couldn't pin down its meaning.

Tim leaned back in his chair. "How many from Court know?"

"Select few, of course. It's protocol," Will replied while he sat on a chair near to him.

"Protocol?" Weiss asked, looking at Tim.

Tim nodded. "Big news is kept under wraps until authorities have enough info to give the population at large, so as to not trigger panic. If you announce someone is dead and we don't know who did it, but they were killed, you instill panic, fear, and mistrust. But if you have more info to give them when you give them that news, something for their reeling mind to cling on to, you get a better response."

"So they won't announce it officially until they know who did it?" Weiss muttered, frowning. "What kind of backward lazy-ass logic is that?"

"Fey procedure," Will replied, almost smiling.

Yes, something was definitely weird here. They couldn't have just simply fallen into chatting so easily, no questions, no nothing? And why wasn't Weiss asking all the obvious questions, like who the fuck was this guy I'd brought in, why we'd brought a little herd of kids with us to boot?

Weiss sighed and dropped into his chair, leaning back. "So how much time do we have?"

"I really can't say," Will replied, frowning a little. "I'm supposed to investigate any potential involvement of your Council. Part of the High Court is keen on naming Leonard Hughes as contender, and they'd like to have someone to point a finger at for the assassination soon so they can get on with it."

"And the other part of High Court? Who's their champion?" Weiss asked, bouncing a tennis ball off of his desk.

"The other part wants to name me," Will said.

"Fucking idiots," Weiss snapped and burst out laughing.

I blinked for a few times, looked at Tim, who seemed just about as in the dark as I was, then looked at Will and found his gaze on mine.

"I'm missing a lot here, aren't I?" I asked, knowing the answer already.

"You're certainly missing something," he admitted and gave me what I thought was an encouraging smile.

"Care to share?" Tim muttered, squinting at Weiss, then at Will.

There was a knock on the door and someone entered. He was tall, about as tall as me, and had a lanky build—even by fey standards, he was lanky. There was something about the set of his shoulders, the tiny crooked smile, and the way his eyebrows framed his eyes....

"Jeremy," Will whispered as if in pain.

He got up from the chair and launched himself in the direction of the young guy. For a moment I thought they'd go at each other's throats, but then they wrapped their arms around each other and held on tight.

"Jeremy," I whispered, my brain working on that. "One of the supposedly dead kids?" I asked, looking at Weiss.

Weiss nodded, actually grinning. "It was about two years ago. This whole mess hadn't started, but there were signs, intel. Will here decided that the life of his oldest son still alive, and of the rest of his kids, was worth more to him than the plans of a King and High Court he didn't believe in anymore."

"You have got to be shitting me," I said, running a hand over my face. "This whole time, this is who you had at Court? While I was working on sources?"

Weiss gave me the "shut it" look, so I did.

"It's so good to see you, Father," the boy said, still smiling.

"We're all here," Will replied, patting his shoulder. "You look better, stronger. How are you feeling?"

Jeremy shrugged. "Okay. You gave me a good one, I'll admit. But I managed through it."

"Good one?" I repeated. "Would someone please help me make some sense out of this whole thing?"

Weiss sighed. "I see staying with fey even for a couple days made you nosy."

"I did my job as best I could. But I see I didn't know a lot of stuff that might have made it easier," I countered, glancing up into my alpha's eyes.

He looked me over for a moment with his icy blues, then blinked. "Can't argue that point. But if you'd known about Will, you might have endangered him. You did your job just fine, Bert."

"I got some files as well," I added.

"He most certainly did," Will said. "Made me work hard for the extraction too. We went into the actual Archives, believe it or not. I wouldn't have tried it on my own. I didn't have anything on the Court Historian without actually interrogating him—and I had no plausible reason to do that. But Bert here seems to have something major on him," he commented, staring at me weirdly.

"You actually got into the Archives?" Weiss asked, looking at me with something close enough to admiration to have me wag my metaphorical tail.

"I got everything I could on the MH project. I'm not sure what it is we have, but I think we have a lot of it. Someone should start looking through it."

Weiss grinned. "That's my beta! Good job, man! I'm proud of you. Now hand over the info."

My face heated up. "Give me a moment to retrieve it," I mumbled and went into the bathroom.

It went faster than the last time and I felt mildly less mortified about the placement. I scrubbed the butt plug and wrapped it in toilet paper. And boy was I thrilled to be rid of that goddamn thing! I threw the little lube pack from my back pocket into the toilet and flushed it, filled with a sense of victory. Butt freedom at long fucking last!

I wiped my hands carefully and took the flash drive. When I got out of the bathroom, Will was talking to his son, smiles plastered on both of their faces. I had to look at them for a moment longer, just a moment. It made my heart a little bit lighter for some reason.

I gave the flash drive to Weiss. "There's a lot of information to comb through, I think. It was all I could possibly get, though. So I hope it's gonna be enough."

Weiss grinned. "You did fucking great, Bert. Real great."

"What's going to happen with Will and his family now?"

"Do you actually care?" Weiss asked, studying me in that annoying way he had since we were kids.

"Enough to ask, obviously," I mumbled.

"Ask me again when you'll have another answer to that question."

"Okay! Okay, boss. I do care. All right? I care."

Weiss grinned ear to ear. It was a disturbing image.

ten

WEISS GOT up and walked toward the door, signaling me to follow. I fell in step behind him effortlessly, something I'd done ever since I could remember.

Everyone in his office watched us go, Will's gaze lingering on me before it returned to his son. I still had a thing for the man even now, on my own turf, in the relative insanity of my home. So I had to admit I had a thing for him, plain and simple. It scared the hell out of me because acting on that thing I had would mean trusting him, at least a little. I wasn't looking forward to that part at all.

Weiss led me to one of the observed holding cells, and my stomach constricted before we actually got there. I knew where we were going. I didn't want to get there.

Weiss leaned against a wall and looked through the one-way mirror into Tricia's holding cell. "How was it over there?"

I shrugged. "It seems fey are even more fucked-up than we believed. The things I found out about Will's family—makes me sick."

"Yeah, I know. I'm sorry I didn't mention who it was I owned at Court, but I couldn't risk him getting exposed. There was more at stake than a simple intel operation, as you now know."

"You mean his kids' life, or the assassination of the King?"

"And what's going on here too, in the Council. Everything going on is strictly confidential. For the record, Will is not responsible for the King's death."

"Yeah, wind, I know," I mumbled and rolled my eyes.

"What?" Weiss asked, lifting an eyebrow.

"Never mind. It was this whole speech. Forget I mentioned it. I meant he didn't do it himself, in any way anyone could prove."

"Which might be another way of saying he didn't do it at all," he muttered, looking at Tricia as she ate a burger and fries. "She still hasn't said a thing."

"Lucky for us we have a grade-A interrogator on hand."

Weiss looked at me sideways for a moment. "You'd want the Fey Court's Interrogator to question your sister?"

"Don't act like you didn't think about it the moment she refused to talk. Back when you knew you had him but I didn't," I felt the need to clarify.

"It might be a bit... harsh. His methods don't always leave the interrogated person unscathed."

My stomach clenched tight, but I kept a cool face. "She's going to be sentenced for treason, isn't she? Execution is the next stop after that. That's where we're headed, right?"

He nodded without looking at me. "We might as well get what we can out of her until then?" he asked.

I ran a hand over my face. "You know, sometimes I still think I'm going to wake up and realize all of this was just a stupid bad dream. Tricia would be stomping about, huffy about one thing or another, snapping at me while she cut my hair or commented about my rounding stomach."

"I can always compliment the slowly growing sphere-like curve of your stomach."

"Yeah, well, you're butt ugly too," I muttered, just like when we were kids.

He laughed a little and so did I, but my heart wasn't entirely in it. Neither was his. We'd grown up together, Weiss, Tricia, and I, even if he was a bit older than us Coopers. But pack pups grew up together, always. It was part of the basis of our later loyalty, this sense of being a large family rather than a random group of strangers. When we managed to become his betas, it was just like it always was: the three of us running around causing havoc, Weiss being our lead and the two of us playing to his tune to perfection, naturally adapted to work like a team. How could it have come to this? Why did it come to this?

"We're all here for you, you know. I'm here for you," he said in that calm, serious voice he always used when he meant something.

"I know. You always were."

"It's gonna be hard to get over it. But you can do it, if you let the right people in."

I shook my head. "Is it here you give me the birds and the bees speech?"

He smacked the back of my head. "Listen, asshole, I can try to cheer you up by beating your ass too. Your choice. Talking or getting your ass kicked?"

I chuckled. "Now that sounds more like you."

"Yeah. Talking is more Tim's thing, anyway," he said, crossing his arms over his chest. "But giving him and us a chance was the second-best thing I did. The first was Alf. So you should consider giving someone the chance to help you."

"What's going to happen to Will and his kids?"

He grinned and looked at me sideways. "You have a boner for the guy, don't you?"

I shrugged. "He's hot, he's smart, he's well educated, and he's articulate—something I've grown to appreciate a lot."

"What the fuck is that supposed to mean, dickhead?"

I laughed. "Just messing with you. But I do like him. I just don't know if there's anything to be done about it."

Weiss turned around and cocked up an eyebrow. "You fucking kidding me? Of course there's stuff to be done about it. Don't tell me you actually need me to give you the birds and bees speech here."

"He has kids, a lot of stuff they went through…. I mean, I don't know if I could even rise to the challenge, you know? I'm a fucking mess. They don't need that right now. So anyway, you still haven't answered. What will happen to them?"

"Will wants to go back to Court. To finish what's been started, change the High Court now that the King is gone."

"Won't that be suicide?"

He sighed. "That I really don't know. I mean, either the fey figure him out for my informer, or they don't. If they do, they kill him—best-case scenario. Worst-case scenario, they torture him for who knows how long. Wouldn't put that beneath them."

"And if they don't?"

"He'll have to fight Hughes to become King or stay on as their Interrogator."

"I'm guessing his kids are staying here whatever happens, yeah?"

"For sure," Weiss replied without missing a beat. "The rest depends on what Will wants to do too. That was part of our deal, and I always keep my word."

"He should have a go at Tricia," I said, looking at her. "She's as good as dead, anyway."

Weiss patted me on the back. "Wait here for a moment."

I did. I waited there behind the one-way mirror and watched my sister toss some fries around. She had a corner covered up in panels, giving her some privacy when she used the toilet or washed. But the rest of her life was an open book to anyone curious enough to watch. I played with the ring I still had on my finger, the one I would soon give back to Weiss. Then I patted my pocket where I had Will's ring too.

He'd indulged me just to make me feel like I could trust him. He'd already planned his extraction, and I was the right opportunity for it. He had used me as much as I had used him. Somehow that made things square between us. There was a nice symmetry to it, as he said.

After a while Weiss came back into the room. "Security is turned off for both rooms. Don't want any Council members deciding they want this stopped. There will be three witnesses to her testimony. That's gonna make it valid."

He didn't want the Council to see how Will's interrogations went, then. I understood that—from what I heard, they weren't exactly a pretty picture to see. In Fey Court anything he got would be considered truth because fey knew how his magic worked. The Council didn't; they could claim the testimony wasn't valid if they were protecting one of their own. But three witnesses, one of whom was the PBI director, would make it irrefutable.

My sister's holding cell door opened and in came Will, looking radiant, relaxed, majestic, even without his uniform. He'd changed, I could see. The jeans-and-shirt look seemed foreign on him but not unbecoming. Nothing could be unbecoming on him. I secretly envied guys like him. My looking somewhat decent hinged on a lot of consideration regarding my clothes, lengths of sleeves, layering, all that crap. He just looked effortlessly gorgeous.

My sister's nostrils flared and she snorted. "Well, this is new. What are you, fey?"

He smiled, a dazzling picture. "I'm Will. And you are Tricia, right?"

She nodded. "I'd say I was pleased to meet you, but I have a feeling there won't be anything pleasurable about it."

"Perhaps. That all depends on you, though."

She chuckled. "Ah, I see. You are aware you can't do the good-cop, bad-cop routine if there's only one of you, right?"

"I've met your brother, Tricia. He's a very nice guy."

That seemed to throw her off her game. She looked down and to the right, then the left. She shook her head as if her hair were in her eyes like it used to be when we were kids.

"Bert is not nice," she replied. "He's amazing."

I tried to swallow the knot in my throat. "Amazing." I was amazing. I pulled nervously at the ring on my finger. Thoughts started running around in my head. Could I do anything for Tricia? Should I do anything, even if I could? I kept thinking about our childhood, about all those times she deliberately did the exact opposite of what she was told. How she always made that innocent face when she got caught, how she'd laugh with me later on about whatever punishment she had to endure and usually managed to get around.

"You could make things easier," Will told her in a friendly tone. "Tell me what Weiss wants to know."

"And how will it help me? You tell me, Mr. Feyman, how it could possibly help me. And why would I want to give Weiss anything, anyway? He's taken everything I ever loved away from me. He doesn't deserve to get any fucking thing."

Will frowned, so expressive it seemed almost comical to me. "Like what? What has he taken from you?"

Weiss walked closer to me.

"What's the point of this chitchat?" I asked him.

He shrugged. "He gets some baseline or something. I don't know."

The ring on my finger started heating up. "A-ha. He's bringing in the bigger guns now."

"How would you know?" Weiss asked, frowning.

"The ring you gave me heats up when that happens."

"Is it supposed to?"

I shrugged.

"Take it off."

"I don't think that's a good idea. Not during her interrogation," I added in a small voice.

Weiss sighed. "Yeah. You're probably right."

Will's voice started having that strange echo. "Who do you recognize as alpha?"

Tricia growled. "What kind of question is that?"

"Just answer it. Don't fight me on this," Will said in a kind tone.

"Fuck you, sweetheart," Tricia snapped.

The ring on my finger heated up more.

"Who do you recognize as alpha?" Will asked again.

Tricia's gaze became dazed, seeming unfocused. I could see her face clearly.

"Who's your alpha?" he asked again, that echo stronger in his voice.

She shook her head and two fine trails of blood slid down from her nostrils.

I clenched my fists, every muscle in my body contracting.

"Who's your alpha?" Will asked again.

"Councilor Stein," Tricia mumbled.

Will looked at the mirror as if confused. Weiss swore and ran a hand through his hair.

"Could she be hallucinating?" I asked.

"I don't fucking know. But I doubt she'd hallucinate about Councilor Stein of all people."

"It's not the first time her name comes up," I thought out loud.

Will pressed on. "Councilor Stein is your alpha?"

Tricia nodded, a dead look in her eyes.

"Did you know about the MH project?"

She blinked slowly. More blood trickled down her lips and chin.

"Did you know about the marking hormones traffic?"

"Yes. We set it up, Amanda and me. And others."

"At Councilor Stein's orders?"

She nodded and ran the back of her hand over her lips. Then she stared at the blood on her hand, her eyes turning into wolf ones.

The ring on my finger got hotter, almost to the point of pain. I noticed Tricia's eyes go back to her human ones. Will did that. He could control another being to that extent, I realized. He was that powerful. A shiver of fear ran down my spine.

"Was she Amanda's alpha as well?"

"Yeah," Tricia replied, smiling. "We were finally together then, Amanda and me."

"You loved her?" Will asked, all nice-sounding again.

She nodded.

"Did Councilor Stein share her plans with you?"

Tricia blinked slowly. She didn't reply. A new wave of blood trickled down her lips.

"Did she?" he asked her again.

I was going to be sick. I twisted the onyx ring around my finger, thinking about pulling it off. It was the only thing I could think to do to stop this. I had no idea this was how Will interrogated people. God, I had suggested it, but I had no idea.

"New Council," Tricia mumbled. "New power. More power for us."

"Does she have anyone else on the Council on her side?"

"Councilor Nichols."

"Only one?"

She nodded.

"What were you going to gain from this plan?"

"Leaders would go down. We'd get a chance to be happy. With those we loved. Those we loved," she mumbled and started rocking on the chair.

Weiss was gripping the table beneath us. His knuckles were white with the pressure. I looked at those knuckles for a few moments, then I slipped the ring off my finger. Will reacted immediately. He pointed his gaze right at me through the mirror, though he couldn't see me. He blinked slowly once, twice, and a third time.

"Do you want this to stop?" he asked.

Tricia said, "Yes," but I didn't think he'd asked her. He'd asked me. I projected all of my pain and anguish at his beautiful, monstrous face. I projected my desire for him, my fears, my doubts, but most of all I projected my love for my sister and the pain and regret I felt for her situation. I knew it couldn't be helped. But I wanted all of this to stop. To end. I wanted it to end.

Tricia fainted. Some part of me felt her disconnect somehow. Will kept staring right at me through the window, and my heart beat wildly in my chest. I felt her absence in a way I couldn't explain. Her chest kept moving. She was breathing. But she was gone.

Weiss made a call and then ran out of the room. Soon after that MCU personnel rushed in and started checking her. Will got up slowly and walked out of the room. He managed to walk into the observation room, where the door was now wide open after Weiss ran out like a storm. So Will walked right up to me until he was only a mere step away.

"It's over," he whispered, looking into my eyes.

"Is she... dead?"

He shook his head. "She's asleep, in a way. Dreaming nice dreams. Happy ones. I promise you," he said, reaching out and clasping my hands. "Happy dreams."

"And when she'll wake up?"

"She won't. At least this way, you know she's happy for a while. Until she goes."

I felt tears burning up my eyes, and then they clouded my vision. "Why did you do that?"

"I felt your grid, Bert," he whispered, leaning his forehead against mine. "All your emotions exploded into my senses, almost strangling me. All that pain, the anguish... I couldn't stand to feel you suffer like that. I gave her happy dreams until she slips away entirely. It's the only thing I could do."

"That blood... is that how you interrogate? By torturing?"

"In a sense they torture themselves. Resisting my magic causes the body and possibly the mind to break down. I always tell them to just share what I ask. But they never listen."

"You scare me," I told him, looking into those dark, tempestuous green eyes.

"I tend to have that effect on people," he replied and smiled.

He ran his hand through the hair on the back of my head where Weiss had slapped me earlier. I must have imagined it, but somehow the sting that still tingled on my scalp there settled down when he touched me.

"Did you... give her happy dreams for me?"

He leaned in and kissed my cheek. "Yes, I did. But let's keep that a secret, okay? I wouldn't want everyone I interrogate to start asking for that favor."

"Is it hard to do?"

"It was worth it, just this once."

"Thanks," I mumbled, looking into his eyes.

He turned to leave, but I didn't want him to. "Where will you and the kids be staying?"

"I'm not sure. Why?"

"I think I can get you an apartment in my complex," I blurted out. "Or two. I mean, I'd invite you to stay over, but I don't think we could all fit into mine."

He smiled. "That's very generous of you. Thanks. If you think we could stay at your complex, that would be lovely, I'm sure."

"Do you want the Fey Court to think of you as loyal?"

"Why do you ask?"

"You could always go back there. If no one will know what you do here, you could simply return to your life there. If you wanted to."

"But I don't want to. And my children will stay here either way. I'd like to be where they are, by their side, as long as it doesn't jeopardize them."

"Does anyone at Court know they're here for good?"

He shrugged. "I wiped the governess's memory. She saw us packing. Other than her, no one would know. I made sure. As far as Court is concerned, I'm here investigating Council implication in the assassination of our King."

"And it would benefit them for you to find the Council involved?"

"I'd say so. Outside guilty parties would be the best option for the Kingdom. Say one or two of your councilors," he said, looking into my eyes. "Traitors to your Council, traitors to our former King. It would make sense."

"Can you do that? Find two councilors guilty?"

He smiled. "Haven't you already figured it out, Bert? I can do almost anything I please."

I gulped. "Stay at my complex. I mean, it's not all snazzy, but, you know… until we find a permanent solution."

"A permanent solution?"

"To where me and your kids will live. Either you stay here or you go, but they're staying here anyway, right? It was our deal. Weiss agreed to it."

He nodded. "Thank you for that. And you'd stay with them?"

"I promised I would watch over them, keep them safe. I fully plan to do that to the best of my abilities."

"I'd really like that, Bert. Thank you."

I got my phone out of my pocket and searched for the Hollowstar Complex admin number. Good thing we were buddies, because this was going to need some serious privacy.

eleven

WEISS STORMED into the observation room, his eyes changed into wolf ones. "What the fuck happened in there?" he snarled.

"She resisted," Will replied smoothly.

I slipped the ring discreetly back on my finger, hoping Weiss wouldn't notice. It wasn't insubordination; it was damage control.

"Don't feed me that crap," my alpha seethed. "What the fuck happened?"

"She gave us two councilors and a testimony witnessed by all three of us. So it's valid," I said soothingly. "We got something."

Weiss shook his head, probably trying to calm down. "We could have gotten more," he growled.

Will crossed his arms in front of his chest. "I don't think so. Her alpha—"

"Pseudo alpha!" Weiss barked.

"Her *pseudo* alpha ordered her not to share information, I think," Will said calmly. "It's probably why she resisted answering my questions as much as she did."

"Didn't look like much resistance," Weiss snapped.

"Trust me, there was a lot of it. It's why I increased the… pressure."

"Thereby leaving us without our main and only witness," Weiss sneered. He shook his head, breathing in and out deeply. "Don't get me wrong, Will. I'm thankful for your help. I'm just pissed we didn't get more."

"Maybe the files will give us more," I intervened meekly.

Weiss nodded. "Maybe. Tim is looking them over. They had to be in fucking Fey of course," he grumbled. "Makes the whole process of looking them over a lot slower since only Tim can."

"I could help," Will volunteered. "Maybe Jeremy and Susannah too. You can trust them," he assured Weiss.

"They're still kids," Weiss said, looking uncomfortable.

"They are trained and ready to replace me, both of them. As Fey Court Interrogators," Will said, cocking his head to the side. "They haven't been children for a very long time. Trust me."

Weiss stuck his hands in his pockets. "Okay. Thanks for offering. You can bring them in tomorrow; they'll work in my office with Tim. I'll set up a couple laptops for them or something."

"Thank you," Will said emphatically. "You're saving their lives, and they'll be thrilled to help you however they can."

Weiss sighed and turned toward the cell that used to be Tricia's. "Is she… in pain?"

He didn't look at Will, but it was clear the question was aimed at him. Will stuck his hands in his pockets and glanced at me. "She's in a coma. Whatever version of the afterlife you choose to believe in, there's this much I can almost guarantee: when the body and the consciousness separate, the suffering of the body doesn't reach the consciousness anymore."

"You guys get the fuck out of here," Weiss muttered after a while.

"Need me to find you someplace safe to stay?" he said, looking at Will.

"We thought we'd stay at the complex with Bert," he replied smoothly.

Weiss nodded. "It's a secure location, and we can arrange it. Yeah. See you guys tomorrow, then."

And he walked out.

TRICIA WAS taken into MCU care. Naty ruled it a coma. Nobody discussed the cause. As far as official records were concerned, she simply fell unconscious during interrogation—regular interrogation. There would be no way of proving anything other than that. The only relevant fey other than Will and Tim was the current fey ambassador, and she was no trouble at all, Will assured us. I took that to mean she was part of the wind, just like he was.

All of the cameras and recording devices had been blasted out of order in Tricia's holding cell. Nobody outside of us, direct witnesses, even knew who interrogated her. Most importantly, nobody but us knew what she said, and about whom. And we had to keep things that way if we wanted to prove we had two traitors on the Council.

It broke my heart to think Naty's mom was a traitor. Because she'd be taken out soon if she were. She'd be replaced on the Council, sure, just like the other traitor. But nobody would be able to replace Naty's mom—even if she behaved as if her daughter didn't exist most of the time. And outside of friends, Naty didn't have much else because of her lost-in-shifting situation. She had gotten stuck during her first shift and remained so since then. The animal ears and tail made her a loner. Sure, she had some friends, and many of us did truly love her to bits. But she was single, and nobody would jeopardize the strength of their future cubs by having them with a female like that. And now she was going to be the only child of a schemer and traitor. Life just wasn't fair for any of us. But it seemed to me it had been especially unfair to my friend Naty.

MY COMPLEX admin wasn't thrilled, but she could be trusted. I got the Simses the apartment beside mine, a three-bedroom unit designed for family life.

"Are you okay?" Will asked softly when we were in the elevator of the complex, going up to our apartments.

"You know how I am, don't you? You can all relate to it, I guess. Maybe except for the twins," I muttered, looking speculatively at them in Susannah's arms.

"Them too," Susannah replied curtly, staring up into my eyes. "I know what losing a sibling feels like. I'm sorry for your situation."

"How do they…?"

"How do the twins know?" Jeremy asked, smiling softly. "We're the Sims line heirs. We know whatever we choose to. And the mind is curious, especially during the first years. Intense emotions draw our attention. We would balance your grid, if we could read it."

I smiled because the cockiness worked on them for some reason. "And why would you choose to do that?"

"You've agreed to take us out of the Kingdom," Susannah said simply. There was no outright gratitude in her demeanor, but I felt the hostility from earlier in the day diminish considerably. "You brought us into PBI, where we met with a brother we thought was dead. You've given us a glimpse into your heart when father was interrogating your sister. Sincere kindness is a rare gift where we come from. Don't think we don't appreciate it."

I looked at Will, somewhat scared. "And they know you were interrogating my sister because—?"

"Because they can read family connections without being in the room. Just as I can."

I frowned. "Wouldn't you read all of the PBI at the same time, if you're that sensitive?"

"We read whatever we're interested in," Susannah chastised me. "And your Council rules don't apply to us. Just in case you were planning to intimidate us not to do it in the future."

I lifted an eyebrow and turned toward her. "Oh, yeah? Why wouldn't they apply to you?"

"Who's going to tell them we're reading grids?" she replied, grinning crookedly.

I saw her father's ego and attitude in that grin, and despite worrying me, it also made me want to grin back. There was something entirely entertaining about a teen-girl version of Will, I decided. Completely terrifying, but also entertaining.

"Maybe I'll tell them," I replied, frowning at her.

Susannah snorted. "Oh, please! You're doe-eyed for Father. Of course you won't."

"Susannah," Will said after clearing his throat. "We've talked about these kinds of answers. They're beneath you."

She snorted. "As if. Don't act like you're innocent. You read him too, when you had the chance. I know you did. You've got that butterflies-in-the-stomach look in your eyes when you see the guy," she informed him, lifting an eyebrow.

"Susannah!" Will snapped and turned toward her.

"Forgive her, Father," Jeremy said, reaching out a hand to set it on Will's shoulder. "It's been a long day for them, not to mention seeing me again…."

Susannah looked up at her oldest brother with an adoring and completely trusting stare, and it made my stomach clench tight.

"And Father has had a terribly trying day too," he went on, looking down into Susannah's eyes.

"Of course you'd be on his side," she mumbled, her adoring gaze turning to daggers. "Never mind that he almost killed you."

"Father saved my life, and all of yours," he reminded her and leaned down to kiss her cheek.

Hector and Sarah were holding hands and standing close to their siblings. I turned away, feeling the moment was too intimate for me to steal glances at. They were a family, acting like one. I had no business intruding on that.

Will bumped his shoulder against mine softly and smiled when I glanced at him. The gesture made my stomach quiver.

"So you guys hungry?" I asked without looking at anyone in particular.

"Finally!" Susannah declared as we exited the elevator. "We're starving."

Will chuckled. "There's no getting on with a starved teenager."

"But there is some when they're full?" I asked, eyeing Susannah dubiously.

Will shrugged. "On their best days… maybe. A little. Not so much," he finally admitted, grinning.

"Come over for dinner," I said, looking at the kids. "Take a nap or something in the meantime, or catch up and just relax. It's been a trying day for all of us," I muttered, opening up the door to their apartment. I set the key in Will's hand and then walked toward the next door, my apartment.

"We'll be over in a few hours," Will said, smiling. "Thank you. For everything."

I just shrugged. "I do love to have people over and cook for them. This is as much for me as it is for you guys."

"You love to cook, I know," Will said softly, then went into the apartment after his kids and closed the door behind them.

The Sims kids had to be tired, emotionally exhausted from meeting their older brother again, and they needed to lie down and eat something better than bars of chocolate.

I grabbed a large pack of watermelon ice cream from my fridge and went over to knock on their door. I also had plenty of spoons in tow, hoping they'd feel better after a treat until I could get them a proper dinner. And I needed to get the complex shoppers a list of what groceries they'd need, including for the babies.

Will opened the door, smiling. "Missed us already?"

"Figured you could all use a cheer-me-up, maybe? Plus I need your list of groceries for the complex manager. They do our shopping here, laundry, the works. I figured it would be better than running around looking for stuff tomorrow," I added, hoping I didn't seem intrusive.

"That would be great," Will said. "We were just figuring out the logistics."

Susannah settled the twins in the kiddies' room, which had two cribs stuffed in there. She'd share a bedroom with her little sister Sarah while Jeremy would sleep with Hector in the last bedroom. Will was going to sleep on the couch. They discussed all of that quick and easy, and I thought Will seemed glad to give them whatever they wanted. Susannah was clearly the spokesperson for the kids, with Jeremy naturally following and enforcing her lead and the smaller kids going whichever way she deemed fit. It made my heart constrict to watch and hear them talk, the picture of close brothers and sisters. That picture stung my chest like acid.

I'd just gotten my sister into a coma. Fucked-up as it was, that was probably the best-case scenario for her right now. Less humiliating, less painful. I realized now all those talks we'd had about Amanda and Weiss as a couple had always had this discreet, frustrated sheen; that she always sided with Amanda whenever doing so didn't seem like outright insubordination toward Weiss. Especially the last couple years or so. I remembered all those shopping trips Amanda took with Tricia, claiming it was a girls' thing. Were they lovers? Did they consummate their love in stolen moments of bliss? Bliss based on treason. What the fuck had happened to our orderly pack life? I swallowed down bile.

After they put the twins to bed in a wailing, screaming state their oldest sister diagnosed as "just being tired," the rest of the Sims kids, their father, and I sat around the ice cream and attacked it with glee. No plates, no glasses to eat from. Just the kids, Will, and I devouring delicious watermelon-flavored ice cream. As we did I wrote up their list of groceries on my phone, a long-ass list that ended up becoming an even longer-ass list with brand-specific items that went to our building manager via the secure app our geek squad had developed for us. Susannah took charge of the list too, firing off brands on the Yes and Absolutely No list for everything we managed to go through: foods for grownups and the twins, nappies, enough baby-related paraphernalia to scare a grown man out of his goddamn mind. Or at least me. She knew everything, had an opinion about everything, and disliked most options available, having a long list of faults for each rejected item.

"Teens," Will said after she finally decided she'd bossed us around enough and left to take a nap.

That, of course, happened after she had instructed me on everything her siblings did and did not like, what they'd go with, and what they'd most assuredly outright reject. Being schooled by a kid was an entirely novel experience, but somehow I found myself enjoying it.

"How old are they, anyway?" I asked, looking over the menu guidelines.

Jeremy, still hanging around the table with us, smiled. "I'm the eldest, but don't let that fool you into thinking I'm in charge," he explained, chuckling. "Our fierce leader is Susannah," he added, grinning with way too much pride and a hint of sadistic pleasure. "You just wait 'til she gets a couple years older. Then we'll all see real hell."

"She takes after her mother that way," Will said, shaking his head.

Jeremy yawned and went to lie down with his little brother. I took the opportunity to ask a couple of questions that had been bugging me.

"I've been meaning to ask," I began, focusing on the spoon resting on the table. "They don't have the same mother, that much is clear."

Will sat on the couch, lifting his feet up and glancing at me. "Except for the twins of course," he said seriously enough that I realized he was teasing me. "Come a little closer," he said softly and beckoned me with a finger.

I snorted but did go to sit on the other end of the couch. After all, I didn't want the kids to hear what we were discussing.

"How come you have so many children and by different mothers?"

"It's a Sims line tradition. How strong the parents are influences how strong children could get. Traditionally the Interrogator has children with as many powerful fey as they can. The children are all officially Sims."

"And single, powerful fey line up to have Sims kids?" I muttered incredulously.

"Of course not. There are financial agreements, sometimes other favors exchanged as well. They don't need to be single at all."

That left a sour taste in my mouth. "They're kids, not clothes to borrow. What the fuck? Someone just has and gives away a baby that easily?"

Will shrugged. "You might have noticed fey aren't particularly fond of their offspring. You want to know why?"

"Let me guess, it's a power thing," I mumbled, crossing my arms in front of my chest.

Will nodded. "Think about it. Who to better know your weaknesses and be able to use and manipulate you but those you nurture, educate, and train until the Fey Academy takes over?"

"What the fuck, man! They're your kids! Not embittered enemies."

"All the more dangerous because, unlike enemies, children do have ample opportunity to work against you and eventually take you out."

"How come you love yours, then?" I asked, frowning.

"I couldn't help doing so," he said, shaking his head ruefully. "Others love their children too, I'm sure. But we all need to keep up appearances that none of us do. Because even if your children don't turn against you...." He looked at me intently.

"Then others will use them to get to you," I finished that thought. "Jesus fucking Christ. I've never been happier I was born in a werewolf family."

"So was Tricia," he reminded me gently. "It's not where you come from that determines who you are, or what choices you make in life. Sure, it will influence you, your values, your criteria. But what ultimately matters is what's inside your heart. Don't you think so?"

I sighed and ran both palms over my face. "And some, like Tricia, have treason in their hearts. Betrayal."

"Also manifestations of their love for one thing or another," Will said smoothly. "Don't judge your sister so harshly, Bert. Sometimes there are things you simply can't ignore. Things you can't help but do, even if you don't want to do them."

"I'm sorry, but I can't accept that."

"You took your ring off and then put it back on," he said and sat closer to me. "Why did you do that?"

"I was tense. I didn't know what I was doing, just playing around with it nervously."

He leaned closer and pushed a fingertip under my chin, making me turn to face him. "We both know why you did it, Bert."

My heart lurched in my chest, a confusing array of feelings trampling through me. "No shit. And why did I do it?"

"Because love makes us do all sorts of things. Sometimes things we don't want to do. Like protect our traitor of a sister," he whispered and leaned in.

He brushed his lips against mine softly, like a caress. I had plenty of room and opportunity to pull back, but I didn't. I breathed out heavily and angled my head in for a kiss I wanted so bad it made my skin tingle all over.

It wasn't a passionate, intense, insane kiss. It was a calm, tender one, soft and comforting. He wrapped his arms around me without pulling me over or into him, just caressing and holding me close. I felt almost as if my spine melted. I took all he had to give me and gave back at least as much. I yearned for more, made small sounds of frustration every time he pulled back even a little, only to come back hungrier for me.

My blood thrummed through my veins and my heart beat wilder and wilder until it was fluttering desperately inside my chest.

It was all wrong of course. I couldn't trust a fey official, even more so because he'd betrayed his Court. I couldn't hook up with a father of six while his kids were just in the other rooms. But I wanted to. My greedy little heart wanted to enjoy and have him. And I got a small sense of what he meant. I didn't want to want him, but I did. And I couldn't stop myself from doing so.

twelve

I LEFT Will's with a hard-on and a vague idea about luring him into my apartment and having my way with him. That and a plan to buy things I had never, ever used to cook before. Because Susannah, the fierce teen leader of the young Sims wing, wasn't easy to please. But for some stupid reason, I not only wanted to rise up to the challenge of cooking stuff she'd like, but I also aimed to impress her. A lot of things were confusing right now, but fuck me sideways if I didn't know how to cook.

The key here, though, was not going entirely out of my way. I didn't want it to be obvious I was trying to impress. Whipping up a French-names-only meal would have been a piece of cake for me, but it would also have been a transparent attempt at wowing—and a potential disaster since two of my guests were kids under the age of ten. I wanted to wow without seeming to have tried.

There were going to be six of us, including kids. A two- or three-course meal wouldn't do. I wanted it to be more of a family dinner kind of feel, rather than a reception. They'd almost certainly had enough protocol to last them a lifetime already.

So I decided to go with pork-and-beef mix lasagna topped off with plenty of raw eggs to make it nice, crusty, and brown like a pie. It wasn't too pretentious, was easy to make, delicious to eat, and was filling but left room for dessert. When eating with kids, you had to have dessert—at least, that was how it had been with Alf. The little guy always loved tasty treats without being too picky about the name or even the looks of things. That was key to getting a kid to eat your cooking: you had to earn their trust, make them feel sure whatever you gave them tasted awesome. And I'd gotten pretty good at that. And at guessing what someone liked.

So for dessert I went big: tangerine- and dark cherry-covered cheesecake, and what my mom liked to call basket cake—tiny dough baskets you baked set over some tea cups so they'd keep the tiny basket shape, then filled with all kinds of sliced fruit, sweet and bitter, and covered with a dusting of sugar. You set the basket cakes back in the oven for about half an hour until the fruit baked enough to get all mushy and juicy, but not entirely flopped into submission. When the basket cakes cooled off, they went into the fridge so the fruity goodness would be all the better. When served, you could top it off either with a spoonful of whipped cream or with a spoonful of ice cream, preferably flavored so it would complement the fruits you used. So sweet fruits in the baskets, bitter-flavored ice cream, perhaps lemon or even mint. Of course you'd ask each guest what they wanted, so it was best to have a few options ready. Because I'd already fed them ice cream, and I didn't want to be so obviously spoiling them to win them over, I went with the whipped cream version tonight.

By the time I had the table arranged, my dining room smelled quite heavenly. I had sweetened fruit tea cooled off and ready to go, plus some red wine because we deserved a glass or two after the kind of day we had. I also had a pretty smug smile on my face. What I didn't have was baby food, and had no idea what the twins would be good with eating. So I made sure the Sims got their groceries and baby food delivered, including baby accessories like chairs and whatnot.

I had no idea what the Sims dinner ritual was—did they have the babies there with them, someone babysitting them while the others ate, had them fed and set to bed before the actual dinner? No clue. It could go either way. It was the kind of thing every family did differently. When Alf was a baby, for instance, he refused to be anywhere but close to his dad whenever possible. That included dinners. I'd watch over him, sure, but he had his baby chair set up where it would give him a good view of his dad. And Weiss used to make all sorts of silly faces at him during dinner—not all the time, just every now and then. That had made dinnertime Alf's favorite part of the day as a baby. Maybe it still was now, even if they didn't do the whole silly faces thing anymore.

God, I missed that kid. He was really smart and entertaining. Though now he was growing up faster and faster, spending more time at school. Soon it would be time to go out with friends, then girlfriends or boyfriends... or both, if he was anything like his dad.... I sighed. Kids grew up so fast. It was unfair. Every time you got the hang of what to do to keep the kid happy at a particular age, they went on to a whole other stage, and you were clueless again. And when you got your head around this new phase, there they were, embarking on the next.

I straightened up, took a very quick shower, changed into jeans and a shirt, and went over to knock on the Simses' door. Susannah opened the door and nodded for me to come in, which was quite informal and, I thought, therefore progress.

"Father is getting ready. He dozed off a bit," she explained as she walked toward the couch.

Jeremy was rocking both kids gently in his arms.

"You're putting the twins to bed?"

Susannah smiled at them ever so slightly. "Yes. They've been agitated, restless all day. New environment, new people.... It's tough on babies. I'm sure you understand."

I looked at this thirteen-year-old and couldn't believe she was a day less than thirty in some ways. It intimidated me a bit.

I nodded. "Will they be alright here while we have dinner?"

"They'll sleep through it, as they usually do. They sleep all through the night already," she informed me.

Like she was the proud mom rather than their oldest sister—and she wasn't that old herself.

"You like to take care of them, don't you?" I asked.

She looked over at me briefly, then back to them. "I had to. The governess who brought us up is awful at best. Children need to be loved and nurtured when they grow up. Her idea of doing that rivaled being clonked over the head with a bag of bricks."

I burst out laughing, I just couldn't help it. Then I shook my head. "Sorry, that wasn't very nice of me. I'm sorry to hear that, but I do love the way you said it."

She looked me over and shrugged. "Good. Then there's hope for you yet."

Jeremy got up and took the babies in their room. A few minutes later, he came back, just as Will was emerging from the bathroom all dressed and clean and good enough to eat.

"Hey," I said, stuffing my hands in my pockets. "So you guys ready to come over?"

"Lead the way," Will said, smiling oh so deliciously.

I did lead the way, opened the front door, and stood by it as they got in. They wasted no time in sitting down, and I brought over the lasagna from the oven where I had stored it in the hope that it wouldn't get too cold. I saw appreciative faces as I scanned the table, doing the honors and serving everyone. I gave the kids the cool and fruity sweet tea and served Will a glass of wine, then got myself one.

"Thank you," Will said brightly. "You didn't have to go out of your way."

I shrugged. "Don't mention it. I enjoy it. Hope you'll enjoy too," I said and reached for my fork.

"May I propose a toast?" Jeremy asked.

"By all means, son," Will replied.

"To new beginnings," Jeremy said, lifting his glass.

"To new and promising beginnings," Susannah said, lifting hers.

"And to pie, because I can smell it," said Sarah.

Hector grinned and lifted his glass too.

"And to more of these delicious dinners in the company of our delightful host," Will added, looking at me.

I felt my face heat up as I lifted my glass. Susannah and Jeremy grinned at each other, then at Sarah and Hector. We each drank a gulp or two of our drinks, then finally dug in.

I found out new and interesting things about fey during this dinner. For one, they seemed to have healthier appetites than I thought. Everyone went for seconds, and some of the kids went for thirds, actually, though smaller portions.

When I brought out the fruit baskets and topped each off with a fresh spoonful of whipped cream, Sarah and Hector clapped excitedly. Susannah and Jeremy contained their enthusiasm better, but I did see joy glowing in their eyes. And Will had, I think, five of those baskets between his second and third glass of wine.

When we were all done with our desserts, we laid back in the chairs, full bellies making it hard to breathe.

"Oh my gods," Susannah muttered dejectedly. "We can't allow you to cook again," she said, squinting at me.

I panicked. "Why?"

"I'm going to get outrageously fat, that's why," she mumbled, looking down at her plate. "I could never stop myself from overeating. Not with this kind of cooking."

I chuckled. "Thanks."

"It's not funny," she said, making a face at me. "I'd stuff myself into oblivion with your cooking around. Whatever it is you did tonight while cooking, never do it again," she commanded.

"You mean I shouldn't cook the same things again?" I asked, confused.

Will shook his head. "The thing about fey is we can taste more than just the food while we eat. You know they say your cooking is always better if you put love into it as you're cooking? It's an actual thing for us. If you're happy, excited, or nervous while you cook, it changes the taste of the food to a degree. Positive feelings make it all the better. Negative ones take away from the taste."

"So you can taste what I felt as I was cooking?" I asked, shaking my head. "That's a little disturbing."

"It's not disturbing," Susannah corrected me immediately. "It's closeness. Thank you for the wonderful meal," she said and finally smiled brilliantly at me. "Father, we're going back to check on the twins and go to bed. We'll have a lot of work to do tomorrow, and we need to rest for it."

Will nodded. "I'll walk you in," he told them and got up from the table. "Be right back," he told me sweetly.

My heart stuttered. I got the feeling Susannah just gave me her discreet okay to make a go at Will. My face heated up again. Thankfully I still had that ring on my finger. I had worn it while cooking, too, and they still could taste stuff about my emotions in the meal. How would it be if I weren't wearing the ring?

Will came back shortly. "I got them in and locked the door when I left," he explained, dangling the key in front of his eyes.

I frowned. "Why, Will, are you drunk by any chance?"

He grinned, devious and hot as hell. "Not really. Were you trying to get me drunk?"

"That depends. What kind of drunk are you? Angry, happy?"

"Horny. I'm a very horny drunk. But then again, I seem to be horny around you even without a drop of alcohol, so you don't need to make that much of an effort."

He walked up to me, took my hand, and pulled me up from the chair. We moved toward the couch and he pushed me down on it. I landed with a thump and looked up, a little confused as to what we were doing.

"Will?"

"I want you, and you want me. Am I right?"

I swallowed thickly. "You are."

"This is not going to be a one-night stand, if it happens."

"If?" I asked, lifting an eyebrow.

"Okay, when it happens."

"Much better," I said, grinning. "I'm not hoping for a one-night stand either. Though I'm not sure what kind of relationship we can afford to have."

He grabbed the hem of his shirt and pulled it out of his pants, then started to unbutton it. "Let's not worry about that, hm? Let's just enjoy each other and our time together for as much as we can."

"Good plan," I muttered, watching the skin of his torso slowly being revealed to me.

I was totally hard just from watching him. Studying the beautiful lines of his body, the elegant way he moved, how graceful yet strong his fingers were as he undid another and another button from his shirt, then moved to the button and fly of his pants. I gulped and reached for the hem of my shirt, but he grabbed my hands and shook his head.

"Please, don't. Let me."

He left his pants on, button and fly undone, and went to work taking off my shirt and jeans. He caressed my hard-on through my underwear, smiling at me in a way that had my heart stuttering. He rubbed the tip of his nose slowly against my treasure trail, tickling me and making goose bumps rise all over my skin. When he reached my hard-on, he sucked it through the stretched material of my black briefs, wetting up and rubbing the spot where the head of my dick was.

"Mh, that feels great," I said, leaning back on the couch and pushing my hips closer to him. "Would feel better skin on skin, though," I said, grinning.

He hooked his fingertips in the elastic band of the briefs and got them down, watching very closely how my dick caught the fabric, then sprang against my stomach as my member finally got free. He pushed my briefs down my thighs, then tossed them away entirely.

When he wrapped his wet, hot mouth around the head of my dick, I thought I saw stars. He slid down slowly until his lips were against the base. And he swallowed, massaging my underside with his tongue.

I finally managed to push my fingers through his hair, grabbing a handful and holding his head tight as I slowly fucked his mouth. He moaned every now and then, swallowed with greed every time I pushed as deep as I could go. Fuck, this felt like heaven. I stared down at how his mouth worked me and at his disheveled hair. It felt amazing between my fingers: smooth, silky soft. He pulled back, releasing my dick with a wet pop. When he looked at me, I thought my knees would melt. His eyes had gone dark, so very dark, a transfixing stare that made me shiver.

"Let's take this into the bedroom," he said, his voice low, almost dangerous. "Which door?"

I pointed at my bedroom, unable to speak. He got up, turned around, and walked there without another word. I followed on unsteady feet, my pulse pounding so hard it almost deafened me. He was taking his pants and shorts off finally, and I looked hungrily at every inch of naked skin he exposed. The hairless body felt young, taut skin, lean muscles. I expected him to seem twinky, maybe, but he didn't. He was like a swimmer—more muscles to his body than to Tim's, a sturdier build, and a much, much more intense presence. And he seemed taller now that he was naked, which made no sense. When he looked at me, my spine straightened. And I felt it clearly: I was falling for him…. I shivered again.

"I want you to remove that ring," he said, staring right at it.

I glanced down. The ring was the only thing I was wearing now. A protection against his prying reading skills. A protection against anyone's reading skills because he wasn't the only fey around.

"Won't your kids be able to…?"

He shook his head. "They're not allowed to read emotional grids in the evening unless there's an emergency to prompt it."

"But the babies…."

"Wouldn't be able to comment on what they'd read, even if they did," he stated calmly. "Take that ring off, Bert. Let me see you stripped of anything and everything, fully unclothed before me. Let me see your entire self, body, feelings, desires…. Show me the insides of your soul," he whispered thickly as his gaze grew unbearably intense.

I swallowed, though my throat felt dry. The ring had been my security blanket in his presence. Giving it up suddenly scared the hell out of me.

He walked toward me slowly, slinky like a panther. It made me want to step back, my beta response to him unreasonable and slightly shameful. I felt conflicted, as if I were betraying my alpha by feeling this way. I shook my head and looked at the ring again.

"I've given you my ring," he whispered, his lips against my cheek, trailing them softly up and down, from the corner of my lips to my ear, then back again. "Now take yours off for me," he said, emphasizing each word by lightly nipping my jawline between words. "I promise I won't hurt you, Bert," he whispered, wrapping his arms around me. "You can't trust that yet, and I understand. I'm not asking you to trust me. But I'm telling you I won't do anything to purposely hurt you. I won't use your emotions against you. I swear."

I felt small, vulnerable, and scared. All of which was ridiculous. "You wouldn't be able to refrain from it. Because to you using what those around you feel is part of regular life. I'm not blaming you for it. It just scares me."

"You grow claws, sharp teeth, and fur when you shift," he said softly. "I'm not scared you'll bite my dick off because it's part of your regular animal life to bite things."

I blinked a few times. "Did you just say 'dick'?"

"You seem to like that," he said as he rubbed my even harder dick.

It was throbbing, needy to the point of pain.

"We're different," he went on. "We will each experience the other in different ways, not because I'm fey and you're a werewolf, but because that's how everyone experiences everything: differently, on a case-by-case basis. So please just let me experience all of you," he whispered and went back to nibbling on my jaw.

I leaned my head to the side, giving him more access. And then I had this weird thought, this serpent slithering though my soul. It just zapped through my mind. And it made me freeze.

He stepped back and met my gaze. "Are you okay?"

"Why are you insisting?"

He frowned. "About the ring?"

"Yes."

"Because I want to get to know you better. And reading your emotional grid is how I can do that."

I crossed my arms in front of my chest. "So it has nothing to do with the ring?"

"You think I want to steal it?" he asked, looking flabbergasted.

"Well, you can't take it off my finger yourself, and you've shown interest in it."

Will sighed and sat on the bed, crossing his gorgeous legs. "I suspected trust would be difficult for you, but I didn't expect things to be this bad."

"Don't talk about it like it's some big issue, okay? And we're not having this discussion while we're naked and hard," I muttered.

He smiled. "You're right."

And he got up and walked out of my bedroom.

thirteen

THE MOMENT seemed surreal. I looked down at my softening dick and felt tempted to ask it if this was happening. I pulled open the dresser and put on a pair of sweatpants and a sleeveless shirt. Then I took a deep breath and went into the living room. From this point I could actually see the dining room area with the table and plates I still had to clear up. I felt sorry I'd ruined a perfectly nice evening and a possibility to get monumentally laid.

I looked over to the couch and was very surprised to see a very much clothed and oddly not pissed Will sitting there.

"Well, this isn't awkward at all," I muttered, sticking my hands in the pockets of my sweats.

"Would you please sit down with me?"

I didn't want to, that was the thing. Sleeping with him, even getting somewhat involved—sure, that sounded good. Doing any heart-to-heart, though? That didn't sound tempting at all.

"Let's just drop it, okay?"

"Ah. So you were planning on this being a one-night stand after all."

"Why the fuck would you say that?"

"Why else would you be so averse to talking about significant things in your life?"

"Because I'm a guy?" I said in a general "duh" tone.

"Weak reply. Try again."

"I don't share my emotions and shit, okay?"

"Yes, I got that point earlier, in the bedroom."

I shook my head. "Look, this is all wrong. We don't even make sense together. I mean, you have kids, lots of them, you need someone sturdy and ready to have a big family all at once, and I just—"

"Don't. Please don't do that."

"Don't do what, say the truth?"

"Don't use the children as an excuse. You're accustomed to being around children. You took care of your alpha's son until recently, after all."

I turned away from him because seeing that stricken look in his eyes broke my heart a little bit. "That's different."

"How? How is that different?"

"It's one kid, okay? And I've known him since he was a wee bit of a fluffy thing."

I felt exactly like the ass I was being. I knew it was wrong to say it and I didn't really feel that way, though his bunch of kids was intimidating. But if he was so keen on reading my emotions and maybe getting my ring too, and I was this averse to trusting him, then we had no business being together anyway. Wasting his time and getting close to his kids in the process was only going to result in heartache. I didn't need any more of that.

"Why do you feel this need to be something other than yourself?" he said, shaking his head.

"Excuse me?"

"You always mold around someone. You talk more vulgarly around Weiss, but not when around me. You're more impulsive when around him, but entirely reticent when you're with me. Are all of these facets of your personality? Or do you act differently around every single person? You won't let me see what you feel. Who are you? What's the real you?"

"You can't compare the two. My natural tendency is to follow whatever direction my alpha dictates. It transpires into a way of talking and general attitude, I guess. But it doesn't mean I'm as fickle and fake as you make me out to be."

"I'm sorry if it sounded that way. I wasn't saying that at all. I'm just so confused about what you feel. That's why I asked you so insistently to take that ring off. So I could see what you felt and be guided by that instead of what you say or do."

I gritted my teeth and looked away.

"Why hide your personality, your way of speaking, your feelings from me? Is it more than just a trust issue in general? Is it an issue you have with me personally?"

"Now you're just getting full of yourself. What do you mean I hide my personality and way of speaking?"

He sighed. "Are you really not aware of doing it, or are you just playing dumb?"

"Well, everyone is dumb compared to the strategic genius Fey Court Interrogator!"

"I'm not a genius. And in case you've forgotten, I left the Court. With you."

"What you wanna say is that you already had a deal with my alpha and didn't deem it necessary to mention that. Then you used me as an excuse to leave, *Sir* Sims. It's a very different fucking thing," I snapped.

He got up and walked closer. "See? This is what I was talking about. This is your natural way of speaking. This is your personality. You only show me your true self when you're mad."

"I'm not mad, I'm fucking pissed! Pissed!"

I stormed back into my bedroom, needing some space.

Of course he walked in there after me. "I'm not trying to get close to you to use you. I don't want your damn ring. I just want to get to know you, to get close to you."

"Why the fuck would you?" I snapped and finally looked into his eyes. "Why? Why would you?"

God, he was gorgeous. He was lean, amazing, well mannered, well educated, and had plenty of responsibilities while in a difficult time of his life, if I had to guess. He didn't need a chubby trash-talking werewolf who had never in his life dated the same person for more than three weeks at a time. And he would read these feelings as soon as the ring came off. And he would know how horribly fucked-up I was. How flawed I had to be.

One guy leaving you, two of them, five of them, was one thing—all of them was another. All of them damning my stubborn defenses and my unwillingness to share myself with them. It stood to reason I really sucked at the relationship part. I didn't want him to see me that way—the way I saw myself. I was the lame, lonely, insecure guy who took care of other people's kids because he was never busy enough not to, who had no personal life outside of his pack and only had one real relationship in his life—the one with his sister. Now I didn't have that either. I had nothing. I was nothing.

And I had this epiphany that Weiss must have thought me good for nothing after all. Because he had sent me out to get him information he probably could have gotten without my help. He wanted to make me feel better, and knowing I was such a loser, he gave me a job he could get done behind my back, maybe. Which meant he was still my friend, wanting to help me feel better, but a fucking liar too.

Will walked closer and grabbed my hand. "Why would I want to get to know you? You can't be serious, Bert. Because I'm falling for you, that's why. What kind of question is that?"

"I don't know. I think I'm having a breakdown or something."

"Just please talk to me about whatever it is that bothers you. Okay?"

Well, shit, I couldn't. I already seemed like a big enough idiot as it was.

"I'm so sorry about ruining tonight," I muttered pitifully.

"You didn't," he said and pulled me into his arms. "You're stressed out, dealing with a lot of pain about your sister. I understand."

"God, I wish I could have a do-over for tonight."

"How about we do just that? Some other night. There's no need to rush into things. We'll just get to know each other under these new conditions. My life has changed a lot too in the last day or so. So we'll figure things out together, okay?"

"You're way too awesome," I said and sighed. "How about you sleep over, though? I mean, actually sleep. You've seen the size of my bed, and I just couldn't forgive myself if you slept on a couch while there was room for you here. I mean, I hog a lot of space, and the blankets, but, you know."

He chuckled. "I'd love to sleep over. I'll just let the kids know I'm sleeping here, okay? So they won't worry."

He took out a phone and I guess texted something. Then he smiled. "Okay. Can I borrow a T-shirt?"

"Sure. It will probably be too large for you, but—"

"Would you stop that? It'll be great. Now could we please get into bed?"

"Do you still want to, uhm…?"

"I'll always want to, but I'd like us to wait until you feel comfortable enough around me to take that ring off. Don't get me wrong, I'll nurse a boner the whole night sleeping with you, but I'd like our first time to be more than just blowing off steam."

I frowned. "So you're turning down sex for more meaningful lovemaking at some later point? You're a very, very weird man."

He chuckled. "I know. But I'm sick of inconsequential affairs. I want to be with someone I count on and rely on. Someone who isn't using me to get to something or someone better. I think you could be that person."

"I could."

But the question was, was I going to actually be able to? I had no real answer right now.

"You're not scared of me, though, right?"

"Pffft! A werewolf, scared? Never. Why would I be?"

He leaned closer. "Because of my magic. You've seen what I can do. Believe it or not, many are scared shitless of that. And I do cuss too, just so you know. I just try not to because I don't want the children to hear it and then repeat it."

The image of Tricia having that nosebleed went through my mind. The idea he could turn him and me into fruit flies twice and turn us back into our normal shapes. The fact he could make pretty much anyone do whatever he wanted. I shivered. It scared me all right. But it didn't scare me away, for some reason. He hadn't cast a spell to make me take off the ring, though he could. Just kept asking me to. Asking why I wouldn't. Trying to make a connection instead of driving me to give him what he wanted. He wasn't trying to boss me around. Maybe that was so new and disorienting I didn't know how to react. And I wanted to let him in, though I was scared. So that meant I did trust him to some extent. We had something to build on. That or I was entirely self-destructive.

THE NEXT morning was, in short, hell. My balls hurt, I was hard as a rock, and I woke up with Will's arms wrapped around me and a nasty pain in my neck. That was probably due to whatever strange position I had slept in. It was my first time sharing a bed in a long time. While I missed some parts of it, some I could do without. But I did like waking up to Will's perfect face. And seeing him open his gorgeous eyes was the kind of moment I'd always remember for the rest of my life.

He got a shower first. Then I went in. We agreed he'd get the kids over and I'd fix them some pancakes because now I had a good enough excuse to have pancakes for breakfast too without feeling guilty: I was making them for the kids! I missed that part of taking care of Alf. My growing belly had been doing well without the pancakes routine, though. I promised myself I wouldn't make a habit out of this. Susannah might try to stab me to death in my sleep if she got less bony. The very idea made me grin.

When the kids came over, I had a stack of pancakes ready for them. Susannah glared at me as she ate, Jeremy seemed to love them, and Sarah and Hector stuffed their mouths. If I had to guess, Sarah was going to spend a lot of time brushing her teeth again, because I was sure pancakes went into those braces with a vengeance. But by the delighted looks on their faces, it was totally worth it. I only ate about three and watched Will eat four. We had coffee as the kids finished up eating.

"So Jeremy and Susannah are coming in with us. What about Sarah, Hector, and the twins?"

Will frowned. "Do you know anyone that could babysit, maybe?"

"I'd love to, but Weiss said I should come in too. I can ask a friend to watch over them."

"Thanks. We can hire this friend of yours for a while, just until we figure things out."

"She wouldn't want to take the money. And she might not be available at all times. She works front desk for another complex like this one."

"Oh?"

"She's the sister of another PBI agent, Travis Chandler. She's great with kids, though I don't know if she's watched over four of them at one time."

"Make the call, and we'll see."

Tatiana was actually thrilled to try it and claimed she'd have everything under control. When she arrived Susannah inspected her for a few minutes, grilled her about baby care, and then nodded, giving her approval.

"Well, I like her," Tatiana muttered, grinning. "Bit of a psycho vibe, but very in charge. She'll grow up to be a knockout too."

"I'm sure of that," I replied, smiling.

"So these are friends of yours? Fey friends?" she said, looking them over.

"Yeah. But you have to keep this a secret. The father, Will, would like to hire you if you'd be available. He's new in town, and until he makes sense of everything, he might need someone to watch over the kids."

She frowned. "A fey family this big wants to set up home on our territories? There's a juicy story to ferret out here," she declared, taking a big mug of coffee. "So where will we be, the kids and I?"

"Next door. You've probably got everything you need there. If not, you know what to do."

She grinned. "Harass the complex manager of course. I'd love to. Now shoo, I can manage. I'm not busy until eight tonight, so try to make it home by at least seven. Cool?"

I nodded. "Will do."

And then we were off. Susannah disliked my car of course, and commented on the lack of room for the baby seats we'd have to install. I looked at her in the rearview mirror and just grinned at every comment. Because they all made me feel like she'd adopted me as a permanent fixture in her family, which made my heart swell with emotion. And it made me feel less paranoid about the whole thing.

Going through security at HQ went smoothly. Weiss had instructed them himself on his way in this morning, it seemed. We got into the elevator and arrived in his office pretty early. But he was already there with Tim and four laptops, not counting his and Tim's computers.

"Morning, everyone," Weiss said when we went in. "Tim has already divided the information on the disk in four parts, two bigger, two a bit smaller. I'll want you to read the text and translate it for us."

"The whole thing?" I asked, frowning.

He nodded. "No way around it. This way we can use any relevant info as official proof too. I'm just not sure about…," he said, looking at Susannah and Jeremy.

Will stepped forward. "My children will never breathe a word of anything they translate or read about in these files. I guarantee."

"Can you?" Weiss asked, frowning.

"He can," I replied before Will could have a chance to. "Can't he, Tim?"

Tim nodded. "Will's magic is the most powerful in the Kingdom. He can condition anyone to do, say, or not do or say anything. His kids are well trained by now too. I'd say close to agent level, in fact."

They sat down to work, and Weiss nodded for me to follow him out. I did, and we took the elevator.

"What's up?"

He hit the emergency button and the elevator stopped moving. "Can we trust Will all the way?"

I frowned. "You're asking me? You said you owned him."

"I helped him save his son's life, and I kept him safe. But now his son is no longer in my custody, he's in his dad's. Could he decide to play us for fools?"

I crossed my arms over my chest. "I'm not sure there could ever be a definitive answer to that."

"Did you get anything useful out of him?"

He meant "did you fuck anything useful out of him?", which I had done for him with Richard. He never outright told me to do so, because the opportunity had presented itself by chance, but he certainly never said I should stop doing it. And now he was counting on me hooking up with Will, it seemed. Which, truth be told, I wanted to do anyway.

Will's words went through my head. Was I always following Weiss's directions without even being asked to, with no personal filter? Was I too dedicated to doing anything he might want me to do? Maybe I needed to take a step back sometimes, get things through my own filter, weigh in on actions I had to undertake. Would that count as rebelling against his authority? But I would never be able to have a life of my own if my sole purpose was to follow my alpha's will. There had to be a line somewhere. The question was, where and how to draw it?

"I'm not sure I got anything useful or new," I replied, playing with the ring on my finger. "He said he wants to leave his kids in my care here, whatever happens with him. I think that's a good reason to think he wouldn't do something to jeopardize their welcome among us."

Weiss ran a hand over his face. "You know what bothers me?"

"What?"

"If the two councilors are traitors, won't they try to get rid of Will and the kids? Because they could pry the truth out of them?"

"Well, shit. I didn't think about that. It would leave traces behind, though. Would they risk it?"

"I don't know, would it leave traces? If they use some of their marking hormone-affected lackeys?"

"I don't think they could get to Will and the kids. If they do, there's a pretty good chance the Simses won't be the victims."

He sighed. "How the fuck will we tell Naty about her mother if she actually is a traitor?"

I scratched the back of my head. "Listen, if her mom is a traitor… she won't like it, but she will understand what needs to be done. She's one of my closest friends, Weiss. Naty cares very much about this pack, even if she's considered a pariah."

He growled. "She's not a fucking pariah."

"The two of us don't think of her like that, but you know very well that others do. And you can't change what people think. Not unless you're Sir William Matthew Sims," I added, smiling faintly.

Weiss leaned against the wall. "Is he really that powerful?"

I nodded. "He turned the two of us into fruit flies to get into the Archives. And again to get back out."

"Fruit flies," Weiss repeated, lifting an eyebrow.

"Yeah. They have an insane amount of security there, by the way. And aside from him, nobody else has enough power to do such a thing. Even for him it was tiring."

"Well, shit. That's one buzzing operation, then," he commented, grinning and shaking his head. "But it means he's a lot more dangerous then I might have initially thought. Tim warned me last night that I have no idea what kind of creature Will is. Does he seem likely to turn on us?"

"That's a good question. I don't have an answer for it."

"I think he likes you," Weiss said, looking at his shoes. "Tim says Will's life has been horrible. Everyone at Court tried to use him. Even the partners he had feelings for eventually asked for things he wasn't willing to do for them. Tim thinks it's why he loves his kids so uncommonly much for a fey. They were the only ones who didn't use him."

"What are you saying?"

"I'm saying he looks at you in a way that makes it obvious he really is into you. And you look at him exactly the same way when you think nobody is paying attention. And if I could see that so clearly in less than four hours spent together, it's obviously a thing. I know your relationships have been… few and far between, and short. It's a curse our lifestyle and position in the pack cast on us, I think. But your duties to this pack, to me, don't mean you should be alone, Bert. You deserve to be loved. We all do, I'm thinking lately."

I didn't want him to ask me to use Will. But somehow I had a sinking sensation he would. So I thought I'd better lessen Will's market value, in a sense. I didn't want to use him.

"The fact that I'd earn our pack a very strong ally would also help," I muttered, tapping my foot. "But only if we can be sure he'd be an ally. And who's to say he's not playing us to get his son and then bail?"

"And go where?" Weiss asked, looking into my eyes. "I said the same thing to Tim last night. Will could never return on Kingdom ground with his son, even if they don't suspect him of any ties to the King's death. Which he had no hand in," he stated as I opened my mouth to comment. "The point is he can't go back there. And I don't think he would leave his kids here with you, with us, and return there. It would make sense that he'd either try to make a place for himself here, or that he'd take the kids and go somewhere else. But where? The elves would never receive him. Any other community wants nothing to do with fey, especially strong ones like Will and his children."

"So you're saying we can trust him because he has nowhere else to go."

Weiss shrugged.

"But does that mean that we can trust everything he says, though?" I wondered out loud. "I want to keep the ring on until we figure it out, one way or the other."

"So you can keep yourself more secure if you try to get info out of him?"

Not exactly. "Yeah."

"Not because you're afraid he, or any other fey, might read some emotions you have? Tim suggested you might develop an attachment to it, now that you'll have to deal with fey on a regular basis."

I nibbled on my lower lip. "Maybe. Could I keep it?"

"Tell you what," Weiss said, rubbing his chin. "If it were mine to give, I'd simply say keep it. Not mine, though. I can sell the idea to the owner if you become an official couple with Will. The fact that it helps you keep him in line, so to speak, and therefore useful to our pack and Council, would justify you keeping it."

"So if I don't mate him sometime soon, you're taking the ring away."

"I'll have to," he said, looking me straight in the eye.

It wasn't that I didn't like Will. Or the idea of a very big family. It wasn't even that I thought he wouldn't go in that direction. Maybe he might. The issue was I was a hot mess right now. And it was the worst time to make huge decisions like this. Plus having that kind of family would make my life a lot more complicated. Mixed emotions and loyalties, maybe, something a beta couldn't afford. Or could, but I didn't see a way to make it happen myself.

"You're my beta," he said as if sensing my train of thought. "You're also my friend. I'm not giving you orders here, Bert. I'm simply making sure you're open to possibilities, tactical or not. I'm taking care of you like a fucking mother hen," he added, grinning.

I grinned back, though I was scared shitless. Fuck me sideways, a caring, touchy-feely Weiss was the sign of the apocalypse. It didn't fit with his character. What did fit was trying to get me to do what he wanted me to. And for the first time in a long while, the idea bothered me.

fourteen

OUR FEY allies worked for a couple hours in Weiss's office. In the meantime I did some damage control about the Tricia situation.

Will had an official reason to be here: he was investigating potential ties to the Fey King's assassination. People could assume he brought his kids to keep an eye on them since the Court was obviously not that safe right now. I wasn't too sure what the pack and Council knew about Jeremy and his presence here, but considering I hadn't had a clue about him, it was reasonable to think others would know even less. I wanted to find out how a young fey could be kept under wraps, but that was a discussion I'd have to have with Weiss in private at some point.

Regardless of what the pack and Council knew about Will's family being here, what they shouldn't know was that Tricia was interrogated and broken in the process. The two possible traitors on the Council might take action if they suspected anyone was onto them. So I sold the story of Tricia hurting herself in order to get into MCU custody, a weak try at shirking responsibility for her treason.

Sadly it wasn't hard to put that spin on things. Everyone in the pack hated her. They seemed to hate her even more than they did Amanda, which seemed weird at first. But as I thought about it, it made sense. Tricia wasn't as high profile as Amanda. She wasn't as strong. As the weaker target, she was the preferred one for venting out frustration and hard feelings on. She'd been a beta, after all. Her role was to serve, to assist, to back up and support. In a way she had done that. Just not for her proper alpha. Of course I couldn't dare voice that thought.

Part of the spin involved talking to Naty Stein. I was secretly looking forward to seeing her, though the idea her mom might be a traitor cooled off a lot of my enthusiasm. I found her at her desk, tapping away at her laptop.

"Hey, Naty."

She looked up and smiled. "Bert! You came by, finally. Coffee?"

I smiled. "Anytime, all the time. Thanks."

I texted Weiss quickly, asking if I should broach the Councilor Stein topic with Naty. My thinking was she'd find some way to help us find out, one way or the other. Weiss wasn't too sure about it, but after some thought, he okayed it.

I took a couple of gulps of coffee. "So what have you been doing with yourself while I was away?"

She chuckled. "You were gone for a few days."

I set a hand over my heart and winced. "Does that mean you didn't even miss me?"

"It means I think you have more to tell than I do," she said, fluttering her long lashes.

The thing about Naty was that people overlooked her beauty and charm, her honesty, her sense of humor. What most of them saw was the midshift phase she was stuck in. But Naty was a lot smarter than many gave her credit for. She ran the MCU with an iron fist, though wrapped in a velvet glove. She always knew everything relevant about everyone she came into contact with, and she had shown a strong moral compass for as long as I'd known her. She was also of a very forgiving and generous nature, made obvious by the fact she was friends with me.

I told her about Will, about our first meeting, the time we spent together.

She smiled widely. "I think you two have a thing for each other. A real thing."

I nibbled on my lower lip. "That scares the shit right out of me. Naty?"

"Yes?"

She looked at me in that serious way she tended to use when she sensed there was something stinky coming up. Shit, how to break it to her?

"Weiss would like to call a Council meeting in a day or so."

She frowned. "Is there something I could help with?"

"You know things have been tense since the Anti-Abuse Act."

She nodded, her brows furrowed in curiosity. "Predictable. But I see fewer household injuries in the MCU already. That's a good sign."

"Yeah, for sure."

"Does Weiss want me to work on a report about that? Like a status update?"

I shook my head. "We were wondering if maybe you've noticed something strange about your mother lately?"

She pushed her glasses up her nose with her finger. "Stranger than usual, you mean?"

I smiled awkwardly. "Exactly."

"What is this about, Bert?" she asked, leaning over her desk.

"I need to ask you for a favor. And you won't like it. But I hope you'll trust me enough to know it is necessary."

She blinked rapidly and her ears started fidgeting. "What do you need?"

"We need your mother's blood. Fresh sample."

"For?" she asked, eyeing me suspiciously.

I took a deep breath. "Checking if there's a certain compound in it. And it needs to be a secret that you get the blood, check it, and get whatever the results are."

"You're starting to scare me. What's going on? What do you want me to test it for?"

"Any traces of marking hormones from the samples we already have, including Amanda's blood and Tricia's."

Her face lost all color. I was glad she was sitting down because I was pretty sure she would have fallen to the floor otherwise.

"You think she…?" She trailed off, shaking her head vigorously.

I leaned forward and grabbed her hand. "Honey, I wouldn't ask if we didn't have a serious reason to check. Can you do that? Will you?"

She leaned back in her chair, fidgeting to adjust her position, probably so her twitching tail would be less uncomfortable. "You have reason to believe my mother betrayed the Council and all of us?"

I nodded, trying to look as sympathetic as I could without coming on too strong. Naty wasn't big on displays of affection. It was one of the reasons we got along so well.

"So you want me to check if she made Amanda and Tricia her pseudo pack?"

"Exactly."

She turned to look out the window. "I guess I'm in shock because I'm not as shocked as I would have liked to be at the very idea."

I patted her hand and then crossed my arms on her desk, leaning toward her. "What does your gut instinct tell you?"

She shrugged, still glancing away. "My mother hasn't been that close to me. She's a very ambitious woman, as you know. A child like me…. I'm sure I was a terrible disappointment. She never said so. But it didn't need saying. My point, Bert," she said, now looking at me with huge, sorrow-filled eyes, "is that I don't know her well enough to know either way. My mother and I are virtual strangers. We share a house, we share memories, but we politely ignore each other beyond civil conversations during the rare dinner we have together."

"Oh, Naty… you're an amazing doctor, and you run the MCU like nobody else could. I hope you know you're valued and appreciated."

Naty smiled. "Thanks. I know. I've grown out of trying to impress my mother, or get her to acknowledge me. She could very well have led a rebellion from inside our dining room and I wouldn't know."

"Will you help us?"

"If she's found guilty of treason, I guess the question is do I want to be perceived as having sided with her, a potential accomplice, or as the child who betrayed their traitorous mother?"

I ran a hand through my hair. "That's the kind of answer only you can give yourself."

"How did you choose?"

Her gaze cut straight through me, making my breaths shorter, the beating of my heart more alert. "I didn't have the choice."

"I wish I didn't either," she whispered. "I don't like her, but she's my mother. I love her."

"Whatever you decide, I trust you to keep this a secret. Honey, I know I'm asking for a lot here. Just think about it. If you want to help us, maybe we'll prove she's innocent."

Naty pushed her glasses up her nose again. "Innocent? Yeah, right."

We looked at each other and smiled, even if faintly. We both knew what she'd choose. Naty Stein had always done the right thing. When we were kids, I was her first crush. For a while there I thought I had a crush on her too. But in time I realized I had more of a buddy crush on her, and we'd been friends since then. I couldn't count the number of alcoholic binges she rescued me from, the number of parties gone bad she picked me up from—never a snide remark or a lecture. Just support, unconditional love. And that made me feel worse about being an ass than any lecture ever could. That was the kind of person Naty was: responsible, smart, and dependable. She was going to help us, even if it would break her heart to bring her mother down.

I needed a shot of disgustingly sweet cappuccino after that discussion, so I grabbed a big mug of it and went back to Weiss's office.

"Well?" he asked when I went in.

"She'll think about it until tomorrow the latest and then will say yes."

Will glanced up for a moment, his brilliant gaze giving me butterflies. "You can read people's minds?" he asked, then smiled softly.

"I trust my knowledge of people around me."

"Does that mean that you trust them?" he asked, returning his attention back to the laptop's screen.

Tim was watching me discreetly, Weiss was studiously looking away, and Susannah frowned at Will, then focused on me.

"Never trust people," she instructed me curtly. "Trust their motivation, their character flaws, their weaknesses. Those are reliable. Nothing else is."

I nodded and took a good swig of cappuccino so I wouldn't have to say anything. This teenage girl knew way too much about people and life for her age. Maybe that was why her standard facial expression was a frown occasionally spiced up with a glare. Unlike many other fey, she seemed to like to use facial expressions, and very expressive ones at that. A defense mechanism, maybe. Or just her way of rebelling against a world she was forced to put up with and live in. I looked at Jeremy, at his serene expression, and for the first time, noticed a scar on the side of his neck, discreet, but in a shape I knew very well. My gut clenched.

"Weiss, do you have a minute?" I muttered.

He nodded and we exited the office.

"Saw that, didn't you?" he asked, stuffing his hands in his pockets.

"Jeremy is not officially fey anymore, is he?"

He nodded. "It was the only sure way to have his loyalty and not worry about his father going back on our deal. He wouldn't try to get a werewolf and pack member of mine back, much less as a Sims Interrogator. Court would never accept him back into its graces."

I leaned on a nearby desk and looked down into my cappuccino cup. "Will we do the same with the rest of his kids? If they're to stay here?"

"Yeah."

"Will you bite them?"

He nodded. "Far as I'm concerned, the kid is like my own. All of them will be, once bitten."

"Even the twins? They can't be more than one year old."

Weiss glared. "Are you questioning my fucking actions, Bert?"

A shudder traveled up and down my spine. "I would never, boss. Just wondering, that's all. I mean, if we're keeping them, I'll have to make some arrangements."

Weiss stepped closer, coming into my personal space. "You are my beta. Never forget that. I sure as fuck won't."

I couldn't look up into his eyes. He was throwing off too much of a dominant vibe for me to manage it, and I didn't even want to try. I glanced down, shoulders hunched, as submissive a pose as I could manage without moving. Pack life was like this. Hierarchy in a pack was like this: blunt, direct, in your face. I liked that. It comforted me. What I didn't like was how his doubts became my doubts, how his desires became my desires out of reflex. I had to stop that from happening.

Weiss stepped back, sighing. "You sure you want to take on his kids? You don't have to if you don't want to."

I sipped a bit more cappuccino, then managed to look up at him. "Will the Council know about us keeping them?"

"Not the fucking Council's business, is it? Not until we know for sure who we can trust. Either way I'd like to take the kids over to my place. And I'd like you to move in too. Alf has been busting my balls about missing you."

"What about Tish? Won't the little guy be sad his favorite aunt won't be his company anymore?"

He growled. "I can't fucking wait for her to leave. She's fucking up my peace of mind at home."

I chuckled. "Big sisters tend to." And as soon as I said it, of course I remembered Tricia and lost all humor. But I didn't want Weiss to think I was giving her too much thought, so I kept talking. "How's Celia working out?"

"Not sure. Didn't do anything wrong of course. But I don't trust her entirely. Now that you're back, maybe I'll take her out of my home."

"Could I make a suggestion?" I asked sheepishly.

"Jesus fucking Christ, now I have a herd of suggestion makers around me. Fine, say it," he snarled.

"Maybe you haven't given her a chance yet. Maybe you should."

"You're the trusting type now? Since when?"

"I was thinking more along the lines of us having Tim's and the Simses talent around from now on," I confessed. "I mean, sure, they're kids, but Jeremy and Susannah don't strike me as the childish type. I'm sure Jeremy can work for us the kind of magic Will can, even if not as strong, maybe. And he's on our side. Right?"

"He is," Weiss answered, grinning. "You're right. We don't have to trust anyone as long as we have living, breathing lie detectors in hand. And now we know their reading or manipulating emotional grids will go undetected since the new fey ambassador is on Will's side. They're valuable assets to the Bureau, to the pack, and to the Council once they know for sure we have them. All the more reason to have them stay at my place. Plenty of space, and Alf could use the company."

I frowned. "Is he feeling lonely?"

"Weiss alphas don't feel lonely," he growled. "I just don't like the wimps he spends time with at school. Too much human influence."

I smiled. He meant "too little uber-testosterone influence," if I had to guess. Company like the Sims kids would be great for our little alpha in the making, that was true. And it wouldn't hurt to have them develop a real bond so they'd be able to work together in the future. The fey situation could shift into outright war at any point, in my opinion. If and when it did so, whatever we could use to our advantage would be great. It sounded cold and cynical to call the kids assets, but strategically, they were just that. And I knew Weiss would use whatever weapons were at his disposal if he needed to. That didn't mean he'd willfully put the kids in harm's way, though. Despite the tough appearance and the general barking, growling manner, Weiss wasn't a total bastard. But he could be every now and then, when the situation called for it. Just like I could too. Like we all could. Which brought me to....

"My contact at Fey Court is probably useless now. When we use the info we got, Richard won't go anywhere near me with a ten-foot pole. That source has been compromised. We need someone else, right?"

He looked toward his office door and grinned in that fucking disturbing Weiss way. "Let me worry about that. In the meantime I need you to run two errands for me."

I finished the rest of my drink in one big gulp. Weiss's errands never were about picking up dry cleaning. "Sure, boss. What do you want me to do?"

He leaned in closer and looked around thoroughly before finally speaking. "You're breaking into Councilor Stein's and then Councilor Nichols's homes and setting up cameras. They are coded and spelled against detection. Only Tim and I can access the broadcast and record it. You have a fucking load of cameras in this bag," he said, producing one from his locker, which was located next to the office door. "I want them placed so I'll see every angle of every fucking corner of every room in their homes."

"That means spying on Naty too," I muttered, grabbing the bag.

He shrugged. "Not the person of interest in this investigation. If she decides she's on our side, then she won't mind us looking through her life."

I scratched my nape. What if she decided otherwise? Did Weiss think she'd betray us, tell her mom about our suspicions? A knot of unease settled in my stomach. This was for the best, I reasoned. Besides, we all lived on PBI property, and if PBI wanted to plant cameras in our homes, it very well could. The thought of being watched made me nervous, agitated. What if there were already cameras all around? I shook myself mentally. Of course there weren't. Weiss would have known about the traitors if everyone were being watched. And how to keep track of so much data? We'd need at least half the number of people watched just to check what was recorded, right? Now was not the time to become paranoid.

"I trust you to do this for me," Weiss informed me. "You won't fail me. You never did. You never will."

I nodded. "Sure thing, boss. Count on me."

I strolled away, holding the bag of tiny cameras. It was very fucking heavy. About as heavy as my heart about spying on my best friend. Before making stops at either Stein's or Nichols's house, I had to make one at Weiss's home. This was a job for my famous baking skills.

fifteen

A COUPLE hours later, I had a sour-cherry mousse and chocolate soufflé in my arsenal, and the bag of cameras was neatly divided into two pouches. I stopped at the gate of the Nichols residence and grinned at the security guy as he checked my ID. Standard procedure, just like at Weiss's residence. Due to my beta status in the pack, they'd just check my ID and allow me entrance. That was a lucky thing because, if I were a simple pack member or PBI agent, they might also search my bags, car, and probably probe my ass just to be sure I wasn't carrying anything dangerous aside from my fine dick.

The gates opened as the security guy called up to the house to inform them of their guest. The Nichols vampire clan was a pretty numerous one, but very few members were in actual residence. Nichols was a grandsire, not a simple one. It meant he'd sired many vampires who had, in turn, sired their own clans that remained under Council authority.

He was one of the oldest vampires in our territories, which was one of the biggest reasons he had become a Council member. That and the fact that, had the Council denied his request, he could have caused us all a lot of fucking trouble. Grandsires could call on their "offspring" at any time, and they would call on their own, mobilizing at least sixteen quite numerous vampire clans. Sure, we could take them down if we had to. But we didn't want to. Werewolf-vampire politics were sensitive as it was. Both our races were accustomed to ruling. In territories outside ours, they tended to be enemies, in fact. Our community required a delicate balance. Nobody was about to fuck it up now after Weiss had worked on finessing it so goddamn hard for years.

One of the little-known facts about Nichols's current consort was the fact she binged on sweets whenever she could. The next thing she did was run to the toilet and throw up everything, not because it didn't agree with her system, but because she was hopelessly bulimic. The very notion of gaining any weight sent her into a vomiting frenzy. I knew her well from a Bingers Anonymous group Weiss had found out she went to, back when Nichols had first made the request to become Councilor. I was a binger, especially when it came to sweets. I didn't throw them up after eating them, but the obsession with food was genuine. It hadn't been hard to get close to Clarice Nichols. And it wouldn't be hard to get inside her house now that I carried this very appetizing gift.

She opened the front door and took two good sniffs, and her eyes gained that manic twinkle. "You come bearing divine gifts," she murmured sultrily.

It wasn't that she liked me all that much, but I was positive she fucking loved the way the sweets smelled.

"Freshly baked," I whispered like we were talking about drugs.

Which, partially, we were.

"I just came back from the lamest ambassador stint in diplomatic history," I said brightly. "I needed a pick-me-up. And after I baked them, I just thought of you. Thought you might like to have a tiny piece. And maybe we'll support one another so we only have the one piece," I said, sounding all hopeful.

She nodded in this solemn, entirely ridiculous way. We'd binged our way through more homemade deliciousness than I could gauge. Each and every time it happened under the same pretense: keeping each other on the wagon. It was bullshit, the size of which you couldn't even begin to measure. We weren't anywhere near the fucking galaxy of the wagon.

We went inside, directly toward the kitchen. She took out two tiny plates and spoons and a huge knife.

"You look well," she lied.

I looked fat. Because I was fat. And I wasn't going to look in any way different anytime soon either. But that was relatively okay. I loved food, good figure be fucked.

"You look amazing," I replied in kind.

She looked like a fucking skeleton despite her kickass healing power. She didn't throw up only sweets, though. She threw up everything she consumed, including blood. Her consort force-fed her his blood every now and then because it was the most potent and meant she had to eat only a little to lead a relatively normal life. Of course, everything was very relative when it came to Clarice.

"Here you go," she muttered, eyes glazed over as she stared at the soufflé.

We ate two fucking cakes, tiny portion by tiny portion, exchanging mediocre pleasantries and assuring each other one more bite wouldn't kill us. It couldn't have, in truth, so we weren't actually lying.

I felt bad about this binge session, as I felt every time I encouraged her illness. But it was the only solid thing we had on Nichols directly, and Weiss was always a very careful, somewhat paranoid fan of having things on people. While encouraging her illness was despicable, allowing Nichols to potentially try to tip the balance of power into his own direction was a greater evil, as far as I was concerned. Besides, Clarice could have gotten help many times over if she was ready for it. Eating the occasionally monstrous amount of sweets with me wasn't what hurt her case.

We leaned back in our chairs, both of us petting our sweet-stuffed bellies.

"Dear Lord, I'm so full I can't breathe," she muttered with that afterglow only a true binger could sport after eating.

"I think I'm about to burst," I replied, grinning like a maniac.

Then I reached into my backpack and retrieved a box of laxatives. This was my fake emergency method for binging. I took about five pills from the bottle and downed them with a glass of water.

"Can I use your bathroom?" I asked as if this was our first rodeo.

She smiled. "Of course."

Then she walked me toward one of the service bathrooms. I stood there, silent, and waited until I could hear her heels click into the other one. I heard the lock fall in place and knew I had about twenty minutes to set the cameras up. I took the chance to put the first one in this bathroom, then went about each room. The cameras were tiny things, about the size of a quarter. Small rooms got one or two, larger ones four to six. In ten minutes I'd covered the downstairs and ran my way up to the second floor. A belly full of cake didn't help at all, and I was sweating like a pig on a skewer, but I hauled ass and set up the rest of the cameras I had in my backpack. Then I ran my way back into the bathroom I was supposed to shit my way into oblivion in, and waited for Clarice to come out of her bathroom.

When she did, I could hear the radio she'd turned on to cover the sounds of her throwing up. I took some paper towels and got out of the bathroom, wiping my face as if exhausted. Had I taken five laxatives of the label I had in the bottle, I'd look just about as spent. To her knowledge I took them regularly, and as soon as I ate, I'd manage to shit copiously.

We smiled at each other as if nothing had happened and went back to the scene of the crime: the kitchen. She poured us each a glass of delicious lemonade, and we sat back for a moment.

"So now you're back to babysitting duty?" she asked me in a crackly voice.

"Yeah," I said, doing my best to repress any wave of guilt trying to swallow me. "It's better for me, anyway. A lot more time spent at home."

"We're homebodies, you and I," she said, putting on a ghost of a smile. "Gone to any meetings lately?"

I shrugged. "Didn't manage it."

"Me neither. The house is becoming a fucking circus," she said and sipped some lemonade.

"Oh?"

"Consort's feeling lonely," she said while staring at the dirty dishes in front of us. "I'm sure he wants to replace me. All these visits," she muttered, shaking her head.

Clarice was always sure. She was also usually paranoid and ridiculously insecure. But she wasn't blind or prone to flights of fancy, so the visits weren't imagined.

"Maybe he's just nostalgic. Were these visits by people you know, maybe? Old friends of his or yours?"

"His precious sires," she spat. "I always knew he was selecting them with this in mind. Replacing me. Getting rid of ugly, stupid, useless Clarice."

"Hey." I reached out and patted her hand. "You're not useless or stupid. And you're fucking gorgeous!"

Or she used to be, at some point. Now she looked tired, worn out. She wouldn't the moment she stopped throwing up, of course. Her body would regenerate as soon as she fed properly and actually kept the food down.

"I need to rest, Bert," she said and got up. "Can you walk yourself out?"

"Of course. Can I just use the bathroom one more time?"

She nodded and walked out of the kitchen.

I went to the service bathroom she'd thrown up in and placed the last camera. I avoided looking at myself in the mirror while doing so. She looked worse and worse every time I saw her. It wasn't my fault. It was her fault for not doing anything to help herself, her consort's fault for not giving a fuck and not doing something to stop this nonsense. I walked back into the kitchen and washed the dishes, including the ones I had carried in full of irresistible sweets. It wasn't my fault.

When the kitchen was clean again, I felt better. I left, plastering on a smiley face for the security guy. He nodded as I passed by the gate. Half of the cameras were up. Now I just had to text Naty and put up the other half behind her back, in her own home, while she was away. It wasn't my fault. But I felt like a fucking dick.

Need your pressure cooker. Can I pick it up? xD

She texted me back within a minute.

Sure. Called security to let them know. Save me some good stuff! :D

You've got it, honey. Ttyl xoxo

Being obsessed with food had its perks. Getting into the Stein residence was ridiculously easy. The security chick at the gate smiled and waved me in, knowing I was a regular around here. It sent a tiny stab of guilt through me, but that was nothing compared to how guilty I felt about setting up the cameras, including in Naty's bedroom and bathroom. The very idea someone would watch her when she thought she was in her moments of privacy…. Even if it was only Weiss, and he didn't ridicule her for her midshift issue, I just couldn't do it.

I aimed the cameras a bit crookedly in her bedroom and bathroom. Just a bit. Enough so she couldn't be seen going in and out of the shower because she had solid walls around it. She was no traitor, and her mother would never use her bathroom. Naty never got out of it naked, and never changed anywhere else but in here, just to be sure no one could accidentally see her naked. If Weiss had a problem with that, he could come in here and change the angle himself. He was going to chew my ass out over it, but this was as far as I could go.

I found their cook in the kitchen. She never did cleaning, made it a point of pride, and only opened doors when no one else was home. She had been Naty's nanny a lot of years ago, so she was an old and mumbling thing Naty and I both adored. But she could barely walk around, so I knew she'd give me no trouble at all. I sent her on the wild pressure-cooker chase because I knew it would be in the cabinet just outside the kitchen, in the lobby I already set up the cameras in. I set up the last four in the kitchen in a hurry, putting up the last one just in time.

"What you doing up there, boy?" Mrs. Gem mumbled at me. "You have me run round the house, searchin' up the damn pot, and now you climb furniture? You gone out of your good mind?"

I grinned. "I saw a spider."

She made a face. "You better have killed that thing, boy. I'm no spider killer, you hear? They don't pay me enough to do contract jobs round here," she muttered sullenly.

"No worries, I got rid of it."

Technically it was about a bug… of sorts. I took the cooker, said good-bye, and drove away. My stomach felt full of rocks. And now I had to go cook something with the damn pressure cooker so I could lie to my best friend about my reason for being at her home. But at least I'd cook her a stew I knew she loved, which would make it up to her, even if only just a little bit.

A COUPLE hours later, I went into HQ and brought lamb stew in beer sauce with oranges, onions, and carrots, a bit of fresh parsley sprinkled on top, and two bottles of Pinot Noir. When I got into Weiss's office, the fey dream team looked exhausted, Weiss might have gotten a boner from the smell of my casseroles I'd brought, and Will looked just about ready to cry. I texted Naty to come join us because I was sure she was still at work.

It was tough to manage eating that delicious stew out of plastic plates, and Pinot Noir deserved better than to be drunk out of paper cups, but by the time we were done eating, I thought everyone seemed pretty thrilled. I had brought Jeremy and Susannah homemade lemonade with honey and cinnamon, a family recipe Cooper kids have loved for generations, because Pinot Noir was not an option for them. After finishing the meal, we were all stuffed full and looking pretty pleased, if I could say so myself.

On her way out, Naty leaned in close to me and whispered, "I'm with you, Berty. Let's talk tomorrow, okay?"

I smiled and kissed her cheek. For a minute there, the lamb stew didn't sit right in my stomach, but I took another sip of wine and everything felt better.

Weiss looked at me and cocked his head toward the office door. We went out one at a time as the fey translating team started exchanging comments and opinions on typos and such that they found in the files they translated.

"She's in?" Weiss asked casually as soon as we stepped out of his office.

"Yeah, just told me so. I knew she would be."

"Me too," he deadpanned. "And the other thing?"

"Done, boss," I assured him and grinned.

He patted me on the shoulder. "Fuck, I missed having you around. You've always been my favorite, Bert. I know I can rely on you."

I swallowed thickly. "Thanks, boss. I'm sure the cooking doesn't hurt either," I added.

"You've single-handedly added four inches to everyone's waistline, man," he grumbled. "Worst part is I'd sooner die than turn down any of your cooking."

I chuckled. "Thanks."

Will walked out of the office, his phone to his ear. "It's going well," he said, looking into my eyes. "They've accepted me with more ease than I anticipated. Must be Timothy's presence that's softening them up," he added.

Weiss lifted an eyebrow and I just stared. Will wanted us to hear his side of the conversation, that was obvious.

"I have a few directions to follow. Yes. Oh, really? I'm most honored," he cooed. "Do you have a specific timeframe in mind? That seems reasonable, I agree. Oh? He was the former King's favorite, that's true. Will we have to stake a claim, then, both of us? I'm looking forward to that. Yes, good night."

He made sure the call ended, then looked at both of us. "I'm expected to make a claim for the throne, and so is Leonard Hughes."

"What does that mean, making a claim for it?" I asked, frowning.

"Contenders have to stand up before the High Council. They measure up their magic, and if they are deemed fit, then there's a fight to the death between contenders."

"So you're going to try claiming the fey throne?" Weiss asked, cocking his head to the side.

Will clasped his hands behind his back. "It would look strange if I didn't, especially since I was told more than half the High Court wants me to become King. I obviously won't lose to Hughes," he added, smiling oddly.

"What about your kids?" I asked.

"I can justify having brought the children with me here, out of security concerns. I believe I can justify leaving them behind too."

"How will you do that?" Weiss asked, looking at me for some reason.

"I will claim to have interrogated someone important from the PBI. Interrogated and harmed in the process. As revenge, werewolves—savages that they are—will have attacked my children, biting all of them. A noble fey would leave them behind without a doubt. They'd be tainted, ruined, and officially not fey since being bitten. So I'd leave them behind with the barbarians who have now claimed them," he added, blinking slowly.

"You're saying you want them bitten?" Weiss asked, still looking mainly at me.

Will nodded. "It's the only way I can be sure of their safety. Indifference from the Kingdom, care from your pack. You will bite them, won't you? Make them pack members?"

"You are aware the first shift is horribly painful, right? Possibly lethal?" I asked, stepping closer to him. "Do you want your kids to suffer through that?"

Will looked into my eyes, those green pools pulling me under. "I don't want them dead, Bert. If they come back with me, they will be dead within the week, if not sooner. Ever wonder why Timothy has no living siblings to be heir to the crown? If Interrogator prospects have it tough, throne heirs have it many times worse. I won't have my children killed, Bert. If that means some pain, then so be it. It hurts me too, all of it. But it can't be helped. I'll be there for their first shifts. Timothy went through it just fine. So will my children. They are strong and healthy."

I crossed my arms in front of my chest. "So let me see if I get this straight. You'd leave your kids, the most powerful magic users in the Kingdom after you, presumably, behind. And you'd go stake a claim for the throne and most likely win. So you're saying we're pretty much helping you become the next Fey King?"

"In a way," Will said, turning away and walking back into Weiss's office.

"That doesn't sound right," I muttered.

Weiss looked at me and ran a hand through his hair. "Question is: did he want to strategically place his kids in the pack so he can be King and have potential spies here, thereby playing us the whole time? Or is he just that fucking smart that he planned ahead and knew all these twists might arise, having thought of ways around them?"

I clenched and unclenched my fists. Will loved his kids. I was sure of it. Why wasn't Weiss?

"He is definitely that fucking smart," I muttered. "I'm not sure about the rest. He's helped us so far, right?"

"Right," Weiss replied, watching as Will talked with Jeremy and Susannah. "Tim did random checks of the translation via his laptop, and they are accurate, he says. So they didn't play us on that."

"He wants the kids as part of this pack. To keep them safe, or to play us from the inside once he is King?"

"Fuck me if I know," he grumbled. "But you're going to find out somehow. Okay?"

"Okay," I replied automatically.

This was what I was afraid of. And I was going to do it, I knew. Because I never could say no to my alpha, and I doubted I ever would be able to.

"Get Will's kids over to my place. We'll do the biting ceremony in private, tonight," Weiss stated and went back into his office. "Whatever he plans, the kids will be safer here. And we can use skilled new pack members."

I ran both palms over my face, hoping to chase all my worries and frustrations away. Was I falling for a strategic genius who was fucking us over, using his kids as future spies, and ascending to the fey throne? Or for a caring, self-sacrificing father who was doing his best to keep his kids away from the demented Fey Court? Fuck me sideways if I had a clue.

sixteen

WEISS PLANNED interrogation teams for the next day. Using the info the fey translating team provided us with after the translations, we had solid proof one member of the first three Leader Murders victims' families or clans each had been involved in the MH project. The names were Mrs. Hemington, mother of the first victim, Susan Hemington; Violet Pax, consort of the second victim, Henry Pax; and Jefferson Wong, consort of Paula Wong, third Leader Murders victim. The fact they were looking for chemical equivalents to alpha or sire hormones was a clear indication they were planning for their natural leaders to be taken out of the picture. And unless they knew there was a plan for that to happen, they wouldn't have gotten involved with anything to jeopardize their standing.

So they looked guilty; hopefully they'd give in and admit it too. The three members who we had on file were going to be interrogated by Travis, Rick, and Timothy to confirm motive as much as possible. They were all scheduled to get in the waiting area at the same time, and then Weiss had left instructions for them to be left waiting for an hour, at least. To stew in their own juices. Hopefully by then Will would manage to assist with part of the interrogations, just to make sure they were telling the truth. But if the kids' biting ceremonies didn't go well or took longer, they'd have to manage the interrogations without Will's help.

Naty texted me that she had gotten a vial of her mother's blood and was now testing it against the samples we had of the marking hormones, comparing it with Tricia's and Amanda's blood samples. We had pretty advanced tech, so the answer to that was going to be coming our way soon.

I drove Will, Susannah, and Jeremy to Weiss's residence. Then I went back home to collect the twins, Sarah, and Hector. Alf's aunt, Tish, took him upstairs for ice cream, movie night, and whatever else they needed to do until we were done with the biting ceremonies. The new beta, Celia, accompanied them before Will and the kids went downstairs to the biting room.

Every time I saw Celia around, I felt a spike of hatred pierce my heart. Rationally I knew it was stupid. She wasn't guilty of anything aside from being more capable than the other beta contenders. And once Tricia had been found guilty of treason, her beta position was rendered vacant. I fucking knew all of that. But Celia's presence felt like an insult for some reason. It might have been my imagination only, but I thought she avoided eye contact with me. Which made me think she either felt bad about taking my sister's place as beta, or she thought I was a traitor too and avoided contact to avoid confrontation.

It was times like these the ugly demons of betrayal truly tormented me. Moments when anything and everything about a situation that seemed wrong was somehow connected to the stain of treason. I was either angry or feeling guilty, if left to my own devices. All of it only made me want to prove myself to be the perfect beta for Weiss. I would walk into a blazing fire if he needed or wanted me to. And I knew that wasn't entirely right either. But I couldn't help it.

In a way I wanted to have someone else to dedicate my time and energy to. Like Will's kids, maybe. It would help me get a healthier perspective on things. To distance myself from pack politics and my role, or lack thereof. And if the biting ceremonies went well, I'd have a bunch of new werewolves to look after and help adjust. They'd be Weiss's subjects, like the entire pack, but he'd leave them in my direct care, of that I was sure.

The bite and first-shift process could be a troublesome one, especially where teenagers were concerned. The relative instability of their hormones carried into the change they went through, altering the chemistry of the first shift, intensifying states, feelings. It could lead to more complications than biting a child or an adult. It made me worry about Susannah, a fact I did my best to conceal.

Will had explained what was happening, discussed things with them in Weiss's living room. They were mostly informed, even if Hector and Sarah were too young to truly comprehend what was happening, and the twins were babies, so they couldn't get a say in it. Susannah didn't seem thrilled about it, but she did state in that regal, grown-up tone of hers that there wasn't any better option available.

Jeremy walked with them to the special room downstairs. "It's going to hurt," he said, holding her hand. "The actual bite will hurt less, and an hour or so after that, you won't feel much discomfort. But when the shift starts, it's going to hurt. A lot. You need to allow your body to go through it," he said, looking back at Hector and Sarah. "You just let your body do what it wants and breathe through it. When it's over, you'll feel so much better. And then we'll have a lot of fun together; we'll run around in the woods at night and hunt rabbits together."

The kids giggled and Susannah rolled her eyes, but they all seemed to relax. Weiss carried the twins in his arms, walking behind Jeremy and the older kids. They were going in together since Weiss was pretty sure he could control the crowd with ease. The twins were going to be the first, then Hector, Sarah, and Susannah would go last. He would allow about twenty to thirty minutes between each bite, so he could focus on each one of them when the actual shift time came. Becoming their alpha and taking them into the pack would be easy once they shifted. Cubs gravitated toward adults by nature when those adults were dominant like Weiss was. And there was nobody more dominant than Weiss, that was for fucking sure.

Will and I sat at the dining room table. He looked worried but contained. He didn't fidget, pace around, or worry his hands. He simply sat there, this stoic, statuesque expression on his beautiful face. It worried me, but I didn't dare say anything for a while, not sure what the hell to say at a time like this.

Jeremy came back up, stuffing his hands in his pockets. "Door is closed. In about five minutes, it's going to start."

Will nodded. "Could we move into the living room? I'd like to sit more comfortably."

His gaze was distant as they made their way to the living room, his voice a monotone with that odd echo effect. The onyx ring on my finger was heating up fast.

"Casting a spell?" I asked, playing with the ring.

He blinked slowly and nodded, then sat down on the sofa.

Jeremy sat opposite of him. "Want some help, Father?"

Will smiled, though it was absent. "Not with this."

"What exactly is 'this'?" I asked Jeremy.

"Father is transferring a part of the pain from the shifts of my brothers and sisters to himself," he informed me, smiling oddly. "It can't be simply taken out of the equation. But it can be partially transferred via magic without interfering with the first shift or harming their later ones. They will feel no side effects and less pain. He, however...."

"He'll feel a goddamn lot of it without the relief at the end of the shift," I muttered in awe and frustration.

It was real pain, I knew that much. And he was taking it all on himself if his spell would work. My heart beat faster and my stomach tightened. That was going to hurt like a motherfucker.

"Will, do you have any idea what kind of pain we're talking about? Especially if it's times five? Are you out of your goddamn mind?"

"My children will not suffer as much if I can help it," he said calmly.

"Your heart will goddamn give out! You could have an aneurism! Losing you won't help them, you moron!" I screeched.

He turned and looked at me. "Are you worried, Bert?"

"Of course I'm fucking worried, you idiot!" I screamed.

He smiled. "Thank you for caring. But I'll be fine, I'm sure."

"I'm sure you won't be, you pompous ass! At least give me half the pain. I'm used to it. I do shift a big fucking lot. Why didn't you just say you wanted to do this? We could have divided it between five of our people, used to it as only a werewolf would be."

He shook his head. "My children are my responsibility. And who would want to feel some random stranger's pain?"

"You're not a stranger to me," I snapped. "Share that pain with me. I'm not being cute here. For fuck's sake, you could die!"

Jeremy frowned. "Father, at least let me take part. Please. I'm a grown-up. I'm a werewolf. It's a world of pain; he's not exaggerating. The first shift is a million times worse than the second and any one thereafter. Times five, it's more than anyone could take. Don't put yourself at risk, please. We need you."

Will sighed. "You two are trying to take away my glory."

This was more proof that he honestly loved his children in that selfless kind of way great parents do. He wasn't using them or planting them as spies so he could become the new Fey King and use them for intel. I was sure of it, just felt it in my gut. He truly loved them. Will Sims was an amazing and admittedly scary man. My heart leapt in my chest. I had this vision of me simply jumping him on that sofa, tearing his clothes off, messing up his hair, licking him all over at least twice.

"Bert?" he asked.

I shook my head. "Sorry, what?"

"I asked if we could divide it between us. In case something goes wrong with me, I need to know there will be someone who can take the rest of my children on. Jeremy can't be part of this."

I nodded. "I get that. Okay. It's going to hurt a big fucking lot. But I can take it. I hope you can too."

Will's gaze went distant again, and the ring on my finger went almost unbearably hot. After a few seconds, it began cooling off.

"Spell cast?" I asked.

Will nodded.

"Okay. First thing, we're going to drink a lot of fluids as soon as possible."

Jeremy got up and jogged toward the kitchen.

"Second thing, we're moving into the bathroom. There will be a lot of sweating and throwing up. I'd hate for it to ruin the living room," I muttered. "If the babies are first, it's probably going to take about an hour for the pains to begin. Blood circulates faster through their systems since they're tiny. It's also a faster shift, so it'll be good warm-up, I guess."

"Bert?"

"Yeah?" I replied, looking into his eyes.

"You're sharing my pain today. By choice. With nothing to gain except my gratitude."

I smiled. "I'm a hopeless moron, I know. You're welcome."

He got up from the sofa and kneeled in front of me, resting the warm palms of his hands on my knees. "I've fallen so terribly in love with you, Bert Cooper."

Well, shit. I opened my mouth to say something, but nothing came out. He just kept looking up at me, actually smiling. Jeremy returned with a few bottles of water, set them down beside us, and awkwardly turned around to leave.

"Once my children shift, they are officially werewolves and part of Weiss's pack. To keep my children safe, I plan to go back into the Kingdom and do as the Court expects. It's the only way I'll know for sure what the High Court plans, that my children will remain safe here with you. This is not a decision I've taken lightly. And if I could do anything else that would be as efficient, I would."

"How about staying here too?" I tried again.

He shook his head. "If Leonard Hughes becomes King, he will do what the High Court planned with the former King. They will keep attacking this community, weakening the Council until it's taken over by their pawns. And they will come after me and my children because they'll fear such a gathering of powerful magic users, even if ex-fey. It would give them a great pretext for attacking, in fact."

Jeremy returned and cleared his throat. "What if they don't know you're alive?"

Will sighed and went back to sit on the couch. Between swallows of water, he said, "While we could keep secret the fact that one or two fey live on Council territory, a lot of us.... That would be virtually impossible to keep under wraps. Tim's presence here wasn't that good of a reason since the Court knew him to be a very weak magic user. Our family, on the other hand... the Court would be terribly interested in all of us. In the risk our presence might pose to them."

Jeremy sighed. "If Weiss can work out a way for all of us to stay here, you think he wouldn't be able to fit you in too?"

"How would we make the High Court lose interest in all of us?" Will shot back and shook his head.

"What if we make them believe you've lost your magic abilities?" I thought out loud.

Will frowned. "And how would we do that?"

"Correct me if I'm wrong, but once fey are bitten to change, they are outcast. Does the Court keep track of them?"

"No," they replied in unison. Then Will continued, "Once they become outcast, they are no longer deemed worthy of being part of fey history. It's as if they've never existed. But that won't—"

"Give me a second, here," I interrupted. "So they have no idea what happens to fey magic once fey change into something else, like a lycan or a vampire or a werewolf?"

"Not really," Will conceded. "There's only an assumption that they will most likely die or lose all their beauty and power. It's a way of thinking very ingrained in Kingdom society, almost guaranteeing no fey would want to put themselves in danger of being bitten."

"So if bitten they could believe you've lost your magic?"

"Considering our strength, they'd want to check. Or would need to notice some circumstance in which use of magic would help and it wouldn't be used, making them believe the ability is lost. More so if Leonard Hughes becomes King. The first thing they'll do is put into motion the plan against this Council, endangering my children in the process," Will explained again, seeming to lose his patience.

"So your idea is to become King to stop the High Court from invading Council territory or attacking us? If they're this set on it, I don't think you can stop them, can you?" I muttered.

Will seemed to consider it. "Probably not."

"So you'll have to find a better excuse for going after the job," I said and winked.

It probably threw him off because his eyes widened. "I never said I was actually going for it. Bert, are you trying to say you don't want me to leave?"

"What the fu… nk—" I ended the word differently so it wouldn't be a bad one, stealing a quick glance in Jeremy's direction to find him rolling his eyes—very un-fey-like. "—does that have to do with anything?"

"So you truly don't want me to go," Will concluded, smiling.

"I didn't say that!"

"You didn't deny it, though," Jeremy chipped in.

"Hey! Don't gang up on me!" I snapped.

"Still not denying it," Will commented. "If you don't want me to leave, you could just say so."

"As if that would make any difference," I muttered, brushing some imaginary lint from my pants.

"It would, yes. We won't be able to see each other if I leave and end up becoming the King or getting killed in the process, is that what you're thinking?"

"Of course not!" I replied immediately.

Too soon. I could see the smug bastard was now convinced I was a lovesick puppy. Which I might have been under different circumstances. But I wasn't. At all.

I tried for a strong comeback. "My point is if the High Court is set on this anti-Council plan, whoever the King is, they'll get their way. If you become King and oppose them, it will look suspicious to them. They'd investigate. That might put your kids in more danger. So the only actual way to get them to give up on the anti-Council plan would be to replace the High Court members."

"They're appointed for life," Jeremy grumbled.

"Well, then. Their lives should become conveniently shorter," I said, looking into Will's eyes. "If that happens, new members would follow the plans of the previous High Court?"

"I highly doubt it," Will admitted. "But if the new King would want to follow through with that plan, then they might agree. And Hughes would love to follow through. He's already invested in it, took part himself."

Fucking fey, there was no way to get them to drop the bone. And they thought us werewolves were beasts.

"What if neither Hughes nor you become King? Who'd be next on the short list?"

Will crossed his legs. "With a new High Court? They'd come up with proposals. I wouldn't know. But anyone else aside from Hughes would care a lot less about ex-fey being here as long they are not a direct threat. And they might be less inclined to attack the Council if we ruin the inside job opportunities. They'd have to start over with schemes since the MH project went rather sideways now due to your new Anti-Abuse Act. It's not enough ground for inciting substantial inner tensions, and getting new allies from the Council would be very hard work. A new King and High Court would want something glorious to invest themselves in, something that would go well, make them look good. So if we eliminate the traitors from your Council, take out the High Court and Hughes... then we might have a chance at some peace and quiet, all of us."

"You'd need to be at Court to do that. Or do you trust the fact that someone else would get involved?"

"I highly doubt that," Jeremy piped in.

"There are those who would approve of such actions for the better of the Kingdom," Will replied smoothly. "But they wouldn't dare act on their own. In order to make this happen, I would have to be there. I'm sure that once a new circle of power is established, the Court would overlook our departure or our part in the previous circle's downfall."

"And you can count on that?" I asked, having a bad feeling about the sound of it.

He nodded. "The sooner, the better."

"You shouldn't seem to be responsible, though. Or punishing you might be exactly what the new A-team would need to make a good start," I said, getting up. "Let's continue this chat in the bathroom. I think it won't be too long now, okay?"

Will nodded and followed me. "Jeremy," he said, "stay here in the living room. We'll call if we need you."

His son nodded, and I thought he also grinned as he went to sit on the sofa. He turned on the TV and settled comfortably.

"I think my son likes you," Will said, smiling while he closed the bathroom door behind him.

"Of course he does. I'm charming and I can cook. What's not to like?"

"Agreed, but I don't mean generally. I mean he likes you as potential mate for me."

"Oh, shut up. We can't plan the demise of several powerful circles and people and do romance at the same time. It's tacky," I added.

He smiled. "If we can find a solution so I could stay here too with the children, possibly with you, I'd love to. And I wouldn't settle for anything less than making you fall head over heels for me, and becoming your mate. You do know that, right?"

"The kids would love you to be with them, that's for sure. They are very grown-up for their ages, and probably well equipped to defend themselves. But this is a new place, with new people. However badass they might be, they are still kids—yours. They'd want and need their father beside them. My being around you guys or not isn't relevant. We both know that."

He walked closer and I stepped back, toward the wall. "Don't," Will said. He kept stepping closer. When he reached me, he ran his palms over my chest slowly, intimately, in a way that made me shudder. "Don't you dare say that. Your being with me and my children would be not only relevant but delightful. I wasn't kidding earlier. I've fallen for you. Every time we're together, I fall a little bit more. I think about touching you and kissing you and tasting you all over. I think about making love to you, about sleeping beside you, wrapped in your scent and the heat of your body. I dream about spending our days together with the children. I want us to build a future together, a happy one. Don't tell me you feel nothing of the kind. Ring or no ring, I can tell you do. That trinket can't hide what your eyes tell me when we look at each other."

I cleared my throat. "This isn't a good time to—"

He leaned in and kissed me, the fey bastard. It almost made my knees give out. I immediately ran my fingers through his hair and pulled him closer, desperate for more. The kiss deepened, my heart going insane in my chest. Fuck me sideways, I was falling for him too. Falling hard and fast. The whole thing was hopeless. And he was going to leave, I just knew it. He was going to make me lose my mind, and then he was going to up and disappear back into that world of beauty and ruthlessness and hunger for power. I clutched at his torso, desperate to keep him right here, within my reach. Even if just for now, for a moment.

We kept kissing like that for a while, wrapped in each other's arms, caressing, pinching, teasing. It felt like heaven, total heaven, and I didn't want it to end. But then the first wave of pain hit. We both gasped, then slid down to the floor.

"Oh wow," Will wheezed. "This is going to be quite something."

"I told you so," I muttered, cracking my neck. "And it's only the beginning. You'll wish we would have gotten more people in on the sharing, you'll see," I informed him without a trace of smugness about having been right.

This evening was going to hurt like a mean motherfucker.

seventeen

WILL SLUMPED against the bathroom wall. He'd just thrown up for the fourth or fifth time. I'd lost count during a particularly nasty bout of pain. We were both covered in copious amounts of sweat, chests heaving with labored breath. I couldn't remember exactly how long it had been since it started. All I could think about was how much more pain was coming. I kept speculating how long it was until Susannah's pain kicked in. That was going to make all of this a picnic. I could think of nothing else.

My mind worked like that; I couldn't help it. It kept projecting perverse images of me writhing in agony, crawling on the bathroom tile, throwing up and sweating rivers. A sick part of me was looking forward to it. To the ease of knowing it had all passed. If I kept thinking about it, I would drive myself fucking nuts. This was nothing short of torture. And I had volunteered for it too. Somehow that thought didn't help at all.

"We need to get our minds off of the pain," I said in a rough voice.

"I'm not sure how that could be even remotely possible," Will replied gruffly.

"Tell me about your kids."

"What about them?" he asked, sprawled out on the cold floor.

"Always wanted to have a big family?"

He closed his eyes, setting a hand over them. "Fey don't think about children as having a family. They are more a means to an end."

"What end?"

"Immortality and glory. Long life spans aren't good enough. We want to have everlasting glory. It's our most sacred duty to try to attain it."

"What do kids have to do with it?"

"They are the way we prolong our skills and improve them. Selective breeding, one might call it."

"Sounds so cold."

"It's meant to be. We have a lot of children, so after they fight among themselves, the best one or ones make it."

"Is that why you had children?"

He sighed. "I had no real plan. I was supposed to have them. So I did."

"Did you think about staying with one of their mothers?"

"No," he replied easily.

Way too easily.

"Cared about any of those women?"

"Not in the slightest. I only cared about their health, power, beauty—as mothers to my children."

"Do you wish you hadn't had the kids?"

He lifted his head and looked at me. "I would never think such a thing. I love my children. I loved them all from the moment they were born. I will love them all until the moment I'll stop breathing, and perhaps even beyond that."

"But your youngest are barely one year old," I protested. "You must have realized how wrong it was to keep having them in that world."

"By the time I had the twins, I was determined to get my children away from Court. I just wasn't sure how to do it, exactly. Then the Weiss opportunity came up. I didn't waste the chance."

"Yes, but—"

"Did you think about having children, Bert? Ever wanted to?"

"Not really," I admitted. "I mean, I like kids, I guess. I like Alf, and your kids are great too. In this overly mature, intimidating sort of way," I muttered. "But great. I didn't get the urge to have any of my own. I don't see myself as a single parent, and so far no one solid enough to be my one and only showed up. So kids were never on my mind. I guess I'm too selfish or something."

"I'm the selfish one, not you. All of this is my fault. I blame myself for allowing my children to grow up in that culture. For not educating them accordingly, at least. I should have done something long before Fey Court rules took away my oldest son."

"This is your penance," I guessed out loud.

"No. This is me taking care of the ones I love. And since we're on the subject—I didn't equally divide the pain transferred."

"I knew it, you bastard!" I gritted out through clenched teeth. "I was sure we were having too different of a time, you throwing up so much more than me."

"You want to equally share even the throwing up?" he asked with a ghost of a smile on his face. "It must be true love, then."

"Oh, shut up!"

Another wave of dizzying pain shot through me. I contemplated the idea he was going through even worse and winced. I'd burned through my "brave, manly suffering in silence" phase. Now was the time to groan and shudder like a baby. Will and I crawled on our hands and knees toward the toilet and puked. It might have even been a poetic moment had it not been so disgusting.

IT WAS late at night when it was all over. We were both exhausted, lying on the bathroom tile. Jeremy had washed our faces, given us glasses of water. But we were both spent. Good thing Jeremy was pretty strong. He managed to carry us into the living room and set us down on the sofa. We slumped there like jellyfish stranded on dry land.

Weiss came out of the basement with the twins in his arms. "All went well. Say hi to the new additions to our pack," he informed us and grinned. "The kids will stay here with me for a while to get them accustomed to pack rules and shit like that. They're safer here anyway. I'll get them settled in rooms so they can sleep off the excitement of the day, then we'll get some rest." He frowned and looked at us, one at a time. "Why the fuck do you guys look this spent? I hope you weren't fucking each other's brains out during this whole time. Not on my favorite couch!" he growled viciously.

I held up a finger; it was the most I could manage. "No fucking. Long story. We'll tell it to you later."

He nodded tightly. "Fine. Weirdos," he mumbled and went upstairs with the twins.

Tish would have to deal with the twins. I simply couldn't lift more than a finger.

I MUST'VE passed out because I woke up with a start and found myself slouched on the same couch, only with something heavy settled over me.

On closer inspection it proved to be Will, snoring lightly and holding on to me in a touching yet smothering way. I wiggled a little, trying to get more space. He mumbled something and held on tighter.

I shouldn't have, but I took advantage of this moment and ran my hand through his hair very, very gently. I was afraid he'd wake up and stop my progress. Or rearrange his hair in his sleep like some weird sleepcomber. His hair felt gloriously smooth against my skin, still slick with sweat. It was a little sticky too in places, but I didn't care. I combed my fingers through its length, all the way to his nape.

Maybe I was imagining it, but I thought I detected the scent of his skin. Under the tangy smell of sweat, his and mine, I thought I could pick out his smell. It made my pulse quicken, and my morning wood started growing at an alarming pace. Well, shit. If he was going to wake up, we'd have one of those elephant-in-the-room moments. Not that my wood was elephant sized, though it was a good-sized package. And of course that idea made me think about his package, what I'd felt of it, seen of it, what I'd imagined. I was so ready for a personal introduction.

Will stirred and lifted his head, blinking bleary, gorgeous green eyes at me. "Morning," he mumbled.

"No morning breath for you, huh?" I muttered.

He shook his head and grinned like a kid.

"You bastard," I muttered in mock spite.

"Were you planning on kissing me?" he asked, perking up.

I rolled my eyes and discreetly pulled my hand out of his hair.

"No, don't," he said, rubbing his scalp against my palm. "Do that some more. I loved the way it felt," he rumbled.

I swallowed thickly. "If Weiss comes down those stairs and finds us stroking and petting on his couch, he might have a seizure."

"Let him have it. Please," Will whispered, staring at my lips.

I ran my fingertips through his hair again, this time with more purpose. My skin tingled from the contact. My nerve endings tingled from contact with him. The weight of his body on mine made blood rush through my veins. I leaned in and kissed him, allowing myself to forget about everything else. There was something dark and nasty looming in our near future. But I ignored it. I ignored everything and just focused on the texture of his lips. On the way they parted for me. On the feel of him reaching for my tongue with his. On its slide into my mouth, the sensuous feel of him slipping into me. Fully hard now, I grabbed his arms and pulled him against me.

"Bathroom," he whispered softly between kisses.

He got up, still holding my hand, and dragged me into the bathroom we were sick in the night before. It was dawn now, I could tell by the light streaming through the window. The soft glow filtered through the blinds and fell over Will's face as I pushed him against the wall. I closed the door and locked it, then reached right into Will's pants. His erection was hot, throbbing, and so deliciously hard.

He wasted no time and grabbed hold of mine, first through the fabric of my pants, then taking it out. We rubbed each other in a frantic pace, hearts thudding against our chests, the vibrations going through our bones and echoing in each other. I angled my face and went in for a frantic kiss as we increased the speed of our hands. Precum pearled on the head of my cock, and I felt moisture at his tip too, spreading it over his length.

We were both panting, shivering, leaning against one another. I could hear some noises outside in the hallway. I heard some voices farther away. It made my heart beat faster and I stared into the dark eyes before me. The vague notion we might get caught excited both of us. I felt my balls tighten, and soon we were both spurting, our streams of cum mixing as we leaned forehead to forehead, glans to glans. I took my hand away from his dick and licked my fingers clean slowly, looking into his eyes. He shivered and did the same, moaning a little at the taste. I just had to kiss him right then, a slow, tender exploration of his mouth, his taste and mine mixing on the tips of our tongues. I wanted this kiss to last forever. The taste, the warmth, the way it made my stomach flutter like an army of frantic butterflies were sparring in there.

"Now this is a good morning," I whispered and grinned.

He chuckled. "Couldn't agree more."

"We're a team from now on," I said in a small voice.

I was half-afraid the words would break as soon as they were spoken. They were delicate things and the outside world was too brutal for what I felt right now. But I did feel it. And I didn't want to keep it a secret entirely.

"Does that mean what I think it means?" Will said in just as small a voice.

I nodded.

He leaned in and pecked my cheek, then rubbed his lips against the skin for a moment, as if losing contact would break his heart. "Let's wash off and go back out there. The day is going to be interesting, to say the least."

After we did we found Weiss sitting in his favorite living room chair, eyeing the couch suspiciously. "I say you two fucked this morning," he hissed, squinting at us both in turns.

I grinned. "Not really, boss."

"Then why the shit-eating grin, huh?" he shot back, rolling his eyes. "And the smell. You smell newly mated, you dirty horndogs. Have a change of clothes you can get into?"

I nodded. "I have some clothes in the bedroom I use when I sleep over. And Will could borrow some of Tim's clothes, maybe, even if Will is slightly taller?"

Weiss looked him over. "I think we have some he didn't even wear, yeah."

"We could ask him directly," I said.

"No, you wouldn't be able to right now. He never made it back home last night. They've been interrogating family members of victims of the first three Leader Murders. And there has been progress. But you need to shower and change clothes so we can haul ass over there. Move it," he barked and walked toward the kitchen.

I went for the bedroom I used sometimes when I stayed the night here, and Will found Tish and managed to get a change of clothes. We showered separately and found each other in the living room again. I drank in the image of him in Tim's soft fabric slacks and delicate shirt under the dark-brown leather jacket. He wore dark-brown leather shoes and his hair was slicked back and darker in color than usual, probably still damp. He gave my jeans, sweater, and leather jacket outfit a slow once-over and grinned.

Weiss stomped in, coffee mug in hand. "You lovesick puppies ready to head into the office? Tish and Celia will stay here and watch the kids. We're taking two cars, just in case we need to separate. See you at HQ," he said over his shoulder and walked out of the house.

"Is he always in this good a mood in the mornings?" Will asked slowly, shaking his head.

"He's probably just crabby over not having slept with Tim last night. But then again, he is usually grumpy, so it's hard to tell. Tim makes him a happier, more relaxed dude, though, that's for sure."

Will smiled. "Let me say good-bye to the kids, and we'll be on our way."

I nodded. "I'll wait in the car. But hurry. If Weiss is this uptight, the development must be significant."

In a few minutes, we were headed out of Weiss's residence and toward HQ. While I drove us there, Will ran his fingertips over my free hand from time to time, and took the chance to smile at me every now and then. It felt very couple-y, and it made my stomach tighten into knots—the good kind of nervous, though.

When we reached Weiss's office, we found him growling and pacing about while Tim, Rick, and Travis leaned against the two desks, looking utterly exhausted.

"Morning, guys," I said.

Will nodded at everyone.

"Any news?" I asked Travis.

He nodded. "We have confessions from Mrs. Hemington, Violet Pax, and Jefferson Wong. Finally got answers about the three Leader Murders cases."

"They all wanted to take their places as leaders?" I asked.

Travis nodded.

I breathed out a sigh of relief. "At least we have that part solved. What about the second batch? The pentagram murders?"

"No confessions to be had there unless the traitor councilors care to give us one. James is dead, the doctor who was supposed to give Amanda her execution injection was found dead, Leonard Hughes has no discernable reason to name his conspirators—we're pretty much stuck on that one. But we've got the conspirators from the first case, at least."

"Any of them give the councilors away?" Will asked, clasping his hands at the small of his back.

Rick shook his head. "But Sands says they don't need to. Between Tricia's interrogation and the files we got, they're nailed."

"I've sent retrieval teams to both councilors' homes," Weiss said between gritted teeth. "They should be in any minute now."

"No official charges first? Taking them directly into custody?" I wondered aloud. "That might make the other councilors suspicious."

Weiss shrugged. "I can't risk tipping them off. They might have gotten rid of evidence already if they suspected anything about Will's presence. Either way, they'll confess if he interrogates them, won't they?"

The evil gleam in Weiss's eyes told me he particularly hoped they'd resist Will's questions, just like Tricia did. A part of me couldn't help but feel the same. But as soon as the two suspects were brought in, the rest of the Council would come down on us hard. And I wasn't looking forward to that particular moment.

Naty walked in. "Morning," she said halfheartedly. "Wanted to see me?"

Weiss cleared his throat. "Morning, Naty. We'll have two suspects brought in shortly. I want you to take blood samples and test them against the samples we have, and check the files you'll find on this drive," he said, handing out said drive. "One of these suspects is your mother. Can you manage that? Or should I ask some other MCU worker to do it?"

Naty's lab coat fidgeted, a sign she was twitching her tail like mad underneath it. "No, Director. I'll manage it. I already have a sample of my mother's blood. I've been working on it. It contains marking hormones. Want me to run it again when she's brought in?"

"You should take a sample once she's brought in so she can't claim later on that it wasn't her blood."

"Will do," she muttered.

She squeezed my hand, smiled a little sad smile at me, then walked out.

My heart squeezed tight in my chest as I contemplated what Naty was about to go through. I ran out of Weiss's office and caught up to her. "Naty?"

She turned around. "Yep?"

"Want me to come with? For moral support?"

She shook her head, then pushed her glasses up her nose. "Thanks, Berty. But I can't seem weaker than everyone already thinks I am. I'll do this, and I'll do this right," she said, seemingly more for her benefit than my own.

"Are you sure?"

"Yes. Yes, I am. But thanks for offering. It means a lot to me."

I nodded and watched her go. Today was going to be an exciting day, to say the least. The other members of the Council were going to be outraged at our ideas, theories, discoveries, and even proof. They would fight all ideas, all conclusions, all facts, trying their best to find some scenario in which two of them hadn't turned their backs on everything the Council stood for, on all its members, on the whole community, even. They were going to do their best, but they weren't going to find alternatives to these scenarios. Instead they'd find the cold hard truth: we were close to destruction because of an inside job. It wasn't that shocking, I supposed. After all, who better to attack you than those closest to you?

I could feel the moment the two councilors made it into HQ with guard escorts. The whole building buzzed with whispers, then some shouts sounded in the distance, arguments. The two councilors were taken into separate interrogation rooms. Will was going to work on one, then the other. And we were going to watch two of the most respectable members of our community either attack everything we thought they believed in, or lie through their rotten teeth.

I couldn't wait to see the whole show unfold either way.

eighteen

THE REST of the Council was now invited to assemble. Considering they were told what for, I suspected they all would make it here pretty fast. Weiss called Will over to his laptop to look over the feed of the cams he had me install in the Stein and Nichols residences.

"What the fuck?" Weiss growled, punching wildly at laptop keys.

Tim sighed. "That's not going to fix it. Mind if I try?"

"I have no fucking time for techy shit, anyway," he grumbled. "Go at it."

Tim sat at Weiss's desk and tapped a few keys, frowned, tapped a couple times more. Still frowned. "Bert, mind stepping closer?"

I did and looked at the screen. It was neatly divided in two, one larger and covering half the screen, the others tiny screens, probably one for each camera. The neatness was the good part. The bad was each screen showed nothing but static.

"I know I set them all up right. That little red light was on when I left them there. It means they were on, functional, and running, right?"

Weiss stomped to the window, grabbing a new tennis ball on his way. I had a bad feeling about where that ball was going to end up.

"Could they be out of power or something?" I asked, looking desperately all around.

Tim shook his head. "They were fully charged and had juice to run for at least five days."

"Could something have ruined their signal, maybe?"

Weiss growled. "They're running! What are you, blind?"

I gulped. "But why—"

"If they would've been off, you'd see a black screen, a tiny 'no signal' message in the corner here where they're all listed," Tim explained. "The static means they are all running. And while one or two could suffer from tech interference of some sort, for whatever freakish reason, all of them, from two separate residences—"

"I get it. Slim to no chance of that. Could both councilors have some jamming device, antisurveillance sort of thing?" I tried again, hoping to sound less moronic.

Weiss turned halfway toward me. "They knew they were doing things that they weren't supposed to. Maybe they suspected someone might, at some point, try to spy on them. So they could be jamming signals, I guess. Might make sense they'd have the same type of device, in fact."

"A device could be detected," Will intervened. "Countered, in fact. I can think of something else that could work a lot better on Council ground. Something that wouldn't be detected, most likely, and almost surely not countered."

"Like?" I asked.

"Magic," Will and Tim said at the same time.

"Who the fuck would've done that for them?" Weiss grumbled, pacing about.

"Maybe Hughes, back when he was still the Fey Court's ambassador here," Tim said, leaning back in the chair. "There's no way to know when they got this done. We've only discovered it now, but it could be a year old just as easily as five years old, for all we know."

"True," I muttered. "But wouldn't that affect their inner circuit security systems too? I don't imagine Councilor Stein and Councilor Nichols going without security. Especially if they've been planning these fucked-up things for a while."

Will shrugged. "If it was Hughes, a smaller-range spell would've been a better choice. He's not that skilled. But targeting sources that transmitted information outside of the home might have been doable for him."

"If it was Hughes, like we suspect, it's not that weak a magic. He almost certainly played the magic role in the pentagram murders we investigated," Tim said, getting up. "He managed to cast a spell strong enough to undo the nose of our tracker, Rick Barton. And he has a fine nose, in case you were wondering."

He walked over to Weiss and reached out to take his hand. I wasn't sure if it was for his own comfort or for Weiss's. Maybe both. But the gesture made my stomach clench tight. The idea someone could have such an impact on someone else's life gave me weird mixed feelings. I wanted to have that too. I was terrified of having it.

I looked at Will and caught him already staring at me. He smiled that small but brilliant smile of his. It almost gutted me. Fuck me sideways, I was falling hard for this guy. I was aware of the inevitability of it all. I just needed something to give me the confidence to take that extra step and simply jump in headfirst. I wanted to feel justified in indulging in the sweet madness. I wanted a mate. That in itself was insane enough. But I needed a bit more to take the final step.

Will clasped his hands at the small of his back. "I'm not saying Hughes is incompetent. Not at all. But a spell that would last for months or more, and that would cast such a wide net of action, would need too many resources. He might have enough to keep a spell of this magnitude going if he were here. But he's not. Hasn't been for a while now."

"You're making my fucking head spin. So it can't be magic?" Weiss asked, frowning.

"If I were to do anything with magic to protect my home from video or audio surveillance, I'd prevent seeing, hearing, and recording. I could sustain the magic with my presence and resources. Long distance from me, though, I'd need to anchor such a spell in the residents of the house I'm trying to keep safe. And preventing technology from functioning requires a lot more magic than preventing creatures from doing something. So long distance I might choose to blind anyone watching a recording of a certain household, rather than prevent the devices from actually recording. Less energy that needs to be used, and possibly something I can base on nonmagic residents of the house with greater ease. When I meet each of the councilors, I might be able to detect any spell anchored in them. And if I do detect one and undo it, then you might be able to see the recordings."

Weiss sighed. "Couldn't you just have said that, but in a simpler goddamn way?"

Tim patted his shoulder and smiled. "He's dumbed it down, actually. It's a whole science at the Fey Academy."

"I don't fucking care about science right now. More interested in results," Weiss grumbled.

I walked closer to him. "Maybe my being there could help him check, or something? I mean, if the ring heats up when magic is cast, maybe it picks up on traces of older spells around those affected by magic too."

Weiss looked and me and smiled a little. "Worth a try." Then he looked down toward my ring. "But what if the ring actually interferes with Will reading those magic traces?"

I gulped. Of fucking course he'd want me to take the ring off. He wanted me and Will to become a thing, after all. Allowing him to read my emotional grid again would help that along. I didn't want to be read. Not now, and maybe not later on either. Not by him. I didn't have an issue with Tim reading my emotional grid; I trusted he wouldn't blather on about it unless it was a life-or-death type of situation, and that was highly unlikely to involve my feelings. Will reading them, though—that scared me. I'd be too exposed, too vulnerable before him. In order to have enough confidence about taking such a major step as becoming mates, I wanted to feel like we were on somewhat equal footing. How the fuck could I feel that when Will was such a powerful magic caster? His power was one of the reasons Weiss wanted me mating him, after all. I needed to have some leverage here. My leverage was the ring.

I gulped. "Maybe it would go better without involving me. Reading the councilors themselves. Might be better for me to just stay out of it and—"

"What if I just checked Bert first? See what comes up. He has been in these houses recently, right?" Will asked.

"He was," Tim replied. "You think you could find traces of magic on him because of that?"

"Every spell leaves a magic trace, like a fingerprint of sorts. Maybe Bert picked up a whiff of it," Will explained, looking at me.

"Then sniff his magic traces or whatever the fuck it is you need to do," Weiss muttered.

Will stared at my ring for a few silent moments. It wasn't heating up, so he wasn't doing anything.

Weiss sighed. "Bert, do you trust me?"

"Yes," I answered immediately. "What kind of question is that? You're my alpha."

He nodded. "Do you trust Tim to keep things confidential?"

"I do," I answered just as fast, but in a suspicious tone.

I didn't like where this was going.

"Do you trust the fact that I would break every fucking bone in anyone's body if they did anything to fuck you up?" Weiss asked, putting a hand on my shoulder. "'Cause if you don't, you should. You've been my friend since we howled at the moon for the first time. Alpha and beta or not, I will destroy whoever fucks with you."

"Not in a literal sense," Tim explained, smiling fondly. "Sexual intercourse is not only permitted, but encouraged," he told Will, winking.

Goddamn winking? What were we, second graders?

"I'm enjoying all the peacocking, but don't get overly excited on my account," said Will, smiling a little. "I'd sooner chop my fingers off than do anything to hurt Bert. And I'm not sure he'd allow me close enough to, anyway."

"This feels suspiciously like asking my daddy if he'll let me go to prom with you," I muttered.

Tim grinned. "Daddy and I say you can."

"Very funny," I gritted out.

"Take the ring off, then," Weiss said. His eyes turned whiter, wolflike.

I shuddered. "Why?"

"So it won't interfere with his detection of magic," Tim explained as you would to a toddler.

And just like a toddler, I replied, "Nuh-uh!"

"I'm concerned you might have developed a magic codependency with the ring," Tim tried again in that soft tone he used during counseling sessions. "If its purpose is to make you feel like it's vital to keep wearing it, then it's affecting your life and choices more than it should. Prove it to us that it's not affecting you, Bert. If you do, you can keep wearing it if you want to."

"You think it's making me feel like I need it more than I do?"

"It might. It's been working differently than the previous owner knew it did. That shows the ring has a lot more power than we gave it credit for. Let's just make sure it works for you, not against you. Okay?"

God, I didn't want to take it off. I looked down at it on my finger, caressed it gently with the fingertips of my other hand. It was so beautiful. It felt so natural on me. Why take it off?

"Bert," Weiss snapped. "Are we doing this fucking thing or not?"

"Ready whenever you are," Will said, leaning against Weiss's desk.

They couldn't take it away from me. That was why they were making me take it off instead. What if they tried to steal it? I was going to take it off just an inch but not entirely off my finger. That had to be enough. And it hit me the fact I thought that way at all didn't seem entirely right. Maybe it was affecting me. Making me scared and paranoid about those around me. But could such a beautiful thing do any damage? My mind flashed me an image of my beautiful sister, of Amanda—even more beautiful—doing a lot of damage. Beauty could definitely cause damage, I decided.

I inhaled deeply and closed my eyes. If I was going to take the ring off, I wanted to be as collected as possible. Or maybe being nervous would help me disguise the humongous crush I had on Will? Wasn't willing to bet on that. I opened my eyes slowly and slipped the ring off my finger an inch. It felt wrong. Like pulling my skin off, trying to pull a bone out through a pinprick.

"How about we try it without taking it off first?" Will said, blinking slowly. "Maybe the ring won't affect the reading. After all, I'm not reading his emotions or anything related to how he felt when in those houses. Simple traces of magic that are not related to him."

Weiss squinted at the ring, growling lightly.

"Be my guest," I rushed to say.

I felt the ring heat up but not unbearably so. I decided that meant Will wasn't using as much mojo as he had in previous situations.

"There is something, but you were in the houses for too short a time to make a lot of sense of it," he said, crossing his arms in front of his chest. "Taking the ring off won't change it. I don't feel it interfering."

"Would you be able to tell when it does?" Tim asked, seeming to perk up in a way he rarely did outside of counseling sessions.

"I've run into the ring's action a few times already. I think I can tell when it's acting. Just like Bert can tell when there's magic going on," Will added smoothly.

Tim was riveted. "Can you? How so? Any latent magic that has woken up?"

I held my hands up. "Nothing like that. The ring heats up when someone is doing something magic around me. That's all."

"But not when you come into contact with already-cast magic?" Tim insisted.

I thought about that. "Not then, I think. Only when it's being cast. Or it would have been permanently burning my finger while I was at Fey Court, right?"

"True. It never did that with its previous owner. Well, that could turn out to be helpful, at least," Weiss said, looking at my hand like he wanted to bite it off.

I shrugged. "That's what I thought."

What I thought was I'd rather gouge my eyes out than take that ring off. It wasn't right to do that. It was far, far beyond my fear of Will reading my emotional grid. And for the first time since I started wearing the ring, I felt sure there was something kind of wrong going on. That wearing it was doing something it wasn't supposed to. Question was, who the fuck could I ask about it? The ring's owner was a big question mark. Weiss wouldn't have a goddamn clue but would make me take it off anyway. Tim didn't know more about it either. That left Will. But he didn't know the ring that well, I reasoned. Telling him wouldn't help. The ring's owner was the best person to ask. All I had to do was find out who that was, then figure how to ask them about it without losing the ring. Fat chance of that happening.

"It would help to have the surveillance materials for the councilors," Weiss said, pacing around the office. "The confessions themselves might not be strong enough evidence. They might not trust Will and his results."

"The two guilty councilors could claim this is all a charade to frame them. Even the Fey Archive material could be considered a forgery, if that's the case," Tim said. "I will vouch for the authenticity of the translations, but they might claim the material in itself was tampered with. Councilor Stein's blood showed traces of marking hormones, but she could claim it wasn't her blood even if we take new samples. In case that happens, having something like video or audio evidence too could push the point through. Even if different bits of proof might seem weak and circumstantial on their own, if we have a lot of them, they might be very convincing. We need that surveillance intel."

Will sighed. "If we had to make the point that someone in a high rank was a traitor at Court, we'd only need to make a somewhat valid point about it. Everyone would believe it, and the party in question would have to prove otherwise," he said, walking toward the window and looking out. "Your Council members won't want to believe they were betrayed by their own. But there's always that one thing, or a sum of them, that would make such a claim seem less outlandish."

Tim nodded. "We need to make the point in a way that would give it the proper importance."

"Here we go. Fey mindfucking at its finest," I said, stuffing my hands in my pockets.

Weiss ran his hands over his face. "I know I'm gonna regret this. I hate it when you go all fucking evil mastermind," he said, looking at Tim. "But go on, let me have it. What do you guys think we should do?"

Will looked at Tim as if acknowledging who owned the fucking evil mastermind crown.

Tim walked around Weiss's desk and sat down, crossing his legs. "For such a claim to be taken very seriously, the accusation should be supported by people who are perceived as very loyal to each of them. In Councilor Stein's case, the only person close enough to her and having a positive enough image among community members and councilors alike would be Naty."

I gulped. Shit, I didn't like where this was going. "But pack members don't like her very much. Are you sure Council members do?"

Tim nodded. "She's been obedient to the Council. Efficient while working under its directives. Instrumental in developing the Anti-Abuse Act the Council has now embraced. They trust her reasoning, her judgment calls. And thanks to her involvement in the MCU, she knows all of the councilors personally, has made a good impression on each of them individually. Would she do it? Support the accusation that her mother is a traitor?" Tim asked me.

I shrugged. "It's one thing to not rebel against it when proven. A whole other to support it when it's still to be proved. She might do it, but I don't like having to ask her."

"I know she's your best friend," Weiss said, sounding so very tired all of a sudden. "I love her too. If we didn't have to do this to clean house, Bert, I would never involve her. But this is a make-or-break moment. And I'll be damned if anyone will break us," he growled.

I gulped. I couldn't help it; my natural response to Weiss's dominant manifestations was to submit. Liking it didn't have a fucking thing to do with it.

"I'll ask her," I said miserably.

"No, you won't," Weiss replied. "I will ask her to back up this pack and do the right thing by us. This is not a personal favor. This is official PBI and Council business. She can shine like a hero or let her mother take her down with her. It's her choice. And my duty to present it to her."

"Isn't she part of your pack?" Will asked. "And her mother? You could simply use your alpha influence over them."

Weiss exhaled loudly. "They're not part of my pack. Councilor Stein doesn't like anyone having any power over her. She never joined us, though she's a born wolf. She didn't want her daughter to be part of the pack either. Claimed it was better for them to not burden us due to Naty's condition."

"Aren't werewolves pack creatures, though?" Will asked, turning to look at us.

"We are," I said and sighed. "But Councilor Stein was always more of a loner. Becoming a proper alpha would never happen for her, so I guess she refused to be under anyone else's thumb."

"And now she found a way to be a pseudo alpha to a pack of her own," Tim muttered. "Framing the issue this way will help increase credibility. Naty presenting the evidence might seal the deal."

"I'll make sure her devotion will be rewarded," Weiss stated. "And I'll ask her to do it."

I would have been disgusted with myself for bringing this kind of news to my best friend, but if Weiss had asked it, I would have done it. It made me all the happier I didn't have to.

"What about Councilor Nichols?" Weiss asked.

"Well, that's tougher," Tim said, leaning back a little in the chair. "All of his sired vampires are known to be loyal, but power struggles are common when dealing with a grandsire like Nichols is. So either one of them turning on him could look more dubious than righteous, even if we convince one of them to present the evidence. We'd need someone everyone sees as unquestionably loyal to him, who wouldn't have anything to win by his demise."

"Like his consort," I ventured.

"I think she is unquestionably loyal to him," Weiss muttered. "What would make her turn on him? Would anyone even believe her? She seems stoned half the time."

"She's bulimic and anorexic," I said in a small voice. "Not stoned."

"What's her pressure point?" Weiss asked, looking into my eyes.

"Jealousy. She's haunted by the idea Nichols would replace her."

"Is he replacing her?" Will asked.

"I don't know. He's been having meetings with his sired. It only made her be more suspicious and convinced he's looking to take one of them on as consort."

"We could use a spell to make her feel sure of it, but it would fade in time. It might fade sooner than intended. And it might drive her into desperation," Will said in a somber tone.

"I'm not comfortable doing that," I muttered, looking at the tips of my shoes.

"Me neither," Tim said.

"What about Councilor Stein?" I asked, glancing at everyone in the room. "She would betray anyone to get out of this mess. What if we talk to her first and give her subtle hints she's a witness? She'd pin everything on Nichols, and if I know her at all, she'll have stuff to prove her claims. Then Naty comes into play, proves her mother's involvement with blood results. We have Tricia's testimony and hopefully we'll have some video too."

"Sounds doable," Weiss proclaimed. "Let's get to it. All this talking is getting me pissed. More doing, less plotting. Go."

He turned around and walked out of his office, probably going for his comfort thing, coffee. Or Tim. Or coffee, then Tim. Or at the same time. Whatever. Tim followed suit as expected.

I rolled my eyes. "So someone's due a talk with Councilor Stein. We'll watch from the observation room so you can scan her for that spell thing. It would be awesome if we can use some video as evidence."

"Lead the way," he said and smiled.

I couldn't resist a request like that. So I led.

nineteen

AFTER TAKING a five-minute break, we did a door-to-door search and found Tim and Weiss talking to Councilor Stein in interrogation room three. We went into the observation room, and Will got right down to his mojo thing. I could tell; my ring went all hot on my finger.

I shut up, thinking he'd need his time and focus. So I just leaned back against the wall and crossed my arms in front of my chest. I looked through the one-way glass and watched my alpha and his mate trying to work Naty's mom. I recalled all those times I thought I saw something dark slithering in her gaze, all the bad feelings her presence gave me that I had ignored. All because I didn't want to believe I might be right.

It scared me to think about it. To think about all the signs Tricia might have shown she wasn't loyal to us anymore. Signs I might have ignored based on the same reason: I didn't want to believe anything like that could be true. How blind we were about those around us—and how scary it was. All the stories about people turned monsters always seemed this faraway outlandish notion that would never have a thing to do with you personally. That made the notion of getting involved with someone new a hugely scary-ass prospect.

I looked at Will surreptitiously. We didn't get involved because we wanted to, did we? Not really. We always got involved because we couldn't help it. And maybe traitors did what they did because they couldn't help it either. It was all a series of things we couldn't help but get into. Partially not our fault. Tricia's actions were not entirely her fault. I felt justified about feeling this way. It felt fair to forgive her some sins because of what she had no direct control over. I couldn't forgive her actions in their entirety. But maybe in time I might be able to accept she made her choices according to her options and the things she couldn't help. I would never forgive her betrayal of the pack. Of me. But I didn't have to forgive her. Just accept she did what she had. I was slowly getting there.

"So why are you so reluctant to take off the ring?"

Will's voice brought me out of my head with a pleasant start.

I looked at him sideways. "What makes you think I am?"

He turned toward me, brilliant smile dazzling me. "I'm learning to read you without the help of the emotional grid. The horror of it, huh?"

I swallowed. "Stop peacocking."

He snorted.

"Well, I see you're taking very well to expressions, sounds, and such to make people know how you feel about things. Very un-fey of you," I mock chided.

"What can I say? This world of yours is rubbing off on me."

An image of us rubbing each other off flashed through my mind. I blinked a few times, trying to clear my head. "So anything on Councilor Stein?"

"I already undid the spell on surveillance systems trying to monitor her home. It was a spell targeting the viewers, not the actual taping, as I suspected."

"Great, I'm letting Rick and Travis know to go through the stuff, then. They're the only ones Weiss would trust with this, aside from me. And he won't want me to be bogged down in video watching."

I texted Travis about checking the material on Weiss's laptop without fear of decapitation. And hoped I was right on this call. Interrupting him during the discussion would be a stupid idea.

"You're quite good at anticipating Weiss's thoughts and reactions."

"It's part of my job as his beta."

"And whatever he wants you to do, you do? Without question?"

"Of course. What does that have to do with—"

"Also what you think he wants you to do."

"In a way, maybe."

"Should I take your reticence toward a relationship with me as him not wanting you to have one?"

I frowned. "No. Absolutely not. He just gave us his goddamn blessing back there in his office."

"So he does want you to be with me. That's why he made that touching speech about breaking bones back there in his office."

I focused on the tips of my shoes.

"But something is holding you back despite his desire for you to step it up."

I kept staring at the tips of my shoes.

"What would make you hold back on following through with the wishes of your alpha on this? Has he asked you to get... close... to someone before?"

I sighed. "Yes."

"And you followed through?"

I nodded.

"But you're not now. Something is different."

"Are we going to listen to their discussion at any point?"

"No need. We'll find out the results anyway. Right now this is more important to me. What's different, Bert?"

I shrugged.

"Could I dare make a guess?"

"Don't see how I could stop you," I muttered.

"You have feelings for me. That's what's different. It is, isn't it? Why you insist on keeping me at a distance, despite all reasons to do the exact opposite. Why you cling to that silly ring." He walked to me, pressing his body against mine. "Tell me. Say it. Please."

I leaned forward and rubbed my forehead against his. "I'm terrified."

He ran his hands up and down my arms, a gesture so much more soothing than I was comfortable with facing.

"I'm afraid my feelings will come in the way of my role as beta. That they'd be strong enough to realign my loyalty to you first, then to Weiss second. I've already been rebelling more against his authority than I ever have before. I can't do that. It's treason, Will."

He snuck his hands between me and the wall and took me in his arms, kissing my forehead, my temples, the top of my head when I leaned my head down. "You've been working against ever getting in this position, haven't you? All this time you've kept all your lovers a foot away so nothing could come between your role as beta and your heart."

I nodded miserably, humiliated by my weakness. Poor Weiss, having picked a traitor and a disloyal weakling as betas.

"You should give him more credit than that," Will chided, still hugging me tight.

You could have knocked me down with a feather. A tenth of a feather, even, not even a full one. "In what way?"

"Do you think he would leave Tim behind for the pack?"

"Tim is part of the pack, he wouldn't—"

"Because his role is to protect everyone that is his own, yes? You, as a beta, are one of his own. He would protect you, Bert. Just as much as he would protect everyone else, if not more. Because you are friends."

"What do you mean?"

"Should you have a mate, he would never ask you to go against them or do anything to break that bond. It would mean harming you, and as member of his pack, his beta and friend, he wouldn't do that, would he?"

I frowned. "Never thought of it in those terms."

Will chuckled. "If you think about it, it's no different than a kid growing up and getting married. The kid's love for their parents never goes away, right? It just makes room for the love for their spouse. And decent parents would never ask their kid to go against their spouse for their sake."

"What about indecent ones?"

He shook his head. "Weiss meant what he was saying in his office. About breaking every bone in my body should I hurt you. But he also desired what Tim said could happen: us getting together. He doesn't want you to be on your own, Bert. Don't build yourself an unhappy, lonely life and put that at his feet."

"Wow, the famous fey mindfuck at its finest yet again. Effective, though."

"Oh? Can I dare call you my boyfriend, then?"

I shook my head. "I need you to answer a question first."

He sighed, very theatrical for him. "The things we do for love. Oh, stop it with the flinching. It won't be the end of you."

"I can almost guarantee it's what Romeo and Juliet said to one another in the beginning."

"Your question was?"

"What will you do about the Fey Court? How do you intend to get rid of them? Do you plan to leave your kids here and get yourself killed?"

"So you want the answer to one of those questions? Do I get to pick which one?"

"Not funny," I snapped, slapping his hip. "I can't bear the thought of…."

"I know. I know, Bert," he whispered and kissed the tip of my nose. "Fine. I'll tell you. But you have to promise me something. You have to promise that I can rely on you. Can I?"

"I thought we'd have that well established between us. We can rely on each other."

"Thank you. I'm going back to Court, yes. Under the guise of contending for the title of King. I'll declare all my children lost to wolf bites, rendering me the last of my line. Then I plan to take out Hughes and the High Council. There are many at Court who don't agree with the former King and his High Court. Once the High Court is gone, new members will be appointed. I believe they will want me to become King. For some the fact I'll have been as strong as taking out the High Court will make me the perfect new King. But too powerful for others. I believe they'd be more willing to let me go because I'd be too much of a potential threat to the new High Court. I think they'd be very open to a new King that won't be me.

"All I need to do is give them a good reason to take me out of the running at that point. Something like claiming to having been bitten by a werewolf, for instance. Stating it as publicly as possible. I'll lose my status as fey and any claim of mine to them or of theirs to me. The fey Sims line will be forever lost. They might perceive me getting bitten along with my children as the line defecting to the Council side. But hopefully the relief of a new circle of power will deflect their attention, at least for a while. So I'll come back here to my children. To you. To us, as a family. If you'll have me."

My temples were throbbing. "You're delusional."

He stepped back. "How so?"

"If you think I'll have any of this lone ranger bullshit, you're out of your fucking mind. You're not going anywhere without me. Not even to the great beyond. Got that?"

"You said I could rely on you. I rely on you to keep my children safe."

"No need. They're not on their own now. They're part of the pack. Weiss took them in, for fuck's sake. It's the Fort Knox of security. And who will bite you, then? Publicly while at Court?"

"It doesn't need to be true. I can simply claim to have been bitten by a Council assassin, for instance."

"Because that's what we'd need. Extra tension between the Kingdom and the Council."

"I'll think of something else, then," he said, smiling. "Maybe feigning to be dead, using the same spell I did on Jeremy. They'd put my body in the Sims crypt. Easy enough to get out of it, simply disappear."

"You seem to have given the first part of this plan a lot of thought. Very little to the coming back part. It's fishy."

He shook his head.

"Get over your martyr bullshit. I'm going with you."

"As?" he asked, lifting one perfectly shaped eyebrow.

"I don't fucking care. Your magic-owned slave. As emissary of the tuft of doom. Whatever works. And I'm bringing you back very much alive. You hear me? I'll bring you back here alive or die trying."

"Impressively invested in my well-being for a man refusing to give in to his feelings for me," he muttered.

"Shut the hell up. I'm bonking you over the head and dragging you back to my lair."

"Promise?"

I growled. He chuckled, his gaze going all gooey and sweet. It made me want to tear his clothes off and do everything humanly imaginable to him, plus a couple things more. I angled my head and moved in slowly for the kiss. It wasn't hunger driving me. Not right now. Right now it was the simple need to have his taste give purpose and meaning to my very breath. I wondered as it did just that if it was something everyone went through. If every now and then, when life seemed fucked-up enough, they turned to their lovers to give everything meaning with simple things: kisses, hugs, nights of pure passion. Was it a kind of life support everyone had been enjoying except for me, all this time? I sure as hell wasn't going to let it go now.

Someone opened the door to the examination room, ruining my moment.

"What the fuck is this, sniffing each other's butt at every corner?" Weiss growled. "You slackers have nothing better to do than suck face every time you're alone?"

"That's what boyfriends do, isn't it?" I asked and grinned.

"Well, I'll be fucked," Weiss muttered. "I've got a lovesick beta. About damn time. Now get your asses out of here. My office."

"Weiss," I called after him, left Will behind, and caught up with Weiss's long strides. "Will caught the spell thing. He undid it. I got Rick and Travis scanning the video of the Steins."

"Good, good. Stein got talking, in case you were busy sucking face and missed it. Turned against Nichols. Gave us passwords for files on her laptop. I had Naty go pick it up. I trust her to deliver it safely. If the fantastic two team can get us something video or audio on Stein herself, we're pretty much tight."

"Did she say anything about Tricia and Amanda? Or the rest of the family members involved in the Leader Murders?"

He nodded tightly. "Show of good faith. She gave me a family member or clan member for each of the three victims in the first Leader Murders case—the same three who confessed to claiming abuse to get hormones from Amanda and then got their leaders killed. Corroborates with the rest of the evidence we have. For the pentagram murders, she said the victims were picked at random, no real reason. They were getting desperate by then. Of course she blamed Nichols and Morris James. Convenient since James is dead. And she implicated Hughes too."

"Why would she do that, if he's likely to become King?"

"He's not, in her opinion."

I frowned. "Who is, then?"

Weiss looked straight ahead. He said "Sir William Matthew Sims" in a perfectly flat tone.

It alarmed me more than his pissed-off general demeanor.

"Do *you* think he's angling for it?"

Weiss looked around, opened the door to an office, and when he found it empty, he beckoned me to follow. After I did I closed the door. Then studied his pose, his expression, the tight line of his lips.

"You're having second thoughts about trusting Will," I stated. Didn't need to ask; it was too obvious for me not to know.

"What if he was looking for a way to place his kids somewhere else so they wouldn't be in his way? Without killing them. Just removing them from his way. He's known to be stronger than Hughes. Everyone expects him to best him and become King, it seems. What if he's playing all sides to get everything he wants out of all worlds?"

"What brought the suspicions on again?"

"He did something magic last night. I'm not sure what, but while his kids were all shifting… there was something fucking weird going on. Their shifts went way, way too easily. He might have messed with the process to stunt them somehow."

I cleared my throat. "About last night—"

Weiss growled. "You know something? Fucking enlighten me already!"

"It's not what you think. I'm sure it isn't. He did do something magic. He relocated the greater part of the pain of their first shifts to himself."

Weiss paced around the office. "What evidence do we have to support that claim?"

"I shared part of it. He divided it between us, less to me, though I asked for half. I knew feeling all of it would kill him. He said he'd divided it fifty-fifty. But I could tell as it went on that he was having a much harder time than me. I asked, and he did fess up to it."

"And you didn't think to inform me?" Weiss growled.

"I meant to, but I didn't get the chance since last night. I was wiped out after the shifts, and then this morning, we rushed over here and—"

Weiss's eyes shone brighter for a second, his wolf threatening to come out. "You don't fucking put yourself in danger without telling me, Bert!" he shouted.

"You were down there with the kids. And it was my own decision. I did it because I—"

"'Cause you love the fucker. I know. I can smell it all over you. On him too, I think. Pisses me off."

"Because you can't trust him?"

He sighed. "Because I don't want you to get hurt. I've lost too much lately. I'll be damned before I let anyone harm you. I trust you with my son's life. There's no higher vote of confidence."

"So does Will," I said as kindly as I could.

"What else don't I know? And don't you dare hold any fucking thing back, Bert. Or I'm going to be pissed."

"Uhm, there is something."

He cracked his neck, wrapping his bulging arms over his chest. "Do fucking tell," he said in that eerily calm way he spoke when supremely pissed.

"He has a plan. About his get-out-of-Kingdom card, if you will."

"Go on."

I did.

Weiss listened silently, a pensive look in his eyes. "Okay. And he wants you to stay behind?"

"With his kids, yeah. I won't, of course. I simply can't."

"You would leave us for him?" he asked, seeming entirely too neutral.

"Not leave you. Just go with him on a mission. Then come back, both of us."

"If you survive," he added, looking away. "What if he double-crosses you at the last minute?"

"I don't get it. You trusted his feelings for his kids before, enough to use him as a source at Court. Now that you have all of his kids, you don't trust him anymore?"

"He was predictable before. His actions made sense on a certain line of thought and action. He's throwing curve balls now. I can't trust someone who's unpredictable."

"Travis and Rick are plenty unpredictable," I piped up. "Doesn't seem like you don't trust them."

He snorted. "Oh, you have it bad for the man. I do trust Travis and his judgment, and Rick by extension. While Travis is unpredictable in action, he is reliable and has proven it over the years. Will Sims is an unquantifiable mass."

"What would make him trustworthy?"

"Bringing you back alive," he replied without wasting a beat.

"How about we give him the chance to do that?"

He shrugged. "I know what it's like to fall for someone. I won't ask you to leave him or go against your heart. After living with Tim these past months, I wouldn't be able to deny anyone the joy I get to experience every day. It's not my desire to hurt you. It's also not my desire for anyone else to do it. But you're able to take care of yourself."

I smiled. "Thanks, Dad."

"Oh, shut the fuck up," he snarled. "If you don't come back, I will go after him. There won't be any nook or cranny in this whole fucking world where I won't look for him. And he will suffer for a very long time before he'll die. No magic will be able to save him from me if you don't come back. Make sure he knows that."

"That's touching. In a psychotic, terrifying way."

"What can I say? I'm in a good mood. We solved three murders today and have answers for the other five. One traitorous councilor down, so we're halfway to cleaning our house. We might actually get out of this clusterfuck in decent shape."

I could see he was feeling more relaxed already. Part of the Council problem was going to be solved. It wasn't perfect, but things were going to be somewhat resolved. I couldn't feel his relief yet. I was looking at a possibly suicidal mission on Kingdom grounds. Relief was very far down on my list of things to feel. But I was going with Will. I simply couldn't stand the thought of doing anything else. Weiss would have to understand or kill me for betraying my alpha's will. Since I was a born werewolf, not a bitten one, neither he nor anyone else had the alpha voice power over me, being able to command me to do anything they desired. So he couldn't make me do shit against my will. And now we both knew he wouldn't be able to convince me to give up on Will either.

I felt it in my gut I was going to come back with him. And I decided I should trust my gut instinct.

twenty

WE DECIDED it was better to leave without telling his kids what we were planning. They were all recovering and adapting to their new lives. Weiss was going to have a pups-full couple of days. Teaching them to control the shifts was the trickiest thing with young werewolves, especially bitten, not born. Will said good-bye to them without saying anything about where he was going or for how long. I thought Jeremy and Susannah smelled something was wrong, but they didn't comment. Susannah was exhausted, having a tougher time recovering between spontaneous shifts—a recurring issue with teenage bitten werewolves. Jeremy seemed to be wise enough not to ask if not told, though he gave us quizzical glances.

Weiss and Tim didn't like us leaving, but they didn't stand in our way. By the time we left to drive to Court, Will had talked with his supporters on the High Court, complained about his "savagely bitten children," and scheduled a face-off with Hughes for the throne. None of the fey complained. Being kingless messed with their morale and Court efficiency. The Kingdom was in subtle disarray without a clear new leader. Whatever would expedite the process of getting a new King was spectacular by them, apparently. Either that or they were up to something. Since we were talking about fey, it might have been a mix of the two.

We were in Will's car, driving toward Kingdom central: the Fey Court.

"And they didn't ask what the fuck you were doing on Council territory with kids in tow?"

"Using them to make connections of course," he answered, already going back into expressionless-fey mode. "I was privy to the plans targeting the Council change. With ambitions to become King, I'd be expected to get personally involved now. To make an impression with the High Court. Prove myself a worthy plotter and schemer."

"And they'd just take your word for it?"

"Of course not. But they will take tactical logic."

I settled back in the passenger seat. This was going to be rich. "How so?"

"I'm not aware of the specifics, but I am sure there are wolves in your pack still marked by the hormones the Fey Institute worked on. There have to be. No High Court plan would rely on fewer than twenty to thirty conspirators and spies. Your investigations might have proof of about ten traitors, is that right?"

I nodded. "You think there are at least as many involved?"

"I'm quite sure there must be."

My head snapped in his direction. "Are you saying you're sure your actions at PBI were relayed to Court?"

"What they look like from the outside, yes. Me hanging around you, significant pack beta. Me being implicated in actions undertaken by Weiss and his cohorts. Unless someone Weiss trusted to be part of this whole councilors operation has gone traitor, the Court wouldn't know the details, the actual intention behind events. Only the fact some events took place. And the fact that I was somehow involved. Think about it. It could look to them like me manipulating my way to someone the Court previously thought of as impossible to manipulate. Even if my help with Tricia and the councilors is no secret for the High Court, it might look like me getting rid of loose ends about to unravel. Like I was trying to make some room for my influence somewhere Hughes already had it, catching up in order to outdo him. It all depends on what they want to believe. And right now I think they want to believe the strongest fey at Court is on their side."

That was a chilling spin on things. Thinking about things in that light, he could spin anything to look any way he wanted it to. And I had a second there, just a brief, passing second, when I wondered if maybe things weren't exactly as they might look. Could he be this diabolical? He was smart enough to be, that was obvious. But did the High Court think he was ruthless enough? Could they believe he'd throw his kids to the wolves' side, then make his way to the throne smoothly? Something about it bothered me.

"Why would your connection to me be relevant? Weiss is known to be unpredictable and close to impossible to influence. If your Court would think I have enough power to sway his opinion, then they'd have lame intel. Would they have lame intel?"

"Most definitely not. But one's desire for things to be a certain way always influences what one understands of what they see. We're gambling everything on Fey Court's inflated sense of capability and on their greed."

"What makes you so different, then?" I muttered. "If all fey would be that way, why would you be so different?"

"Perhaps I'm not."

My heartbeat accelerated. "What do you mean?"

"I might have an even more inflated sense of capability than all of them. I'm counting on my ability to sway the way they will see my actions and intentions. And then I'm counting on my ability to defeat Hughes and the High Court in a confrontation. I'm being greedy too. Greedy enough to want you and my children safe. Greedy enough to want to have it all. In a sense there is nothing suspicious about my behavior or motives. I'm counting on that to work in our favor."

"My being there with you will only serve as proof that you've made your in with me. Why would the High Court take that as meaning you've got my alpha's ear?"

"Would your alpha allow my presence and relationship with you if he didn't trust me at least in some small measure?"

I cracked my neck, hoping to release some of the tension that was starting to throb in my muscles. "I guess not. Him allowing our relationship means you have some in with him too."

"Exactly. It could be taken to mean I have you both wrapped around my finger, in fact. Otherwise your alpha would never allow one of his betas onto enemy ground in my company, as it were. Your presence makes my influence official."

"Or I could be a mole for my alpha. And my presence could be proof of your ineptitude."

He looked at me out of the corner of his eye. "Not if your behavior makes it clear I'm your lord and master."

I flinched. "What the fuck did you just say?"

"Just hear me out. You being eager to fulfill my every whim paints the best picture concerning my influence with your pack."

"You've got to be kidding me," I growled.

"I'm as serious as death. My influence over you translates into my influence over your alpha."

"Not fucking likely! You wouldn't be able to influence Weiss to burn if you were using a blowtorch on him. Anyone with half a brain would know that."

"Stop feeling about it. Just think coolly. I've been spending time with you and your alpha in the public eye. I've been involved in pack and PBI affairs, Council affairs, in fact. You're coming with me to Court, where I'm supposed to compete and win to become Fey King. Your devotion to me enforces my standing."

"I'm devoted to my alpha, Will. And even he is *no* lord and master over me," I gritted out.

"All the more reason to see you as completely under my influence, should you display such devotion to me."

"What are you getting at?"

He inhaled deeply. "I need you to behave as if I am the center of your existence. As if I am the air you need to breathe, the only nourishment that keeps you alive. The beginning and end of your reason to exist. You must seem to be loyal to me above all else. Above your alpha, pack, Council."

"I'm confused. What the hell do you want from me, exactly?"

"There is a fey rite that communicates these mutual feelings between parts. It's proof of commitment, devotion, and entire dedication to the stronger magic partner from the less magical one."

"You want me to become your slave?" I snapped while my hands began shaking. "What the fuck is wrong with you?"

"And I want your alpha to say he's okay with it too," he added, giving me that almost smile that was starting to creep the ever-living fuck out of me.

"Did you snort some coke or something?"

"I can and will take Hughes out. I will be able to deal with part of the High Court swiftly, but not all of them unless they are reunited. They are bound to have allies of their own outside of the High Court chamber. We'll have only two shots at killing the High Court members, and that's during the throne contenders' competition, or during the coronation test and ceremony. Tradition prohibits access to any other magic users but the circle and the contenders in the chamber while these two things take place. Unless it's a swift action taking them out while they're without backup, we might fail. We might die. Weiss wouldn't allow that to happen."

"I'm getting dizzy. What are you planning?"

"There are some spells I can use to defeat the High Court. I'll need some time to channel the magic I want to use. The kind of time we might need to organize that fey ritual. It would be politically convenient, tactically convenient... and I'm in love with you. So it would be emotionally convenient for me too. To have you as my own by my rites, and be yours by yours as well."

"Are you asking me to magic marry you?"

"Yes."

"And use this magic-marrying thing to get rid of the High Court?"

"Exactly."

"There are less convoluted ways of asking a man to marry you, you know. Are you blushing?" I asked, squinting.

"I was presenting the tactical advantages."

"What if I don't want to have you by my rites, as you've put it? What if I don't want to be yours by your rites either?"

"We can undo the union as soon as you'd like. All it takes is a magic user to undo it. Jeremy could do it, for instance."

I frowned. "Then what's so impressive about it for the High Court, if it's that easy to undo?"

"Only a strong enough magic user can do or undo the union. The less-magical partner would never be able to. And the stronger one would always be able to prevent its undoing, no matter who tried."

I got the chills. "Sounds suspiciously like matings involving leaders from back home."

He nodded. "Except the element of dominance is magic, not hormones. The difference is, while in this union, the stronger magic user can gather and use the magic of the less powerful one. It's why fey regard it as such a show of unflinching devotion. To give up your power to someone else is the highest form of servitude."

"But I have no magic. It wouldn't help you as a resource."

"True. A good reason for them to entertain the notion and allow it to happen prior to the coronation test, when I get that far. But there is magic in your nature, Bert. Shape-shifting is a magic process in itself. It's just not magic accessible to you outside of the shift itself. You benefit from the effects of this magic but aren't a magic user."

"But you are," I said, starting to get his point. "You think it might be a last-resort boost of sorts?"

He nodded.

"Wouldn't they know that too?"

"In a sense, yes. But most fey think that's useless magic. It's why they look down on shape-shifters, for their inability to access a source of power they have at hand. But my line has studied shape-shifters in the past. I think I could harness magic through the union. It wouldn't hurt, that's for sure. Why not use everything at our disposal?"

"Wouldn't my ring prevent you, though?"

"It might actually come in handy. It has strong magic of its own, awarding a portion of it to you. Perhaps because you can't fully grasp or use more of it. But I might be able to access it through you to use it."

"Okay, I get the tactical advantages now. But what are the consequences of this magic-wedding thing for me, exactly? You're way too squirrely about it, only mentioning the benefits it would offer you. In my experience that means downsides for me in these kinds of unions."

He cleared his throat. "Considering the fact that you have no active magical qualities, it would put me in charge of you, in a way. Until I release the magic bonds between us. It's a union meant to give the most powerful partner unquestionable power over the other."

I frowned. "Not sure I want to go under that sort of power-over-me effect."

"One that I would undo immediately after the ceremony. You'd still be my consort, of course. But I would renounce my magic power over you."

"And I'd have to trust the fact you'd do so?"

He nodded.

Well, this was it, then. My final choice: to trust him entirely or not enough. All of Weiss's doubts floated through my mind. All the ways this could go wrong for him and me. This was the leap-of-faith moment between us. That turning point that would forever mark the way things could go between us. Looking on the bright side, if he didn't manage to do what he was claiming he could, we'd both be dead. So I wouldn't have to put up with unpleasant consequences. What the hell, you only live once. And I'd played it safe for pretty much all of my life. If ever there was a time to take a chance, it was this. So I decided I would take a chance. All or nothing.

"Okay," I said.

"Thank you, Bert. This is very important to me. I promise I won't let you down."

"You better not. What's the plan?"

"I face Hughes and defeat him first. It would mean my coronation test and ceremony would follow. The coronation test is the final stage. Then the High Court reunites to test the power of the coronation candidate. An ultimate test, if you will. Once you pass, you are crowned."

"Just to be sure here, you don't intend to actually become King, right?"

"It has never been my intention. What I plan to do is use the test as excuse to take the High Court out. To get out of Court."

"But somewhere between these two moments, you kicking Hughes's ass and you facing off against the High Court, we're supposed to get magic married?"

"Proof of my influence over you and your pack. Reinforcement of our cover. Time and opportunity for me to amass more magical resources than I have at my disposal regularly."

"And stellar opportunity to have direct power over me," I added in as neutral a tone as I could.

"For a very, very short moment. Only until we retire to consummate our union."

I massaged the bridge of my nose. "This better not be all about getting laid, Will. And if you try controlling me, I might not be aware of it, but Weiss will be at some point. And he will kill you. Don't doubt that for one moment."

"I don't. This is the best I can come up with to get rid of the corrupt circle of power and get out of it alive."

"Convoluted as hell."

"Which is why it might actually work."

"For fuck's sake, I have a headache already and we haven't even gotten there."

He patted my thigh. "Look on the bright side. We're going to be at Court for a few hours longer than initially intended, and then we'll go home. If we get out alive. If they're onto us, we'll die quickly, so we won't be staying there for long."

"That is a spectacularly fucked-up way of looking at things. It's also what I was thinking. I need something sweet to get through this. Pull over near the first pastry shop you see. This is an emergency. I can't think well on low blood-sugar levels."

He smiled. "Sure. But Bert, we need to talk about something else."

"What more could there possibly be?"

"The ring."

"What about it? We talked about you using its magic already."

"The collective power of the High Court is great. They work as a magic circle. The more focused each member is, the greater the power of the circle."

"And?"

"To be honest, your true feelings would work for us in this case. You'd be nervous, anxious, afraid…. They would be intense emotions. Maybe they would attract attention when we'd need circle members more distracted than concentrated. I was going to propose you take it off at some point. Not for long. Enough to draw their attention. During a tense or difficult moment, though, when we'd need to break their focus, not while things are calm."

"How will I know when things are tense or difficult? Fey are so hard to read."

"I'll signal you to take the ring off for three seconds at most."

"What's the signal?"

"Me saying 'puff.'"

I ran a hand over my face. "Yeah, that won't be suspicious at all. I can so see fey saying 'puff' left and right."

"It's distinctive enough I wouldn't use it randomly, and neither would anyone else. Seems good enough to me."

"Oh, fine. Puff. Jesus fucking Christ, what I've been reduced to saying."

"Don't be huffy and puffy over it," Will said with a revoltingly straight face. "I'll get you something extra sweet to make it up to you."

"Chocolate soufflé. Up front."

"You drive a hard bargain. But fine, I'm a man of my word."

I leaned over and kissed his cheek. "Thanks. I promise I'll show ample appreciation once we get out of the Kingdom alive."

He grinned. "Now that is good motivation."

twenty~one

ONE DELICIOUS serving of chocolate soufflé and a tiny lemon and mint cream cupcake—okay, maybe two—and we were back on the road. The plan seemed way better now that I had a less doomy view on life in general.

"You're glowing about as much as you did after you came," Will said, adjusting his position.

"Yummy stuff does that for me."

"It's certainly doing it for me too."

"You didn't have any."

"Oh, trust me, I am fully aware," he muttered, looking straight ahead.

I could see his growing bulge and grinned. Once we got out of this whole Court thing alive, I had plans to fuck his brains out and for him to do the same to mine for maybe about a full week. Maybe two if he got me chocolate soufflé again. I smiled at the thought.

"Unless you want us to crash, you need to stop grinning like that," Will said gruffly.

"Well, thanks. Good to know I'm so desirable."

"Are you kidding me? I haven't ever craved anyone a quarter of how much I crave you."

He perched the coffee cup against his lips, sipping slowly. That was his comfort food: coffee. He even called it food. I couldn't mess with his addiction, though. Not while I sported mine nicely rounded along my ass and thighs. But screw it; it was worth every freaking bite and swallow. Especially every swallow, I thought and grinned again.

"Now that's just cruel," he grumbled.

"Sorry. I'll stop, scout's honor."

"You most definitely were not a scout. But okay, I'll take what I can."

The retort died on the tip of my tongue as the Court's building came into view.

"So we're just going in?"

"Yes, we are. Nervous?"

"We're going to confront the most skilled bunch of nutjobs, lie to them, get magic married, try to kill them, and then make it out alive and home safe. Why would I be nervous?"

Will parked the car, reached out to grab my hand, and then kissed the sensitive skin on my wrist. "You did just say you will go through the ritual with me, right?"

"If you've been playing me all along, you can get me killed as soon as we set foot into that building anyway. Getting magic married and possibly fucked before dying doesn't seem all that scary in that context. So why not?"

"I'm in love with you, Bert. You have to know that. To believe it. Do you?"

I tensed. "As much as I can believe anything, yeah."

"Do you feel anything for me?" he asked, trailing his lips over my wrist.

"Hard, if you keep doing that," I muttered and rearranged myself in my seat.

"Please, tell me," he said, looking into my eyes, and then kissed the area he was tormenting.

"I've fallen for you too. Isn't it obvious? Why else would I even be here?"

"Because your alpha asked you to?" he muttered slowly.

"He didn't like me coming here."

"Because he doesn't trust me with your safety. I can understand that. I'll prove to both of you that I'd sooner die than let anything happen to you. And I believe I can get us both out of there safely, or I wouldn't have permitted you coming here with me."

"You wanted to leave the kids with the pack, though," I pointed out.

"I want a better life for them. For all of us as a family. We can't have that on Kingdom ground. So I did everything I could think of to get us the chance at that new life with a side whose chances I liked as our safe home."

"And you helped clean that new home of rats," I couldn't help but comment.

"Proof of my intent to move in."

"Or proof you know how to make it seem that way. You are way too clever and skilled for your own good."

"A curse I have to live with," he replied with glinting eyes.

"Stop peacocking. Just do your best to not make me a widower."

"I promise you this: the only way anyone gets to hurt you is going over my dead body. I may not look like it, but I can be pretty fierce when in combat. Stuff is going to happen in there. Almost none of it will be remotely pretty. Brace yourself."

"We are getting married in a way, though. I hope that will be pretty."

He smiled, a full, brilliant one. "That will be a thing of unparalleled beauty."

"I just hope we don't die after it happens," I muttered under my breath.

As soon as we exited the car, I noticed the change in fey. Every single one of them looked at us, more specifically, at Will. I had the sense everyone and their third cousins twice removed knew who he was and what he was doing today. I was obviously not fey and yet with him, which made everyone without exception give me an almost readable gaze. The Court gates opened, and someone in uniform greeted us as soon as we reached the first security point.

"Sir Sims, welcome back," the uniform-guy said. "The High Court is convened and waiting for you, as agreed. If you'd kindly follow me?"

We did. I was the huge pink elephant in the room so far. Nobody asked who I was. But I didn't expect that to go on for too long. We entered a great hall, very lavishly decorated with wall bas-reliefs, painted super-high ceilings—the place was decadently gorgeous. It suited the idea of fey officials. There were about twenty stone thrones set in a circle in the center of the room. About fifteen of them were occupied. I could see Hughes standing in the middle of those thrones, hands clasped at his back and a somewhat worried look on his face.

"Sir Sims, we're delighted you've returned to us," one of the seated fey said. "Your guest would be Bert Cooper, I assume?"

Will nodded discreetly. "Thank you all for convening on my behalf on such short notice. Mr. Hughes, it is good to see you again."

Hughes nodded. "Good to see you too, Sir Sims. I hear you've been quite busy with our wolf friends as of late."

Will crossed his hands at the small of his back too. "A mess was about to fall on our heads. Someone had to handle it before it ruined all of our long-term plans. You've played a role in creating it, I believe, Mr. Hughes."

"Gentlemen, save it for the confrontation, if you will," the High Court member intervened.

Will bowed slightly. "Of course. But I would like to make an announcement first. Bert and I will go through the union ritual after the issue between Mr. Hughes and me is settled."

"What makes you think you'll win?" Hughes snapped.

Will simply smiled that small, eerie one of his. "A level head."

"Does your companion's alpha agree to this union? It will grant you, as our potential King, direct power over his beta. I imagine it might be taken as too much of an influence in Council territories." The same fey spoke.

"Do you hope to impress us with this boon?" said another High Court member. She sneered slightly while looking in my general direction. I guessed she wasn't on Will's side.

"I hope to exercise my plans to completion," Will replied without blinking. "Influence over the werewolf pack is part of those plans. And yes, the alpha agrees to our union. He might not be fully aware of its benefits," he mentioned casually. "But these benefits concern the Kingdom more than the Council, anyway. I will be enjoying them here as King, after all."

"And will the beta keep his position after he becomes yours?" the fey lady shot back.

"Of course he will. What use would I have of a werewolf otherwise?"

I almost flinched. It took every ounce of control I had to keep still and look stoic as they talked about me as if I were an object of little value. A smear of something stinky on their marble floors, even.

"We will have the alpha's confirmation that he allows this union and the beta will remain as such in his pack afterward," another High Court member announced.

"Of course," Will replied, pulling out his phone. "I will have him on speaker for you, if you'd like?"

"Video conference," Hughes jumped in. "We need confirmation it's not some recording or trick. That Weiss is there."

"It will be arranged," Will said, giving me a look.

I got my phone out and called Weiss. It was the shortest, most daunting conversation of my life. But I had texted him about what we were planning back when I was enjoying that delicious soufflé, and now we simply set up the details for the video conference. A computer was brought in, the connection was set up, and soon Weiss appeared on-screen with Tim at his back.

"Good evening, Mr. Weiss," one of the High Court members said.

Weiss grumbled. "What do you want?"

The fey smiled. "Merely to confirm your desire to have Bert Cooper, your beta, go through the union ritual with Sir Sims. Do you agree to this ritual taking place?"

"Yeah, I fucking do. One of my betas is a good enough match to your Interrogator, soon to be King," he snapped.

"So then Mr. Cooper will retain his beta role?"

"Of course he goddamn will," Weiss snapped. "Will Sims did a lot for us. We will do this for him."

"And what has Sir Sims done for you?" the lady fey asked.

"Helped us get rid of some sour fruit," Weiss replied bitterly. "He was instrumental."

"He's got to be lying," Hughes butted in. "That man would sooner chew his hands off than trust fey with anything remotely important."

"You'd do well to remember my mate is fey, or was," Weiss growled. "Not all fey are as incompetent and cowardly as you are, Hughes."

Hughes gritted his teeth but didn't reply. Things seemed to be looking good for Will and me so far. They hadn't seemed to turn on him yet, at least. That had to be good news.

"Would you be willing to join the ceremony?" the lady fey asked. "To show your appreciation for your beta and Sir Sims's union?"

"I appreciate it just fine. But we're too busy over here."

"As you wish," the lady fey said, almost smiling.

The conference ended. Time was not to be wasted, they decided. I was cordially invited to step outside the circle of fey thrones while Will and Hughes remained inside.

"After the confrontation takes place and I win it, I would like the union ceremony to be officiated," Will told the most talkative fey in the circle.

"I think it better to officiate the union after the confrontation and the coronation one," he replied in a very reasonable and calm tone. "We would like to officiate this union as a regal one, should it be the case. Your consort will become the regal consort, after all. He should be officiated as such."

Will threw me the kind of gaze I knew wasn't good. I had no idea what to do with it, though. Was I supposed to take the ring off? No. No, he hadn't said "puff." I crossed my arms in front of my chest, trying not to run in there and do something.

The fey on the thrones chanted a few words in unison, and I felt something like an explosion in the room. Looking at Will became difficult. There was a wall of what seemed to be vapors going from one throne to the next, enclosing Will and Hughes in the center of those thrones.

"We're sorry to change the schedule on you, Sir Sims," the lady fey said. "But we are rather in a hurry. The sooner the matter is settled, the better. Once you become King, if you do, there'll be plenty of time to take a consort."

That didn't sound like a warm welcome into the family for me.

"My consort is chosen, and I will not postpone our union on your whims," Will shot back.

"Careful, Interrogator. You don't yet have the rank to talk to me in such a way. Especially not while in our circle."

Hughes grinned. "You shouldn't worry about his impertinence, my lady. He won't be bothering us for much longer."

The nerve of that dickhead! Will sighed and the ring on my finger went from warm to a lot warmer. Hughes screamed and fell to his knees, convulsing. But my ring went warmer still, and Will covered his ears, screaming in what seemed like agony. I circled the ring of vapors, hoping to somehow find a breach somewhere. Seeing Will hurt was not in my schedule for the day. At least not while I was standing by idly.

"Stop running around our circle, wolf," the lady fey sneered. "The only reason you're here at all is you're so pitifully magicless. If you dare interfere, you will instantly combust. Don't give me a reason now. I am looking forward to it, I assure you."

I growled and kept circling. Will seemed to hear or feel me; his gaze searched for mine and he stopped screaming. He mouthed "puff," and I wasted no time taking the ring off for a moment. All fey eyes in the room jumped to me, but the circle of vapors didn't waver like I half hoped. It was enough, though, for Will to do something that made Hughes scream savagely, blood spurting from every orifice. It wasn't a pretty view. The spray of blood was contained in the circle of vapors, but Will was covered in red. The High Court members seemed to have been shielded. Hughes's body fell to the floor, permanently silent now, I was sure. The vapor circle dissolved, and the ring on my finger cooled off slowly.

"That wasn't one of the traditional duel spells, Sir Sims," the lady fey muttered, displeased.

"Neither was his crippling tinnitus-inducing spell, but you allowed it, my lady," he replayed in a steely tone.

"A terrible oversight," she said, nodding. "But still—"

"It wasn't one of the prohibited spells either," another of the circle said.

"Yes, but—" she started again.

"I have won this contest," Will interrupted her. "Is there any other claim to the fey throne but mine?"

The lady fey pressed her lips together. Since others didn't speak against her, she must've had supporters. But no one spoke to support her either.

"Very well," Will said, looking at each of the ones in the High Court. "Do you maintain that the union ritual should take part after the coronation test?"

"It would be best," a new voice from the circle replied. "Give the Kingdom something more to celebrate along with the fact we have a new King. A union always makes for sensational celebrations. It will diffuse any pending tensions."

Will looked at me and I nodded. After all, the union thing was a way to reinforce his abilities. He had no need to push for that now. His abilities were evident by the bleeding body on the floor, the great pool of blood around him looking oddly like sun rays in the circle of the High Court. The iron-like scent of blood permeated the air and there was a sweeter note to it, not of a flower in particular, but reminiscent of one, maybe. I wondered if it was the perfume of someone from the

High Court, or if fey blood truly smelled and maybe tasted different than a werewolf's.

"Fine, then," Will said. "When would the circle desire to conduct the coronation test?"

The High Court looked at one another, slowly nodding. One of them spoke:

"Let us do this now, so no time is wasted."

"But custom dictates a breather between—"

"We will do this now." That annoying lady fey cut Will short.

One of them rose to his feet. "Sir William Matthew Sims, Court Interrogator, descendant of the great Sims line. We, the High Court, are now testing your ability to occupy the Kingdom's throne. Should you fail this test, your claim will be forever forfeit, and new candidates will be sought. Do you accept these terms?"

"I do."

I gulped. Will looked at me once, this intense gaze that made me shudder, then closed those brilliant green eyes, and suddenly the atmosphere in the room changed. The circle of fey did something, their eyes closed too, as if in sync. The ring, now back on my finger, started to heat up, but only a comfortable warmth, not the heat of casting magic. Were they amassing power now, as Will had said he would?

The air in the room seemed to shimmer. I thought I saw sparks here and there. The air grew heavy and breathing it in made my heartbeat accelerate. I was getting dizzy. I tried to level my breathing, to slow my heart down, to keep calm. I couldn't help but fall prey to an overwhelming sense of dread, the impulse to turn around and run so strong my leg muscles were twitching and almost hurting my joints.

Will opened his eyes and they were glowing. The High Court members opened theirs, and each pair of fey eyes glowed, more or less intense. Will's shone brilliantly in a way that made his facial features hard to distinguish. The ring on my finger seemed to be vibrating, as were all the bones in my body.

I couldn't help but be overtaken by a terrible feeling of doom. My ring got unbearably hot, and all hell broke loose.

twenty~two

SPEARS MANIFESTED out of thin air. A good dozen of them, all pointing at Will. A subtle green shimmer enveloped him, and when the spears rushed toward him, wheezing through the air, they ricocheted. One of them pierced the chest of one of the High Court members, the lady fey who had seemed to be rooting for Hughes.

I cringed and stepped slowly behind one of the marble columns that surrounded the circle of thrones. One High Court member was down. It seemed like a good start.

Will put his hands up, palms toward the ceiling. A rain of arrows fell perpendicularly on the thrones, some of them piercing flesh and eliciting yelps and curses.

"Offensive magic is not supposed to be part of this trial," one of the hurt High Court members screamed.

"On either side, yes," Will replied, smiling. "Yet it didn't seem to prevent you from throwing spears my way."

"The circle can be granted allowances," the wounded fey replied.

Will shrugged. "Then so can be the coronation candidate."

They were all turning on him. So much for the support he claimed to have from part of them. Or maybe he had known all along they would turn on him, if the time came. And maybe that was why he'd talked about taking out the whole circle, not just parts of it.

Another wave of arrows materialized out of thin air and swept through the circle. This time they came vertically, and at least five other circle members were hit. Two of them oozed copious amounts of blood and didn't move.

"Damn you, Sims," one of the untouched fey cried. "What in the gods' name are you trying to do?"

Bolts of lightning hummed through the air, arching through the circle members and hitting Will too. From him the bolt jumped back at a circle member and then hit the column I was hiding behind.

Will's bright gaze sought me out. I waved I was okay, though I wasn't. Part of my arm was burnt, the current having traveled somehow around or through that damned column. My ring thrummed with energy and it was hot enough to singe my skin. I tore a piece of fabric from my shirt and stuffed it between the metal and my skin, round and round. It was a small comfort, but it took away the edge of that burn.

The ground shook and the columns started to rock and tumble, one at a time. The one I was hiding behind shattered in half, so I crouched behind the remaining bit. I heard Will cry out and I watched as a sword went through one of his legs. I shuddered as he gripped it with both hands and pulled it out. He fell on his knees, but the light in his eyes shone just as brightly. My stomach tightened and I felt nauseated. I crawled toward the circle, hoping to find some solution, some way to interfere. The ring felt way too hot when I got nearer, so I crawled back just in time, the sword flying at me, missing me by a mere inch.

"You stay out of this, pet," one of the circle members gritted out.

I picked up a piece of marble and threw it at his head. Shockingly, it hit the target and the guy fell out of the throne, blood oozing out of the head wound. All of the others turned to look at me. Shit. A dagger materialized out of thin air and flew at my head. I ducked and jumped to the side, taking cover under a chunk of marble column. The dagger flew by me, but not before tearing me a nice little pattern on the arm. It stung like hell and I cursed.

"Stay out of it, please," Will shouted.

Water dribbled down from thin air over the circle members. It hissed when it hit the ground, eating away at the wood and flesh it touched. Acid. It was raining acid. Will was shielded and so were a couple circle members, but three howled terribly and gurgled as the acid got to them. The smell of burnt flesh, close to rotten meat, and the sludgy puddles growing on the floor under the acid victims made me taste bile. Rubble flew about, falling over the acid puddles, covering up the sludge and screams of the victims. Will was now surrounded by piles of rubble and the last standing five circle members. A couple were bleeding; one looked pale as hell. Will didn't look that good either. The glow in his eyes had diminished some. That seemed like a fucking bad sign to me.

I looked down at my ring so I could think. Will wasn't going to make it. I knew he wasn't. I felt it in my bones now, looking at the ones left standing. It occurred to me they had all wanted to take him out from the very beginning of this confrontation. It was why Hughes had been allowed to use forbidden magic or spells, to bring a gun into a fistfight. It hadn't worked. Maybe Will had proven to be stronger than they had anticipated. But it seemed clear to me now he wasn't strong enough.

"Fuck it," I muttered.

I wasn't going to let them kill him. Not without putting up a fight. I was a goddamn werewolf after all. Fighting was what I knew best. I tried to take the ring off, thinking I should hide it under some rubble. Nobody would know. Nobody was paying me much attention right now. But it wouldn't come off. I pulled despite the burns around my finger. Or where I thought I had them. Upon closer inspection I realized there were no wounds there. The ring hadn't left burn marks like I was sure it must have. Had I imagined them? The scent of my singed skin? I shook my head. It wouldn't come off, then. Fine. I just had to shift with it on. I was about to when I heard a voice I never thought I'd hear again.

"Are you the fey's prized pony, then?"

I stared, my jaw hanging open. "Amanda?"

"One and only, servant," she replied, grinning. "Surprise!"

"But you were—"

"Obviously I'm not dead. You've ruined my plan to use Hughes. Bad, bad wolf servant," she chided. "You won't ruin the one where Sims dies, though. I won't allow him to become King, the fucker."

"What the hell does it matter to you?"

"I've invested a lot in this hormones project. Your fucking boyfriend would ruin it. He doesn't understand its advantages. But others do."

"How do you propose to stop him?" I asked and grinned.

"I bet his boy toy getting killed will throw off his game," she replied with glowing eyes.

"Presumptuous of you, Amanda. You should remember you've never fought me, out of courtesy toward my alpha."

"Close to nobody fought you. Because you're a butt-licking lapdog, not a top dog, at that. You think you could fight *me* and win?"

I was sure of that. But I was sure the fighting might break Will's concentration. How could I avoid it, though? "I can fuck you up easily, yes."

"So you're delusional as well as obedient." She spoke as she slowly circled me. "Disgusting combination."

Amanda's fighting style was well-known in our pack. She liked to play with her prey, injure it, prolong the pain and panic. She was a conceited, sadistic bitch. The longer our quality time together was, the worse it would be for Will. This had to be quick. For that she had to be angry, furious, in fact—reckless and rushed.

"You want to talk about disgust?" I shot back. "Your mate didn't fuck you for years."

She growled, her face reddening. "That's because I wouldn't let him, you flea-infested loser."

I snorted. "Yeah, right. He never liked to fuck you much, and we both know it. Don't forget I was there, heard your discussions, saw your life together. I bet he couldn't wait to get away from you and shower even before he got Alf, huh?"

She screamed and threw a pocketknife at me. Got me in the leg, the embittered bitch. I didn't give her the satisfaction of even wincing. I simply pulled the knife out and pocketed it.

"What are you hoping for, here?" I asked to buy a little time.

The initial pain in my leg had to subside a little. I couldn't afford letting it distract me during the real fight that was coming.

She snorted. "See, that's the difference between servants and masters, lapdog. Servants lack vision. I don't. The people Stein sent after me? They were our people. Helped me get here. Hughes and I had an arrangement. I needed his help; he needed mine. Needed me to become the Fey King."

"There are new laws now, Amanda. The Anti-Abuse Act changes things. Why are you still trying to destroy our community?"

"You all turned on me, you sniveling bastards," she growled.

"You turned on us first."

"It doesn't matter now. I want Weiss dead. I won't have any peace until then."

"If I were you, I'd just run. Make a fresh start somewhere."

Her eyes turned golden. "You're afraid of fighting me, you limp-dicked coward. Just as impotent as you always were. You think I didn't know you had a thing for Weiss? Envied me for my place in his bed? I knew, you little shit. I always knew."

"I never had a thing for him. What are you talking about?"

"Isn't that why you never had a fucking relationship? Ever? Always yearning for *my* man."

"He was never yours, Amanda. Not even for a moment. And I never wanted him."

"You and your fuck toy ruined a lot of plans today, Bert. You'll pay for it," she sneered.

I had never liked Amanda. Something about her always struck me as wrong. She was too ambitious, too jealous, too demanding. Then she was too surly, too distant, too manipulative. But she never struck me as insane in all the years I knew her. Depressed, maybe. Unbalanced and unstable, for sure. But never insane. Now she had that kind of gaze. A raving madwoman, thirsty for power and blood, greedy enough to steal and cheat her way to it. She was once a mother, a wife, even a friend to some—though not to me. She was once driven, ambitious, but rational. Somehow she had turned into this lunatic now.

I felt sad for her. For all the wrongs that had been done to her. For all the wrongs she had done herself. But none of that absolved her of her crimes. She was part of a plot that led to death and suffering. She had led to my sister's betrayal, which would lead to her death. I would never forgive Amanda for ruining my sister's life. I didn't want to forgive and forget. I wanted to get even. This was my chance.

"I never understood why Weiss decided to use you as mother to his heir, you know," I said casually. "You always struck me as weak and sorely lacking. You made up for it in eagerness, maybe. But not even that made Weiss ever want you, did it?"

That was it. She wasn't going to run now, even if she might have thought to sooner. Now she was raving-mad. I had her right where I wanted her: overconfident and furious. She tore her clothes off. Slowly went on all fours. Her body shifted.

I put my phone and wallet to the side, got my pants down in a hurry. There wasn't any time for the shirt too. I allowed my wolf out. It shivered with joy. It had been so, so long since he'd been free. I had good reason to not shift unless in dire circumstances. Apart from submitting to Weiss's wolf form, my wolf was an erratic, destructive force. It had even attacked Tricia, despite knowing who she was, despite recognizing her scent. Now all I had to do was unleash him upon Amanda and hope Will would manage a way to defend himself. It was either that or both of us getting killed. Fuck me sideways if I was going to die without putting up a hell of a fight.

My eyes changed. I knew because I saw all the colors in either brighter or more muted tones. Will shone like an explosion in the desert, the burning bright light drawing me near. I shook my head as claws pierced my flesh and my bones broke and realigned. The crack and muscle burn made me howl, and everything before me grew taller as I went on all fours. My last thought was I had to not kill Will. And I hoped I would manage to keep some semblance of control over my wolf mind, though I knew it couldn't happen. Werewolves lost human thinking when shifting. We had the animal's thoughts. In time they tended to fuse or follow the human ones, but the thinking process was animal nonetheless.

But I realized I knew I was in wolf form. I still had my human thinking. I looked around. The ring was gone. But I still felt the burn of magic being cast. I felt a wave of warmth envelop me and saw that weird green light glow around me, the same one that glowed around Will. He was shielding me somehow, I was sure of it.

Which was a good thing when Amanda pounced toward me. Her bite was vicious, but she only tore away a bit of the fur on my chest. I growled and took a good chunk of her side with one bite. It tore easily and she whined. She retreated and circled around me slowly. We tore bits out of each other, our furs bloody and our limbs limping every now and then. She was weaker than she used to be, I noticed. But I could have taken her on her good days. And I took her today too. One wrong turn was all I needed. She went for my throat, but I managed to angle my head so I grabbed her by hers instead. A smart wolf might have lain low for a moment, bided his time. Amanda was frothing at the snout, not smart. She struggled, bit my forepaws, raged. I tore her throat out. Her paws twitched once and then her body was still.

I set my gaze on one of the fey in the circle, one with fewer wounds. I launched myself at him. The run made my muscles tingle. My open jaw was hungry and determined to do damage. I landed on him from behind. Bit out a good chunk of his throat. He didn't have time to do a thing. Just fall, spurting blood on the already red floors. The slippery and warm liquid felt glorious on my tongue. It dribbled down my snout. Tainted my fur. I wasted no time trotting over the slippery sludge of the floors and jumped at another fey.

I wasn't quick enough. He threw a bolt of lightning at me, projecting me clear across the room. I heard something crack ominously. I couldn't tell if it was a bone of mine or something I hit. I didn't give myself time to ponder it. Riding on pure adrenaline, I howled, got up, and ran right back at the bastard. The distance helped increase my momentum, and Will timed an attack at the man the moment I was jumping at him. Distracted, he fell prey to my snout with ease. I bit hard at the back of his neck and pulled until he went limp, the satisfying crack of his neck music to my alert ears. Will's eyes glowed less than they had just a moment ago. It was time for this dance to come to an end.

I lunged for the legs of one of the other two standing fey just as he was about to cast some magic; the hot tingling of his force fizzled as pain clouded his thoughts. He tried to stab my chest with a dagger. I bit and tore away the offending fingers, slashing a bit of my lip in the process. I growled, angry it might break Will's focus.

The last fey gathered a massive amount of magic. Will threw a thick bolt of lightning at him. The magic around him shimmered but didn't focus on a spell. Not right away. All I needed was that one moment of hesitation. I jumped at his stomach with open teeth and a bloodlust I hadn't felt before. His stomach gave under my teeth with a sickening smooshy sound. His bowels fell out after I tore a good mouthful of soft tissue. It was one thing predators knew for sure: when in need, go for the soft spots to inflict the worst damage. The belly was the most vulnerable part of an animal's body. Also of a man. But men carried their vulnerabilities without a shield, so easily accessible when they were on twos instead of fours.

The ball of magic he had amassed blew up as the caster fell to the floor. It sent both Will and I flying through the room. We landed on opposite walls. The adrenaline was slowly fading away now. The pain took its place steadily. And whatever wounds I had, they'd be doubly as bad when I changed back into human form. So I decided I could stay there for a few minutes. Allow my body a bit of time to heal. It did so faster in wolf form. But I wanted to rest beside my desired mate.

I got on all fours and walked toward Will. He lay there as if sleeping. His chest still moved, so I knew he was alive. I refused to contemplate he might not make it. It simply wasn't an option. I pushed my wet nose into his chin, into his cheek. I rubbed his forehead with it, leaving sloppy, bloody marks all over his gorgeous, though scratched and marred, face.

He stirred. I actually licked his face clean, wagging my tail like an eager puppy. Weiss would have kicked my fucking ass if he saw me.

Will moved his head slightly and cracked his eyes open. "Bad fall," he wheezed out.

I whined, the sound shrill and panicky in my ears.

He groaned and tried to move. Didn't manage to. Shit. He wasn't going to make it. I just knew he wasn't. It had been a really bad fall. There was blood trickling out of his ears and nose, the corners of his mouth.

He cracked open his eyes again. "Speed my healing," he wheezed.

I whined, not getting what he meant, and pushed my nose into his cheek.

"Bite," he said between coughs that sprayed out blood.

Was he asking me to? I looked into his eyes. He looked into mine, though the gaze was slowly growing hazy. He nodded as much as he could. I closed my eyes and everything fell out of my head. All but the idea he was dying. I knew of one thing that sped up healing: the bite. But it could very well kill him when he first shifted, as weak as he was. I didn't like those chances.

People came in. I heard voices, shouts. Someone tried to come close to us, but I growled and my fur rose up on my nape and back. Nobody was touching my Will.

"He has no braid. He's not our King," someone said, sounding way too calm for my tastes. "Step aside. Let us take the killer into our custody."

Of course, fucking fey! They were pouncing on him now that he was weakened. I growled louder.

"Bite... me... now," Will wheezed again.

They were many, and I was one. I had no chance to fight them all to keep him safe. And they were going to kill him, I just knew it. Couldn't let that happen. Not now that I knew he was my desired mate. There was only one chance for us, and it meant risking his life. But it was the only thing I could do.

His breath was raspy, slow. I put my snout up and I howled; a long, shrill sound that echoed around the room. And then I bit.

The fey rushed on me, trying to grab Will, to pull him away. I made to bite all the hands reaching for us. They withdrew immediately, probably terrified I'd actually bite them and they'd lose fey status immediately. Will had just lost it. They seemed to realize this and stepped back, as if of one mind.

"Not fey now," one of them snapped, irritated. "No High Court either. We have to reunite the Council of Electives, vote for new members. Go through the whole King selection process all over again."

"And the strongest contender is lost now," another mumbled, strolling away. "More chances for the rest of us," she muttered as she exited the room.

"We should put the beast down," someone whispered.

"And bring down wolf wrath upon us now? When we are without King and High Court? Absolutely not. Let the mutt do as it pleases. He's of no concern to us."

I realized with both relief and disgust they weren't going to help Will or me. Not even take us to some infirmary. I had bitten him in front of witnesses. He just lost the fey status officially. He wasn't their King or anything of theirs anymore. Now if he made it, he would be mine. I'd be his alpha and he would be my personal pack of one.

I growled until the crowd dispersed and I stood guard beside Will as his chest rose and fell steadily. The bleeding stopped. The rattly sound his lungs made slowly abated. I knew they were all good signs.

I could have shifted back into human form and called Weiss for help. He'd come. But it would take time. At least an hour to drive here, locate us. Another hour to make it back to the MCU, where Naty would do what could be done for Will. That meant he'd go through the first shift in the car, if he made it at all. It was a very bad setting. And we couldn't pull over and get out. Random humans couldn't see us at all, even less so in such times.

No. The best idea was to stand by him, whatever would happen. In my wolf form, benefiting from faster healing myself. Whatever happened with him, I would deal with it. I listened to his heart beating. Everything else in the world faded away. My own heartbeat attuned to his. I loved this man. If he didn't make it, I would never be able to recover from his loss. What would I tell his children? How could I live beside them, knowing I'd gone home without their father? How would I explain it to little Sarah or Hector? They would resent me for surviving. I would resent me for surviving. Shrill whines escaped me every now and then. I couldn't help it.

After about an hour, I was fully healed. He was twitching all over. It was happening: his first shift. Maybe it was a good thing he was out cold. The pain had to be horrible. But he'd felt part of the first shift pains of his children, as much as I had or more. It wasn't a new experience for him to go through that pain for himself now. That would make managing it easier. It would help his body not panic and rebel against the changes. Or so I hoped.

The sound of cracking of changing and rearranging bones filled my ears. Music that made my heart beat faster. He opened his mouth and screamed. He screamed in a way that made me howl, the pain almost radiating into my eardrums and from there all through my body. But his body slowly accommodated the pain and his two-legged form changed into a four-legged one. He was a gorgeously blonde wolf, his fur silky and thick, covering him like a majestic coat. He had a lithe body, thinner than mine but not looking frail. Simply more graceful. His beautiful snout was slightly open and his eyes were closed. I nudged his nose with mine and he opened his eyes. My heart almost stopped beating. He had brilliant green eyes, deep and knowing and so immeasurably beautiful.

He tried to get up, but I growled deep in my chest. This was a make-or-break moment. He had to submit to me as his alpha, and I had to allow him to bite me so he would become mine. If he got any funny ideas and defied me, it wouldn't end well. Wolf forms, no matter what our thoughts, were highly driven by instinct. In this more than in anything else, even. If someone defied their alpha, they'd get killed.

Will slowly turned on his bent paws, still down. He reached out to me, holding his nose downward, his tail slightly between his legs. I nuzzled the top of his head and he whined but didn't move. I nipped his ear playfully and he nudged me with his snout softly. He reached for my forepaw and bit the skin there, right where the leg merged into my torso. It stung and a trickle of blood seeped out. He licked the spot clean. I climbed on top of him and bit the fur at his nape, reveling at how the fine fur felt against my teeth. He whined but stood down. When I let go, I felt a thrill of joy bathe my insides and my heart. I howled again, long and proud, and he joined.

He was mine now, and I was his. He was a werewolf. My werewolf mate.

twenty-three

IT WAS surprisingly easy to get out of the Fey Kingdom once we shifted back into our human forms. I'd managed to retrieve my phone and my pants from the rubble of the High Court chamber. Will had to make do wearing a knee-length sweater we retrieved from the chair of a High Court ex-member. But we had the car right outside, so it wasn't like we had to parade through the Kingdom in our improper attire.

Getting some clean clothes wasn't too hard once we stopped by Will's home. I had to make do with some sweats that looked more like hot pants on me and a hoodie that was tight enough to make my nipples visible through the fabric. I didn't give a fuck. All I cared about was driving out of the Kingdom and back onto safe Council ground.

It wasn't difficult to do. Everyone fey ignored us, even avoided us like the plague. In a way, we were. Once we had clean clothes on, we got into Will's car and simply drove off.

I called Weiss.

"What the fuck are you doing?" he growled as soon as he answered.

"Good to hear you, boss," I replied, grinning.

"Is this whole goddamn mess amusing you, Bert? It's not fucking amusing to me!" he growled viciously.

"We're safe, the both of us. Driving out of the Kingdom. Mostly unharmed."

"Mostly?" he snapped. Then released a deep sigh. "If you ever—ever!—do that to me again, I'll rip your balls off and feed them to you."

"Please don't. A newly mated wolf needs his balls."

"What the hell are you talking about?" he snapped.

"Long story short: I bit Will and we mated. He's mine now."

"You bit him? On fey ground?"

"He asked me to. I had to; he was injured. Badly. I'll tell you about it when we get there."

"Fine. Bert?"

"Yeah, boss?"

"Congrats, man. I'm proud of you. If you need advice or just a friendly ear, you can always count on me. Know that, yeah?"

"Yeah. Thanks," I said, then ended the call.

Will smiled, still looking out the windshield. "On a scale of one to ten, how pissed is he?"

"About a seven, on his best days. He won't tear us new ones, though, if that's what you mean. He might threaten to," I admitted and chuckled. "He'll get over it by the time we get there."

"You saved my life," Will said, looking straight ahead. "I hope you didn't bite me out of obligation."

"I wanted you before, I want you now, and I think I always will. I made you mine because of that. Everything else is just details. Did you ask me to bite you just so you could survive and get out of the whole Kingdom business?"

"I asked because I wanted to be yours, and for you to be mine. In whatever way I could. Dying would have been inconvenient, that's true. But you're not a means to an end. You're the prize. My prize."

"We need to pull over somewhere," I gritted out.

We were both hosting epic boners, but fey ground wasn't a good spot to consummate our mating. As soon as we made it out of the Kingdom, though, the first motel we found on Council ground, we pulled over and got a room.

It was a cheap motel room with tacky wallpaper and a dubious comforter on the bed. The room smelled kind of stale too. I didn't give a flying rat's ass. As soon as we closed the door behind us, I jumped his bones. Moaned when his lips made contact with mine. We both shook as we helped each other undress and hissed in pleasure as skin touched skin. Details like a gaping wound or sprained ankle didn't mean a thing now. The taste of his mouth was intoxicating, the strongest inebriation I'd ever felt. Feeling his touch on my skin was like a sugar rush, and I never wanted it to end.

When I entered him, it felt like heaven. Tight, hot, deliciously mine—heaven. We were both exhausted, wounded, and sorely sex deprived. It didn't last long. But then again it didn't have to. This was about urgent claiming of each other. It was lightning-fast satisfaction. I came deep inside him, shuddering and screaming. And when he slowly crawled out from beneath me and managed to slip his way inside me, I groaned and scratched at the wallpaper, tearing small bits of it from the wall. The walls could've fallen over us and I wouldn't have cared. I came a second time as he thrust deep and fast into me, and he exploded with a cry sounding somewhere between despair and bliss.

We fell asleep in each other's arms, chests heaving, bodies slick with sweat, hearts vibrating to the same tune, this new and hypnotizing beat of us.

"I love you, Sir William Matthew Sims," I whispered and held him tighter.

He chuckled. "And I love you, Bert Cooper."

LATER THAT night we finally got to PBI HQ. Naty greeted us at the entrance with emergency kits. She hugged me, then cleaned and bandaged our wounds, fixed my sprained ankle and Will's fucked-up shoulder. We didn't have time to chat now; I knew Weiss was expecting us. We found him in his office, tossing around a tennis ball.

"I hope you won't throw that thing at me, boss," I said as we stepped inside. "I've got a couple sore spots where it could do some real damage."

"You rutting sons of bitches," he growled. "You couldn't postpone the fuck marathon for one day and just come the fuck home?"

"It was an exhausting day," I replied meekly. "We needed a rest before driving home."

Tim grinned, sitting at his desk. "And after what must have been the most harrowing day of your lives, you deserved a little time to yourselves."

"You're lucky Tim found it in his heart to keep me otherwise engaged," Weiss muttered, squinting. "Well? What the hell happened there?"

After we told him the story, he calmed down. Even let the tennis ball out of his hands.

"We got Stein and Nichols," Weiss said after listening to our story. "I used a little creative truth involving Hughes and Will failing to become Kings and the High Court getting killed. Who better to buy into the story of a revolution than those trying to start one themselves?" He grinned.

"Once they thought their fey allies were gone, they both started talking. The whole story. Stein told us about the first three Leader Murders, how they worked on a list of victims for the murders before even getting started. And their list was a lot longer. Rick ruined their plans by figuring out Amanda."

"And how did they come up with that list of intended victims?" I asked, massaging my temples.

"Amanda had a whole crew of disgruntled nonleaders. Everyone on their victims list was written on it by a family or clan member looking to get rid of the leader for personal reasons—that Stein knew, but Amanda was blind to. Mrs. Hemington wanted to get back together with her ex, Susan's father, who was Mrs. Hemington's alpha. But she couldn't because her daughter had alpha hormones despite her gender assignment surgery. The only way to get together with her beloved, in her mind, was to get rid of Susan. According to Mrs. Hemington, her daughter was an abomination. She convinced herself killing her was the right thing to do, anyway. All she needed to talk Amanda into adding her daughter's name to the list of victims were some bruises and a sob story about supposed abuse she was enduring at her horrible daughter's hands.

"Henry Pax's consort, Violet, wanted a new consort without losing her clan. She figured getting Henry killed and becoming a pseudo sire would be the best way to do that. And that was pretty much what Jefferson Wong, consort of the third victim, Paula Wong, thought too. They claimed to be rebelling against abusive leaders, but it's now clear they were lying. They used Amanda's cause to achieve their ends."

"It doesn't mean others weren't abused by leaders, of course," Tim intervened.

"The plan was to incite the community against leaders by and large. To create a sort of civil war," Will said. "That obviously didn't work."

"It couldn't have." I looked at Will. "Now that we are a pack of two, you understand the why, I think."

He smiled. "Too strong a bond to break that easily. Even if it would be abused."

"Which is why us getting the Anti-Abuse Act voted law was one of the best things to come out of the whole ordeal," Tim said, looking into Weiss's eyes.

He nodded. "When that plan didn't work," Weiss resumed, "Hughes upped the game and involved bigger fish. Morris James wanted to take revenge on me, and his accomplices were under marking hormones effect. They still are. It was easier for Nichols since he's an actual grandsire. Stein needed the marking hormones, though. It took some convincing, but we managed to find out for sure that the pseudo alpha was Stein herself, and Amanda was her beta, or one of them. Stein not being a true alpha, she had no problem using her pseudo pack and tossing members aside when they weren't useful to her anymore—like she did with Amanda, for instance."

I cleared my throat. "About that—"

Tim frowned. "What about that?"

"She wasn't dead. When we arrived at Fey Court, she was there," I said, looking into Weiss's eyes. "The team Stein sent after her when Amanda escaped, the one that we thought killed her, must've actually helped her escape. So they were their pack, not ours. Who knows how many of the pack she's turned against us?"

"Fucking rabid bitch," Weiss snarled. "I'll go out there and hunt her down myself."

I gulped. "No need. She attacked me. We fought and… she's dead now."

Weiss turned away for a moment and it scared me. Was he upset? Angry?

"I'm sorry, boss. I had to. She came at me viciously. Kept babbling about how she wouldn't have peace until she'd killed you. Seemed she'd lost her mind, all bloodthirsty and driven by hate."

He looked at me. "Then I'm glad she's at peace now. I'm sorry Alf's mom is dead, but what she'd become…. She wasn't his mom anymore. Not really. Just a nutjob. A violent, scheming, destructive nutjob."

"I think we'll have to take a closer look at our pack members, boss," I said. "We should get rid of all the rats now that we started the process. Pull out the evil at its roots, if we can."

He nodded. "Going through anything like this again could break us."

Tim walked over to him and caressed his shoulder. "You managed it the first time. Whatever might happen, you'll manage it."

They kissed, a brief peck more than a languid tongue-y affair. It made me smile. And reach for Will to kiss him too. I couldn't help it. We were still in our honeymoon phase. But there was something on my mind. "How's Naty?"

"She waited for you at the entrance, didn't she?" Tim asked and frowned.

"She did, but we didn't have time to chat. We were hurrying to come up here. She was functional, but how do you think she feels?"

"Sad," Weiss replied, shaking his head. "She reported her mother's treason to the Council. Went in there with everything, the blood work she'd done herself from two samples, proof it was indeed her mother's blood by using hers as comparison, all the evidence we had from the Fey Archive files, video and audio material presenting her plotting with pack members. Naty seemed a prosecutor more than a doctor. Made quite a nice impression. She's a loyal member of this community, even in the face of adversity."

"She's an amazing woman and deserves more respect and recognition from us," I dared reply.

"She's going to get that, I assure you. Tim and I have made a suggestion with the Council. And they agreed with our point of view. Naty will take Councilor Stein's place on the Council. She can run the MCU too, if she likes, but probably less hands-on than she did up until now. Her merits and loyalty will be recognized as they should be. Anyway," Weiss said after clearing his throat. "Will, welcome into the pack. As my beta's personal pack, you are part of my official pack. We'll have our wolves meet sometime soon. I'll recognize Bert's scent on you, and your own, I'm sure, and we'll have no issues when you recognize my authority. Your alpha's alpha isn't yours, strictly speaking, but you have to respect the chain of command."

Will looked uncomfortable. "Will there be biting involved?"

"I don't expect there to be. A simple act of submission will suffice. Do you think you'll have issues with that?"

"I'm not sure," Will replied, frowning. "I've only been a wolf once so far, and that was when I was hurt. My interaction with Bert might be different than with you."

"I sure fucking hope so," I muttered.

Weiss squinted. "I'll let that slide 'cause it's your honeymoon phase and your first mating."

"Sorry, boss," I immediately said, looking down.

"Don't sweat it this time. And Will, you shouldn't sweat it either. Your obedience to my wolf will come naturally. Worrying about it won't help. You'll do just fine when our wolves meet. Trust me," he said with that intense look in his eyes.

I felt Will's position shift, his shoulders slightly bowed, his look aimed at the floor. It relieved me. I had been worrying about his reaction to my alpha too. But nature seemed to take its course. It would be fine. We would be fine.

"Your kids have gotten out of the rough patch with their shifts," Weiss said. "They don't seem to have a hard time behaving and controlling them. It's a fey thing, I understand. They seem to keep their human thoughts when in wolf form. Doesn't help with the twins, I must admit," he added, grinning. "But everything should work out just fine."

Will nodded. "Thank you. I'm forever in your debt for taking in my children and keeping them safe the way you did."

"Oh, shut up. We're basically family. And on that note, I have to warn you: Alf and Sarah have a puppy love thing going on."

"They're not even ten!" Will bristled.

"I know," Weiss replied, looking defeated. "Man, I wouldn't want to be in your shoes with that army of beautiful kids. But it's only fair that Alf might get one of them when they grow up," he added, looking smug. "They're going to be the beauty stars of the pack."

"Stop talking about my children like that," Will said, massaging the bridge of his nose.

"Relax," I whispered and kissed the side of his neck. "He's just messing with you. Though Alf and Sarah would make a cute pair."

"Don't you start now," Will gritted out.

Which was overly cute too. I rubbed a fingertip on the creases between his eyebrows. "Relax, lover."

He sighed.

"Tell me," Tim intervened, "during your first shift, did you maintain your normal thought process, Will?"

"I think I did, yes. I remember having some thoughts, though I was pretty much passed out. Why?"

"I noticed the same thing myself," he explained. "Do you feel your magic is any different? Stronger, weaker?"

"Stronger, I think. I feel I have more resources. Haven't tried it yet, though."

"While we're on the subject of magic," I cut in, "I couldn't take the ring off. And when I shifted into wolf form, it disappeared but still worked. When I changed back into my human form, it was there on my finger. But it won't come off. I've tried."

Weiss sighed. "The owner said the ring chooses its heart. Supposed to pick its true owner and award them with unknown abilities. Seems like it chose you. It has a mind of its own, in a way. Only you can take it off, and only at times. Maybe when you're not under the threat of death or nervous about something," he added, scratching his nape.

"So I get to keep it?"

"Yeah," he said, shrugging. "All yours."

I smiled. "How did the Council take the news they had two traitors among them?"

Tim sighed. "Not that well. But when presented with all the facts and evidence, they had no choice but to accept the truth. They've canceled their Councilor titles."

"You know, I can get Amanda's twisted logic, maybe," I muttered. "Tricia had a thing for her, I think, so I can get that. I can get family or clan members looking to replace their leader, even, by whatever means necessary. Mr. Nichols had greater aspirations of power, I'm sure, and had means to make that work, being a grandsire. I could get that too. But Mrs. Stein? What on earth possessed her?"

Weiss grabbed the tennis ball again and started bouncing it off a wall. "She said despair made her do it. She was sure her 'flawed' daughter would never make a place for herself in this pack and Council. She had no other kids. She wanted to have access to power. Believed herself better than most. Said she wanted to change a few Council members to get better leverage over her and her daughter's future."

"I call bullshit on that," I said immediately. "She never cared much about Naty."

"I agree," Weiss replied. "Only as potential means to power, maybe. And since she didn't turn out to be that... I think it was greed. Plain old greed and vanity. A terrible combination."

"What will you do about all the ones who participated in the marking hormones research, and then used that stuff?" I asked looking at both Tim and Weiss.

Tim shrugged. "Naty's research lab came up with an antidote based on the formula we got from the Fey Institute files. Once they take that, I thought we could offer them a reeducation program option. Or time in the pen as punishment. I'm hoping they'll take the reeducation option. With the Anti-Abuse Act in effect, things are changing. People need to adapt to the change, to embrace it, for the Act to improve their lives. It might be slower than I'd like, but it will balance things in time."

"Won't help vain and greedy power grabbers, though," Weiss muttered.

"We need to reeducate the whole pack," Tim persisted. "I'd like to talk to the Council about some pamphlets and free classes. What do you think about that, Weiss?"

He shrugged. "I can never say no to you, you know that."

"That is entirely too much information," I said, grinning.

Weiss growled and Tim rolled his eyes.

There was a knock on the door, and Travis and his mate Rick came in. "You guys back safely?" Rick asked, looking between me and Will.

"We are," I replied, smiling. "How are you two?"

"Fucking tired," Travis said. "You had us go through hours of boring-ass video. Not cool, man."

"Sorry. Had to be done. And I knew Weiss would trust you two with it."

Rick leaned against his mate. "Thanks. I'm glad part of this whole insanity is resolved, at least. What happened at Court?"

"I took out Hughes. Then took out the High Court with Bert's help."

"Wow," Travis said, yawning. "And I thought our day was full."

"Amanda was there," I said, knowing Rick would care.

He looked into my eyes. "And?"

"She was raving mad," I said softly, looking at the floor. "It wasn't even about leader abuse anymore. She simply was raving mad, vindictive. Tried to kill me."

"Since she obviously failed, I'm guessing you did kill her," Rick concluded.

I nodded. "Had to."

My conscience prickled a little. I didn't have to. I could have injured her, taken her into custody. Though the Council would have executed her, anyway. I had wanted to kill her back there in the High Court chamber. I had stirred her temper so I would have to. She'd taken my sister from me, from us. It had been a mercy kill, I reasoned. Better to die in a fair fight than be executed before the eyes of your son and your used-to-be pack. It was better for everyone this way.

"At least she's free," Rick said in a gentle tone. "Even of her own demons. I wish things could have gone differently."

"We all do," Weiss said.

Rick looked doubtful about that but didn't say as much. His initial resentment toward Weiss had subsided, but only slightly. Part of the reason was the sessions Rick was now having with Tim. I knew Rick had abuse in his past, and that had somehow overlaid with Weiss's abrasive brand of leadership. True, Weiss had made some mistakes in the past. We all made mistakes. And some of us paid dearly for them, as he did. Maybe with time Rick would grow to appreciate Weiss for his qualities rather than judge him for his faults. I hoped it would happen. Until then, not snapping and huffing at him all the time was enough. And it seemed he was getting there.

"Well, then, I guess what's left to do is get the kids and take them to my apartment," I said, looking at Will.

He smiled. "Yes. We'll take the kids home."

"I have a better idea," said Tim. "How about you leave them with us for the two-week training period instead? Take it as a real honeymoon. You deserve it."

Will frowned. "Won't visiting you all the time be bothersome?"

"Are you kidding me?" Weiss said. "Bert spends half his time at my place anyway. Having you around too won't hurt. Besides, you need to take some time to look for proper housing. You are a pretty big family."

I grinned. "How would you feel about having us as neighbors? There's a free residence a couple houses down your street."

"Have at it. It'll work great for the kids too, I think. Alf will love having wolf friends to play with. It's been difficult for him. Other pack kids are intimidated."

"He intimidates them because he mimics your behavior," Tim chided.

Weiss frowned. "No, because he's a future alpha. And they're weak anyway if they're intimidated. But he gets along real well with Will's brats. They have this uppity air about them. There's no intimidating them," he said with a strange note of pride.

I blinked a few times. "The fact that you're this thrilled gives me the chills for some reason. I hope you haven't been putting strange ideas into their heads."

He snorted. "Me? Strange ideas? Never. I like the brats' attitudes."

"That's what worries me," I muttered.

Will caressed my back slowly, leaned in, and kissed my cheek. "Let's see this house, then. The kids can too since it's so close by. We'd have an easy time coming and going from the Weiss residence; the kids can spend time together. As long as Alf doesn't try to steal the heart of any of my children," Will added, frowning. "Then living so close could be a real problem."

"Don't jinx it," Weiss said, shaking his head.

I smiled. Things had changed so much in the last year or so. Leaders couldn't abuse their packs or clans anymore, by law. If they did they had to pay. Though I'd never spoken on the topic, I liked that change a lot.

Travis had Rick, and they were very good for each other. And a very fun couple to hang around. Also trustworthy and reliable. I had no doubt they'd manage to develop the Abuse Investigations team of two into a full team of many. Rick cared about it enough to be very involved, and Travis cared about Rick enough to move heaven and earth to make things happen as Rick wanted them to.

Weiss had Tim, and he was a godsend to him, Alf, and the rest of us too. Even though Weiss was just as bossy as ever, he seemed to become an even better alpha with Tim by his side. They would no doubt lead our pack and community into a better future. Weiss's determination coupled with Tim's strategic thinking made a killer team.

Naty was going to take her mother's place on the Council, which seemed not only right, but smart since she was such a fabulous lady. Maybe someday soon she was going to find her own mate too. I was hoping she would. I wanted her happy too; she was my best friend.

I had gotten Will and a veritable gang of kids in one go. I was actually looking forward to the challenges of becoming an instant dad of six. With Will's calm approach to everything and my diplomatic skills, I had no doubt we'd live through the teen years of all our children.

And things would be quieter for the Council, PBI, and our community, at least for a while. I didn't think the Fey Court would suddenly find the secret to peaceful cohabitation with other communities, but they'd be busy organizing themselves at least for a while.

The future was actually looking bright.

LIV OLTEANO is a voracious reader, music lover, and coffee addict extraordinaire. And occasional geek. Okay, more than occasional.

She believes stories are the best kind of magic there is. And life would be horrible without magic. Her hobbies include losing herself in the minds and souls of characters, giving up countless nights of sleep to get to know said characters, and trying to introduce them to the world. Sometimes they appreciate her efforts. The process would probably go quicker if they'd bring her a cup of coffee now and then when stopping by. Characters—what can you do, right?

Liv has a penchant for quirky stories and is a reverent lover of diversity. She can be found loitering around the Internet at odd hours and being generally awkward and goofy at all times.

Stop by her website for the latest news or visit her blog for occasional rants. She also regularly spamificates Twitter and Facebook. For The Win.

Be afraid. Be very afraid.
Website: liv.liviaolteano.com
Blog: blog.liviaolteano.com
Twitter: @LiviaOlteano
Facebook: www.facebook.com/LiviaOlteano

LIV OLTEANO

A tooth
FOR
A fang

Leader Murders: Case 1

Three days. Three dead bodies. One newly turned, broken-hearted lycan tracker to figure out the connection.

The one summer Rick Barton takes a vacation, all hell breaks loose. Running from an abusive relationship leads him into the arms of hard-nosed lycan Travis Chandler, who gives him little choice but to become a lycan too and join the Paranormal Bureau of Investigation. Out of options, Rick joins the weird organization, expecting some two weeks of training and an adjustment period. Tough luck, he doesn't get either. On his first day, his new partner offers to promote him to field agent if they get mated—less time wasted on training, more time on the field, and considering Rick is the only tracker the Bureau has on hand when a wave of strange murders hits the community, time is of the essence.

Someone's killing the leaders of the paranormal world and mutilating the bodies. Investigating and tracking clues is enough of a challenge, and Rick must contend with an impatient Council, Travis's advances, and actually adjusting to being a lycan. Only one thing is certain: Rick's new life promises plenty of interesting adventures—as long as he can survive.

www.dreamspinnerpress.com

LIV OLTEANO

A counselor AMONG wolves

LEADER MURDERS: CASE TWO

Leader Murders: Case 2

Five dead leaders, their bodies arranged in a pentagram. Treason, lies, and backstabbing. A make-believe affair that turns into a real mating.

Timothy Sands is a PBI counselor, half-fey, half-elf, with a secret crush on Herman Weiss, PBI director. As a new chapter is added to the Leader Murders, it is Weiss's responsibility to investigate what seems an impossible-to-solve case. The other problem? Weiss is suffering from rages, and his only salvation lies in Tim's emotional-grid-balancing skills. They only have to pretend to be a couple for Tim to use his talents, and he owes Weiss a big favor. Piece of cake, right?

The fey might be involved in the Leader Murders. Someone on the Council might be their ally, and another prominent PBI figure looks more and more suspicious as they investigate. The stakes are upped when Timothy's father, the Fey King, threatens to leave the Council destitute if they don't hand Timothy over to him. Weiss's brilliant solution? Mating Timothy and forcing the Council into protecting him.

There's only one small hitch in that plan: instead of protecting one, the Council might decide to get rid of two.

www.dreamspinnerpress.com

THE HERACIAN AFFAIR

LIV OLTEANO

Space Files R: Book 1

Even years after Rizzo Berg's lover and Dom died in combat, the memories torment him. Following a particularly disappointing date, Rizzo goes to sleep in his apartment only to wake up on a spaceship with tall, gorgeous, alien Captain Conrad D'Ollet of Heracia, a man so deliciously dominant Rizzo's knees turn to jelly.

Apparently the Heracians need help, and Rizzo is a humanitarian through and through. Spending more time around Conrad is totally not one of the reasons he wants to lend a hand.

Soon Rizzo finds himself completely conquered and blissfully owned. But neither he nor Conrad is willing to risk his heart, let go of the past, and dare to believe in a future that won't end in catastrophe.

www.dreamspinnerpress.com

SANDSTORM HEART

LIV OLTEANO

SPACE FILES R

Space Files R: Book 2

Ron Vid is a Celian soldier with some personal demons. Hoping for respite, he deserts his squad and leaves his planet. Working as a mercenary on Asai, planet of sand and wind, he has a reprieve, until the Haffa named Zaoh joins the mercenaries. Celians and Haffas have a history of strife, but when Ron and Zaoh are paired on a mission, their chemistry crackles. After they fight together for survival, it's clear Zaoh wants Ron. Zaoh can be a fierce and dominant lover, but Ron's secrets, and his fear that the Haffa might uncover them, could keep Zaoh from getting his man.

www.dreamspinnerpress.com